THE UNTOLD TALES OF DOLLY WILLIAMSON

AN OCCULT STEAMPUNK THRILLER: PREQUEL TO THE GUILD CHRONICLES

J M BANNON

D1563811

Cover Art by Covers by Christian

Editing by Suze Solari & WriterMom

Please join my mailing list to get free books and news about upcoming projects.

To Mom, who always believed.

FOREWORD

Fredrick "Dolly" Williamson is a young detective sergeant in the detective branch at Scotland Yard. When called on to investigate the murder of an investment banker, he is reminded of past encounters with the occult. Dolly requests help from Sister Rose Caldwell, an expert in the mystical arts. The body count continues to rise and the mystery deepens after the enigmatic necronist guild provides clues to the origins of the murderer.

This tightly-wound thriller is set in an alternative 19th century, where powerful guilds use mechanical power, occult rituals, and alchemy to vie for influence in the courts of Queen Victoria and the ever-youthful Emperor Napoleon.

The Untold Tales of Dolly Williamson is the prequel to the Guild Chronicles, a steampunk fantasy book series.

SPECIAL THANKS

Thanks to Beta Readers

Heidi Wags

Christianna Johnson

SUNDAY, THE 6TH OF JUNE 1858

8:00 AM, 217 KING'S ROAD, BELGRAVIA

During the early hours of Sunday morning, a constable roused Dolly to tell him there had been a murder. Together, they walked to the scene of the crime. The streets of London were peaceful this time of day. Later, the residents would emerge from their homes, stoke the coal beds of steam carriages, hitch up horses to surreys and ride to church or the park. Except for the occasional clip-clop of a horse-drawn carriage or the whine and chug of a steam-driven vehicle making an early delivery, the streets felt tranquil, a rare occurrence. This was London, the world's largest city, the capital of the greatest empire and home to over three million souls.

Hundreds of new inhabitants came to the city every day. Rural folk and immigrants, all looking for factory work and a better life. To help deal with the chaos of the fastest growing city on the planet, the home secretary enlisted Dolly and his fellow detectives with the responsibility of crime detection, a novel concept that had proven its merit by thwarting conspiracies and catching villains that in the past would have gone unpunished.

Fredrick Adolphus "Dolly" Williamson had made sergeant at twenty-eight years of age. Other men had achieved the position in the Metropolitan Police Department earlier than Dolly, but he was the youngest sergeant of the ten men serving in the special detective branch of the Metropolitan Police Service.

More than the day, it was the neighborhood that made this walk serene; King's Road in Belgravia lay far away from the streets swarming with new migrants and country folk seeking to make their way in the evolving world. Rarely were his services needed in this part of town.

The crime scene was located at the townhouse of Sir Francis Chilton, first baronet and the managing partner at the investment bank, Chilton, Chilton, Strathmore & Owens. Chilton and his partners were men of exceptional power. He was the principal partner of an enterprise, where even kings went to borrow money. The Chiltons had the finances that could fund countries going to war or the creation of entire industries, like those of the mechanists. The only financiers in London that perhaps had more money under management were the Rothchilds, but they had far less influence.

Two Peelers managed the modest crowd that had gathered in front of Chilton's townhouse, including a correspondent from the Guardian, Gerald Welch. No doubt some copper tipped the newspaper man.

Dolly pushed past the growing crowd and entered the home. The beat sergeant stood in the foyer, talking with one of the household servants. Dolly walked up to him.

"Detective Sergeant Williamson," declared the sergeant with a tone of respect and relief.

"Sergeant," Dolly replied, looking to him for his report of the situation. Dolly was now the ranking officer on the scene.

"This here is Mr. Cooper, the head butler. He found Sir Francis this morning," answered the beat sergeant.

Dolly turned to the butler and said, "I'll have questions for you later." Dolly then spoke to the sergeant. "I want to see the scene first."

The detective followed the sergeant down the hallway, and they turned right into the private study. A cadaver lay in the center of the room. A dead man unlike any corpse the detective had seen.

The body was kneeling on the floor, arched back with its arms splayed out, chest up. A deceased male, naked above the waistline. A white shirt and dinner jacket were folded neatly on one of the overstuffed chairs beside the body. What was most disturbing was the state of the body. It was gray with skin like clay dried in the sun, cracked and leathery. This sight brought him back to the horror he saw four years ago.

He circled the body, noting no trace of a struggle, no blood spatter or gun shots. Jutting from the rib cage of the deceased man was a remarkable object. A strange ornate piece of wood about a foot long, decorated with odd markings, small bones, feathers, and beads, almost like a primitive magician's wand. The object penetrated his breast, but presented no evidence as to why all the victim's vital fluids were gone.

Dolly paced around the chamber and sniffed the air to sense if there was solvent or chemical residue that may have caused the strange condition of the body. At first glimpse, it appeared to be a burned corpse, but it did not have the smell of a burned body. Rather it had no smell. Scenes from the past kept sneaking into his mind, visions of a man on fire but not dying, laughing and not burning. It had been months since that fellow had visited him in his nightmares and years since the episode.

He glanced over to the constable by the exit. "Send in the Butler." Dolly needed help to understand if things were missing or out of place.

The policeman returned with Mr. Cooper, who remained just outside the study. Upon viewing the scene, Mr. Cooper was overcome with grief. "Do you think he suffered?"

Of course he suffered. He looks like an overdone hen, Dolly thought. Instead of voicing a response, he asked him a question. "How long have you worked here, Mr. Cooper?" Dolly was now on his hands and knees, peering at the carpet below the body for any traces of fluids or evidence.

"I have served at the townhouse for twenty-four years," Cooper replied.

"What causes you to believe the body is your employer?" Dolly asked, looking at Cooper while going to his feet.

"The clothing, sir. Like I said, I have been in service to Sir Francis for a long time. I know every stitch of clothing he owns," said the butler.

"And this is just how you found him. You touched nothing. You did not fold up the shirt?" asked the detective.

"No, sir, I have not stepped into the room," he said.

"Please come in and look around the office. Does anything look out of place or missing?" The butler took a deep breath

4

to steady himself, then stepped into the room as if he were taking the step off a cliff.

The old man paced the room. Dolly observed him, looking for any telling behavior.

"From what I can see, it all looks right," said Cooper. Dolly doubted he could notice anything. The man kept looking back at the mummified remains of Sir Lester, like he would jump up or talk.

"Mr. Cooper when was the last time you saw Sir Francis alive?"

"Now that is the odd thing, Detective. I have not seen him since Friday morning, and I did not expect to see him for a fortnight as the family is at the estate this time of year. He showed up unannounced and without staff late Thursday evening. All alone. I asked him if I should call for temporary help, and he said no. That he was in London only for a short time and had no need to open the house."

"So you saw him Friday morning?" reiterated the detective.

"Yes, I served him breakfast. Then he told me and Mrs. Blake to take Friday and Saturday off as he would not be returning after going into the office."

Dolly stepped to the hall and signaled for the constable to come over to where he and the butler stood. He had been to countless crime scenes and only one had the same eerie feel that this one did. Dolly had kept in touch with the other witness that knew what happened in that cellar four years ago, but he kept contact to a minimum. Seeing her, while comforting, was also a reminder to him of that night of terror. He wouldn't try to go it alone again. Better to reach out now and make sure that there was nothing out of the ordinary and if there was, she could point him in the right direction.

"Constable."

"Yes, Detective,"

"Run a message over to the Yard."

Cooper interrupted, "Detective, the house has its own wire-type. You can message them from here. It's—it's behind Sir Francis's desk."

Of course, they have wire-type, thought Dolly. "Thank you Mr. Cooper. Could you help the constable get a wire over to Scotland Yard? I need a photographer to come to this address and constables to go fetch Rose Caldwell and bring her here. Tell them to look for her in Bethnal Green."

∽

10:00 AM, The Hare and Hound, Bethnal Green

Rose Caldwell looked up when she heard the tinkle of a small bell. She was at the Hare and Hounds Public House, and it was now quiet enough in the pub to hear the doorbell ring when the door opened. That was because it was early in the morning and she had been there all night. When Rose arrived on Saturday night, the pub was full of a raucous group of locals drinking and having a good time. Now Rose, like the few other patrons of the pub, were not eager to see the silhouettes of two constables or the bright mid-morning light come through the door of the public-house.

The constables approached the bar. The barkeep was connecting one of those new-fangled draft handle systems to a wooden keg. Instead of pounding in a wooden tap and gravity feeding the ale, a hand pump was put into the bung. He stopped working and toweled off his hands as he conversed with the pair of cops. The man behind the bar pointed at her, and all three of the men's eyes went to Rose.

The two constables approached her table and stood over her, returning her stare. The senior officer broke the silence. "You Rose Caldwell?"

That question was usually followed by vitriol and accusations of the questioner.

The last few days had been particularly hard on her, and so Ms. Caldwell had been in her drinks for some time. Drink wasn't the solution to her problems but was a common choice in her family when answers didn't come easy. The trouble she faced was not metaphysical but the common one most folks in this part of town had: how to pay next month's rent. Like her father and uncles, she only made matters worse by spending what little she had on washing her problems out of her mind for a few hours. "I wish I weren't," Rose answered.

"Sergeant Williamson asked us to fetch you." The constable that addressed her turned to his partner. "Go see if the barkeep has a coffee for the lady." The other bobby walked back to the bar.

Rose picked up a wine bottle on the table and tipped it over her cup, hoping that there was wine left. There was none. She looked at the cop that spoke and asked, "What's this about?"

The constable glared. "Miss, we're here to collect you and take you over to Saint James to meet the detective," said the constable.

Rose had not talked with Dolly in a year. After the incident at Father Milton's Rectory, she had regular meetings with him, the kind of get-together that war veterans had, not to share war stories but to be with someone that understood and had the same view of the world. When he didn't call anymore, she assumed he had moved on. She missed him, but the thought of him moving on with his life made her feel better about losing his company.

"He says he doesn't have any coffee," yelled the constable at the bar.

"Is he alright?" asked Rose.

"Fine, miss. He is at a crime scene and asked for you," said the bobby.

Sister Rose stood up but had to steady herself as she was still drunk and had not been on her feet for hours.

The Constable grabbed Rose's arm to help steady her and said, "Let's go."

∾

11:30 AM, 217 King's Road, Belgravia

Sister Rose awoke in the rear of the black maria, her head throbbing in turn with the chugging of the drive turbines. Unsure of when she dozed off or why she was in the back of a police wagon again, she worked to piece together the events from the previous night. When the vehicle came to a halt, she peered out the rear window. To her surprise, she was on the street, not in the courtyard of the local jail.

The bobby opened the door. "This way, Miss Caldwell."

Her mouth was parched. Her short slumber in the back of the police wagon had left her one foot in a drunk, the other in a roaring hangover. Her head was in a clouded funk struggling to piece together how she got to where she was. After she stepped down from the carriage, she stretched her back and arms to throw away the soreness. As clarity set in, she realized she was in Eaton Square and that people were staring at her.

Sister Rose was used to getting looks. Rose was fetching, with short black hair, rather than long, put up, and that was just the start of her style that bucked current fashion rules. As usual, she wore riding pants and boots. Rose was never in skirts and bustles. Her blouse was white. Well, mostly white; it looked a little dingy and crumpled from a night of boozing. Rather than staring back at all the onlookers in defiance to the disapproving looks they gave, she reached into the leather purse on her belt and drew out sun spectacles. The darkened round lens spared her eyes from the glare of sun and society.

She could not conceive who's home she was standing before. There was a substantial crowd outside, including passersby and gawkers, mostly society types. Mixed in were a few columnists and several photographers. One shot a picture the minute he recognized Rose.

Walking to the door of the townhouse, a smile came to her face as she saw Dolly Williamson waiting at the transom for her, but he was scowling, or at least she thought he was frowning under his thick mustache. Dolly wasn't wearing his usual bowler hat but was finely dressed for an average English bloke, wearing contrasting plaid pants and a waistcoat with a lightweight summer coat. Always trying to be a bit fashionable, his collar was adorned with a wide black silk tie that was tied in a loose bow. He looked down at Rose as she approached. He stood around five-foot ten, nearly a foot taller than Rose.

"For Pete's sake, constable, you brought Rose Caldwell in a police wagon to the front door," bemoaned Detective

Williamson. The constable went pale. "This will be in every daily in London now," the detective finished, ushering her into the home.

Dolly turned to Rose and grinned as he greeted her. "Thanks for taking the time to come and slum with me, Were you with the queen at Buckingham or Windsor?"

Dolly put his palm on Rose's back and ushered her toward the crime location.

"Swanky digs, Detective," Rose mentioned, taking in the opulence.

"Yes, you are in the Belgravia residence of Sir Francis Chilton," he replied.

"The banker?" said Rose as they walked through the marble-tiled foyer past the grand stairwell to enter the study.

"And this is Sir Francis," Dolly answered. As they arrived at the doorway of the study, he gestured to the withered corpse on the expensive oriental rug.

Rose took in the office. It was an affluent man's study. Rich exotic wood paneled the walls. A large writing desk dominated the room with two overstuffed leather armchairs facing the desk. Behind the desk was a credenza with a stock tape clacker and a type-wire keyset. Most people Rose knew couldn't even write, let alone operate or own one of Mr. House's type-wire sets. The machine looked like a small piano with twenty-eight keys to type a message that would go over Electric Telegraph Company wires to another wire-type set. Upon arrival, the message would print out above the keyboard via an array of brass mechanical components driving a daisy wheel to transfer a message to paper.

She removed her sun spectacles, then took a leather

instrument roll off her belt. Walking past the body, she set the roll on the exquisite tortoise shell desk and unlocked the two clasps that kept it closed. Rose guided the unwinding of the case with her index finger, then surveyed the instruments attached to the case, selecting a silver chain for all the bits and bobs in her collection. Rose put the silver necklace around her shirt collar. From the necklace dangled a dozen monocle lenses of varied colors and dimensions.

Rose took a small incense censer from her purse and lit a match to ignite the incense. There was smoke until she dropped a few drops of tincture from a vial. As the smoke stopped, she screwed down the cap of the censor with a chain attached and began to wave the incense burner in slow arcs to disperse the smoke. As the vapors spread, she used her other hand to choose various lenses to peer into the telltale fog. Her keen eye could detect fragments of the past, intermingled with the present, and future images echoing through the mysterious mist.

Dolly stood and stared. "You know Rose, you look downright silly with that pantomime of yours."

"Dolly, I don't question how you go about your business." She never thought much about how she looked when she was doing this work. "Nothing otherworldly was in here. Whoever killed the man was from this plane of existence or he would have left a snag in the warp and weave of the Aether," Rose said.

The ex-nun inspected the body and the totem with various lens of different color and thickness, looking at the object through an amber lens then magenta. She pulled out the totem, examining the wound site. When done with her process, she closed the censer to extinguish the invisible vapors she was using to illuminate the supernatural.

"Anything?" asked Dolly.

Rose returned her tools to the appropriate places of storage and rolled up the leather and closed the clasps.

"His soul was stolen. I have never seen the totem before, so I can't help with the arcana used, but I'd say primal for sure." Rose stated.

She walked to the door. "Oh, two other things…"

"Whoever did this took their time doing it, maybe all night. That is why he looks like a raisin," stated Rose.

"And the second?" asked Dolly his brow furrowed at the bad news.

"They want you to know how they did it. Otherwise, they would not have left you this souvenir," Rose said as she handed him the totem and left the study.

MONDAY, THE 7TH OF JUNE

7:00 AM, SCOTLAND YARD

The work week was in full swing. Dolly woke earlier than usual when he heard the workers beginning construction on the street side of his three-room cottage. The lane he lived on was being broadened to better serve the growing adoption of steam lorries and electric carriages. A gang of workers ran jackhammers at first light to break up the curb on the east side of the street, widening the thoroughfare. Dolly had a light breakfast and got dressed before stepping out of his house and latching the door.

Dolly purchased a paper from the boy as he made his way up Cottage Place to Westminster Road. On the corner, the paperboy squawked in a high pitch over and over, "Headline: English workers locked out of Prussian alchemical works!"

It was the latest drama in London. The detective's curiosity pressed him to learn the opinions of the columnists and editors on the state of affairs with the trades protest at the gas works.

He gave the headlines a cursory glance then tucked the paper under his arm, planning to have a careful read at morning tea.

On his daily route from Number 12 Cottage Place to Scotland Yard, Dolly strolled along the raucous Westminster Road and crossed the river, turning right on Parliament Street, then on to Whitehall through to Charring Cross with another into Great Scotland Yard, a short walk for a man who walked a beat as a Peeler in 1850 and spent eight to ten hours walking the streets.

The desk sergeant yelled out to Dolly as he strolled into the station-house. "Ay ya there, Williamson, the commissioner said you're to go directly to his office."

"Ta O'Brien" He was sure that the murder of a high-profile aristocrat would draw the scrutiny of the government and the police commissioner wanted answers. Any morning opening with being ordered into the office of Commissioner Mayne was not a good start to the day.

When he got to his office, the commissioner was not there. Maybe there was something more pressing. Dolly needed to get prepared for the Monday morning briefing. Mayne would be there, as usual, to get updates from all the detectives on their cases.

Dolly sauntered off to his desk to put his notes together. He squinted and scrunched up his face when he saw that Mayne was waiting in the detectives' pen going through files on Dolly's desk. The commissioner looked up to see Williamson enter the pen.

"Williamson, I've been looking for you!" exclaimed Mayne.

"Sir?" Dolly answered as he stepped up to his own desk.

Mayne sat in Dolly's chair. "Sit down, Williamson. What's this matter over in Belgravia?"

Dolly set the paper on his desk and pulled out his notebook. "On the morning of June 6th, a body was discovered at 217 King's Road by the butler, a Mr. Cooper. Mr. Cooper identified the individual as Sir Francis Chilton."

"Yes, yes, Chilton's homicide, I know, but this!" Mayne pounded his finger on the newspaper, showing frustration as he struggled to open the paper to page two. "You brought that witch to the murder scene in front of journalists." There it was: a picture of Sister Rose being ushered into the home of Sir Francis.

He had forgotten, and now there was hell to pay.

The commissioner went on. "I couldn't care less about her issues with the Papists and her ex-communication. She is not the first in this country to receive the Pope's wrath, but to bring to the public's attention to the fact that you consort with her ilk... Well, you know, Williamson. It makes us look silly," said Mayne.

"My sincerest apologies, Commissioner. I understand that you may have to bring the hammer down, and be assured this lands on my shoulders as the detective in charge. Those boys picked her up on my request, and they weren't given clear instruction to the level of discretion required," explained Dolly.

"Fortunately for you, the Home Secretary is more worried about this gaswerks business. His government is being questioned by the Crown on this matter. Her Majesty's cousin, King Wilhelm, has voiced concerns to her Majesty that the guild alchemists at the works were in danger of immigrants storming the facility. While the rabble is shouting Marxist and unionist slogans, the Home Secretary holds the belief that this is the work of French agitators out to wreck the alliance and cripple the strength of Her Majesty's air fleet. Walpole called me to his home on a Sunday evening—a Sunday evening! I told him you would work this case like you worked the Fenian affair and rooted out those Irish traitors." Mayne didn't handle pressure well.

As far as being inconvenienced on a Sunday, try getting pulled out of bed to look at a withered corpse. "I can do that sir, I plan to go to the Chilton offices to interview the staff, but I can look into the matter at the works afterwards," answered Dolly.

Mayne leaned back and let out a sigh, his shoulders slumping in relief. "Thanks, Williamson."

"I will get Burton and Keane to wander the crowd at the protest and determine if they can spot anything unusual," replied Williamson.

"That's it, action. Eyes and ears on that rabble," Commissioner Mayne confirmed as he pressed up from the desk.

"Sir?"

"Yes, Detective?"

"Could you wire-type the home office and let Walpole know I plan to interview at Chilton House today?"

"Yes, and let London police know you're in their jurisdiction, in case they want to send an escort." Mayne was one for protocol, and the City had its own police.

"I will, sir."

After the detective's briefing, Dolly composed a wire-type and sent it off to the City of London Police. He proposed having a sergeant accompany him on his interviews. The offer was declined. Finally, he grabbed a cup of tea and read the paper. The front-page story was on the growing protests at the new gas plant, Walpole's paramount concern. It was likely the usual rabble looking to use the issue to gain local influence with common folk to raise money for the union or get votes in upcoming elections. He read the story that followed the lithoprint of the gaswerks gates with a crowd of sign-wielding protesters.

The recently commissioned gaswerks on the banks of the Thames is the sole commercial LQ gaswerks outside of Prussia and the site of growing social unrest. As part of the Wessex Alliance, mechanists constructed a mechworks in Prussia to improve Prussian airship design in exchange for construction of a gas plant on British soil. Both guilds would profit from the compact, but Prussia's compulsion to preserve their secrets has left the English worker out in the cold. The guilds agreed only to the terms of a lucrative deal that improves their profits and influence on the condition that the plants were operated without the local workforce. As London fills with hardworking country folk seeking a better wage promised by these industrialists, what they find instead the new jobs at the Badenworks are filled by Prussians hand-picked by the Alchemist Guild. Currently, the Workers United Party and the Commonwealth Communist Union have begun active protests at the plant with a list of grievances. Hieronymus Brood, a borough councilman and one officer of the Workers United Party, did remark when questioned, "Boatloads of immigrants come to London daily from Ireland and the continent with their pockets empty and their heads full of dreams about earning a wage in factory work. Instead, when they get here, what greets them is a locked gate." Are the citizens of the empire more secure now with this plant on our soil, when no Englishman can enter nor learn the Baden Gaswork's alchemical secrets?

He opened the paper, and there it was next to another article about the plant: a picture of Rose Caldwell walking through Sir Lester Chilton's front garden with two constables. Even Dolly was caught in the lithoprint standing at the open door, fortunately too grainy to make out his personage. Above the picture was the headline:

Witch of London Consorts with Metro to Find Phantom Killer, Gerald Welsh

Dolly read on.

In the early hours of the Sabbath, one of London's elite was gruesomely slaughtered in his home through an unexplainable mummification. Sir Lester Chilton was found dead on Sunday morning in Belgravia. Metropolitan Police was unwilling to come on the record as to who they think is behind the act. This reporter witnessed Rose Caldwell, AKA Sister Rose, being brought to the scene to assist the police in their investigation. She was a witness in the 1854 Saint Anthony Rectory Fire and defrocked after accusing the Papal See of covering up a demonic possession. This can only mean that a Phantom Killer is perplexing the police, and they require the help of the devout occultist.

I'll be Welsh's phantom killer. His eyes moved to the next article.

Will Derby's Conservatives let the Wessex Agreement Stand?
Wesley Post

The Baden gaswerks is of vital national interest. Without Luminiferous Quintessence, or LQ gas, the British ironclad fleet, simply put, cannot fly. While our illustrious mechanist guild, headed by top military engineers, is designing a British ironclad air fleet that can keep Emperor Napoleon contained on the continent, there is one chink in that armor: dependence on LQ. The empire is subjected to another tyranny that of the Alchemist Guild with close ties to the Duchy of Prussia. The Alchemist Guild are so possessive of their processes it required direct intervention by her Majesty Queen Victoria to appeal to King Fredrick of Prussia to coerce them to provide a reliable supply on British soil, the concession being a pact to transfer technology as part of the Wessex alliance of mutual defense. How was such a lopsided agreement made? Prussia will learn our mechanical technology, and we get put on the LQ teat of the Alchemists, leaving our national security in the hands of a few privileged Prussians.

He sensed a shadow behind the paper and lowered it to see a young constable standing at his desk. He was fresh to the uniform, maybe eighteen or twenty, more a clerk than a cop at this point in his career.

He smiled at Dolly when acknowledged. "Wire-type for you, sir."

He took the slip of paper and looked at it, noticing it was from a Mr. Simms at Chilton, Chilton, Owens, and Strathmore, letting him know they could see him at ten AM. The detective had less than an hour to get to the financial district.

"Constable, run down to the motor pool and tell whoever the duty sergeant is—"

"It's Sergeant Smith, sir," the blue-eyed lad interrupted.

"Then, tell Smitty that Dolly needs one of his boys, quick around the front to run him over to the city."

The young copper turned and trotted away to the motor pool.

10:00 AM, Chilton House, City of London

Dolly's steam carriage took him across town from the Yard to the offices of Chilton, Chilton, Owens, and Strathmore, known as Chilton House, a three-story office building that was an icon in the city of London and testified to the wealth and power of the investment bank.

As Dolly sat in the passenger seat of the paddy wagon, he read through his notes and research he could dig up on Chilton and speculated about the influential merchant bank and the family that ran it.

Sir Francis's grandfather, John, had established a business syndicating insurance and finances for merchant shipping. He had the soul of a sailor, and through his readiness to move to where commerce took English ships, he became a trusted source of finance for overseas traders. John Chilton personally started the Hong Kong office and toured the East and West Indies, learning about the risks and rewards of maritime trade. He had two boys, Cecil and the younger Erasmus. Erasmus followed into the family trade, and Cecil trained as an engineer. Erasmus, like his father, concentrated on maritime commerce and later expanded into sovereign finance. Erasmus knew how to deliver higher yields through his intimate familiarity with the industry of a nation, growing the firm to rival the great European financial houses.

It was Cecil that persuaded his brother Erasmus that the Boulton-Watt condenser design would gain acceptance through efficiency and that his brother should be the source of capital for the growing mechanization of the empire. Cecil understood that engine power would replace human power and that machines like the Boulton-Watts steam engine could do the work of twenty men without pause. There had been others who had developed steam-powered engines, but this one was different, with a separate condenser, making it more powerful and efficient than the Newcomen engine.

Cecil became a founding member of Her Majesty's Celestial Order of Mechanical Science, commonly known commonly as the mechanist guild. He was conferred the Crystal Gear for lifetime achievement, not because of his mechanical aptitude but for helping the mechanists access the finances for their projects and priming the industrial revolution. The guild helped to organize funding and advance technology by acting as a forum to share theory. By brokering know-how, those in the mechanist guild quickly grasped what worked and what didn't. They also augmented the mechanical sciences with advancements in metallurgy and precision control.

Mechanists were masters of creating powered constructs that could operate with precision and increasing autonomy. But behind the mechanical wizardry was the power of the Chilton financial engine. Without their money, the mechanists would still be tinkering in their garages.

The carriage let out the hiss of bypassing steam as it came to a halt. "Thanks, laddie," said Dolly to the policeman that drove him over.

The attending footman opened the carriage door. Dolly stepped out of the car in front of a plain building reminiscent of Palazzo Medici. A uniformed doorman opened the door for the detective to the magnificent interior of the bank. The spacious lobby was all white, black and pink marble. Inside the door were two private security guards.

Oscar Owens met Detective Williamson in the vestibule. Second generation in the company, Oscar was a partner, just as his father was back when it changed from Chilton Company to Chilton, Chilton, and Owens. He was a corpulent fellow in his later years, jowly with generous side whiskers yet bald. He wore his banker formals with the enhancement of a black armband for the mourning of a named partner. Along with Owens was his personal secretary, again in a black suit and armband.

"Welcome to Chilton House, Detective Williamson. Let me present Mr. Sims, my personal business manager," said Mr. Owens.

"Good afternoon, gentlemen. I wish it were under better circumstances. I hate to be so abrupt but can we start with an inspection of Sir Chilton's personal office?"

Owens gestured towards the stairs. "The merchant banking and partners' offices are on the second floor."

"If you permit, I would like to interview the staff to get a sense for Sir Chilton's movements and any interactions last week," replied Dolly.

"I will attend to you today and can offer a place for you to run interviews. My assistant will get you that list," Owens continued.

"Thank you. It would also help if you could provide me a list of employees that worked regularly with Sir Chilton?"

"Certainly, please follow me, and we will get you settled," replied Owens.

The detective followed Owens up the stairwell. The stairway was unlike any office building he had been in, more like an opera house or palace. "I noticed that you have security at the door."

Owens stopped mid-stride and gestured to the detective. "While we are a merchant bank, we pride on being full-service for our clients. Besides our merchant, industrial and maritime desks, our foreign account settlement desk has its own wire-type room upstairs. They confirm exchange rates on overseas transactions, and many of our wealthy clients use our trust management to keep their incomes. We desire to have a variety of currency to settle accounts for our clients and to allow for cash withdrawals. Therefore, vaults and guards are a necessity."

"Were guards on duty this weekend?" asked Dolly.

"At all times," replied Owens.

"I should like to speak with the guards that worked on Saturday and Sunday," Dolly said, thinking to himself they would have seen Sir Francis if he was in the office over the weekend.

Owens looked to his clerk. "Can you get the schedule to show the detective?"

"Yes, Mr. Owens."

Glass doors separated the stair landing in the lobby from the partner's wing. Inside the glass doors, the decorations changed from the cold open marble halls to the warm and plush tones of mahogany paneling and thick maroon carpet.

Owens led the party down the hall to the partners' suites. The hallway was lined with oil portraits of the partners, starting from the original founders up through contemporary partners. Sir Francis's likeness was draped with a black shroud. Between some of the portraits were offices of key executives.

The hallway ended in a set of double walnut wood doors that Sims opened to let the group into the partner suites.

Club chairs occupied the public space for waiting customers. Getting upstairs to meet a partner was the first challenge. The next line of defense was the three desks of the personal secretaries. Two had gentlemen seated at them that stood at attention when Owens and the group entered the room.

Owens gestured to the shorter of the two men standing at attention. "This is Mr. Healey, Sir Chilton's assistant. Mr. Healey, may I introduce Detective Sergeant Williamson of the Metropolitan Police. He would like to talk with you and look over Sir Francis' office."

"Yes, Mr. Owens," The man only looked up when he spoke. He was visibly upset, and his eyes were red and watery. He glanced at Dolly. "I am here to serve, Sir."

Owen's continued. "Detective, this is Mr. Chalkley, He is the clerk for the other partners that have offices down the hall. Gentlemen, please make the detective comfortable and aid him. Allow him to use the boardroom for his examination of the staff."

Owens then excused himself. "Detective, I have affairs to attend to downstairs."

"I appreciate the accommodations Mr. Owens," replied Dolly. He turned to Healey. "Can I start with a walkthrough of Sir Chilton's office?"

Dolly was reviewing the office of Sir Francis with Healey when there was a knock at the door.

Mr. Sims entered the boardroom with a worried look on his face.

"Detective, we need you in the vaults."

Sims ushered Williamson past a small cluster of clerks and bookkeepers huddled and talking in hushed tones. They were looking towards the rear of the lobby. They passed through the dark wood railing that divided the general lobby from the space where clients met clerks to handle routine transactions like withdrawals. The two men double-timed it down a large center aisle that led past the six desks in two rows and ending in the back of the main hall. The grand hall was filled with the echoes of the two men's clipped steps on the marble floor.

An archway in the marble wall revealed stairs leading down to the vaults. The top and bottom of the stairs had wrought iron gates that were opened. Dolly followed Sims down the stairs and through the gates. The vault area was cooler due to its location in the basement of the bank. The stairs ended in a landing that had a solid marble wall with a brass sign that read "Chilton House Vaults" and additional brass gates to the left and to the right were both open.

"Detective, this way," Sims guided Dolly to the right, "This is the partners' vault."

Mr. Owens was sitting on a chair, sweating profusely, having some kind of attack. His tie was loose and his collar undone.

Dolly looked at Owens. Unable to catch his breath, he just pointed at the vault.

The huge steel vault door was open. The interior walls of the vault consisted of a myriad of different sized doors for lock boxes. In the center of the room was a simple wooden counting table, and on the floor, were two dead guards.

Dolly stepped into the vault to get a closer look. Two guards both shot in the chest. Between the bodies was a Lancaster pistol. Dolly picked up the four-barreled pistol and opened the breach. The receiver lifted the four brass cartridges out of the barrels, and he saw that two of the Adams .45 caliber cartridges were discharged. *The boys never stood a chance.* Dolly looked out the vault. "Sims, call the London Police."

No footprints in the blood. No one had been in the vault since the shooting.

He stepped just once in the large pool of blood to look across the rest of the vault. He surveyed all the lockboxes. Three were open. Two lower ones that could hold a sizable container were empty. A smaller one, about waist-high, contained ledgers and papers. The contents had an even spray of dried blood and flesh fragments from the exit wound of the victims.

Dolly made his way back out of the vault to Owens and crouched down to ask him a question.

Owens spoke. "The guards—I came—I came down to the vaults to retrieve my papers...

and found them."

"Get a doctor," bellowed Sims.

Dolly looked at Owens, smiled and put his hands on his upper arms, "Mr. Owens, take deep breaths. You will get through this." Dolly turned to Sims. "He is in shock and a state of hysteria but unharmed."

The guard interjected, "I was escorting Mr. Owens as that is the procedure when anyone comes down into the vaults. I was standing at the gate when he performed the combination. He asked me to help him open the door as it mighty be heavy for the old man. That's when we saw them, Jack and Freddie, just lying there."

One clerk chimed in, "They were the weekend guards."

Sims added, "This vault is the private vault for the partners. Only full partners have the combination."

"Let's have order," Dolly boomed out. He thought the best he could offer until London arrived was to get the chaos under control. He turned to the guard. "You are on duty, sir, and need to get the vaults cleared of all these people. This is a crime scene."

The young man took the cue. "Alright, alright, all of you upstairs," he said, waving his arms as if he was herding children off a playground.

All Dolly could do now was wait for the London police to come. Chilton House was their jurisdiction. He reached down and untied his boot on the foot he had placed in the blood. No need to track blood all over the crime scene.

Today would be a long day.

TUESDAY, THE 8TH OF JUNE

10:00 AM, WALTZING PELICAN

Dolly was set to meet Keane at the Waltzing Pelican at ten am. He grabbed a carriage to a nearby neighborhood, then strolled to the tavern from there. He learned it easier to blend into the public walking than driving.

The air in this part of the city was acrid and gritty. The four smokestacks of the gaswerks billowed exhaust from the boilers and gas crackers across the river from Woolrich. Below the haze of smog was the largest London industrial estate made up of the industries supporting Lloyd & Sons Mechwerks, the Baden Gaswerks, and the London Airship Works and Aerodrome.

Lloyd and Sons owned the aerodrome and were awarded the contract to construct the HMS Victoria, the empire's first air-dreadnought. The hull had been laid three years ago and now the world's largest ironclad airship was to be christened in less than a year by Her Majesty.

Dolly's British pride swelled when he peered up to see the

activity on the colossal ship resting in the construction scaffolding. The ship dominated the skyline in this part of the city and that was a feat considering the scale of the mechwerks and gaswerks. His plan was to meet Keane, get his report, then walk the perimeter of the Baden Gaswerks before his meeting with Commander Michael Penfold, the engineering liaison to the Her Majesty's air service and the commander of the project.

The young police officer was in admiration of what this modern world of industry was producing. In his lifetime, he had witnessed his countrymen tame the power of steam, send messages over wires and tap into the eldritch elements. He took one more glance up, watching the workmen rivet and solder a hundred feet above his head before stepping into the dimly lit Waltzing Pelican.

The Pelican was a shift bar. It was convenient to the industrial estate and ranged from the extremes of empty to full based on the changing shifts at the adjacent mills and factories.

Keane was standing at the bar. He was a tall man and looked bigger in his glen plaid suit. For the past few days he had been milling about the crowd that were congregating at the front gates of the works.

Dolly sidled next to him but acted as if he did not recognize him, facing forward at the racks of bottles and the tap handles. Keane smelled sweaty and of tobacco smoke.

"Well, what do you make of it?" asked Dolly.

"What I make of it is this. I've been up all night watching the plant while you were sleeping in the cozy cottage of yours."

The barkeep came up to Dolly, "What you having, mate?"

"A pint and a pickled egg," Dolly threw a coin on the counter, "and a beer for this grumpy fella here."

As the bartender turned aside to pull a draft. Keane spoke, "There's about seventy-five to a hundred bodies around the gates. I noticed two Marxists there stirring people up," Keane continued in a mocking whining tone. "It's the same old bollocks that the guilds are running the working man out of a living. None of the fellas are the type to take pay for this. They're true devotees of the struggle for the common man shit."

"Any of your Fenian brothers?" asked Williamson.

"Not that I could see, but there was no shortage of Irish in the mob." Keane changed the subject, "I heard you paraded that faithless witch through Belgravia."

Dolly took a gulp of his pint, "Ah. I did." Then sucked the beer foam from his mustache.

"You believe that hokum," asked Cullam Keane.

"When I was ten, it was fantasy that a man could fly. Now there are flying ships full of men, so I reserve my judgment on the fantastic and unimaginable. As far as Rose Caldwell is concerned, she was not excommunicated for evil works. She left the church because of what she was prepared to do to stop evil." Dolly finished his egg and washed it down with the last of his pint and sauntered out of the tavern.

It would be a matter of time once he was at the works that he would be identified. Any of the Marxists knew of him from him questioning them after an arrest; others would recognize him from his appearance in the tabloids.

Dolly walked the perimeter of the plant to see if there was any additional access to the plant and to confirm Keane's count of protesters.

The site was enveloped by a formidable stone wall. He could only see in to the works at street grade when the iron gates broke the wall at the midpoint of each side. The protesters were in several clusters: a main group with signs picketing the main gate, then more along the road that wrapped around the perimeter of the wall. There were crowds milling about at all the other gates.

As he made his way around, he came to the same conclusion as Keane; about eighty protesters, with roughly twenty at each gate. The street that circled the plant wall had three perpendicular roads that connected directly to the south, east and west gates. As he approached the east gate, he heard his name yelled.

"Williamson, you come to support the common man?"

He had been recognized, but could not make out who it was yet, so he kept walking.

"Brothers, here comes Detective Sergeant Frederick Williamson." It was Nelson Bruce, a union activist that had worked to get better conditions in the dye mills. A true believer.

Dolly walked up to the communist. "Mr. Bruce, we will not have any trouble here, will we?"

"Sergeant, we need to make sure the grievances of the workers are heard by the foreign task masters." Nelson was making sure that the others heard his propaganda.

"These Hun alchemists need to have proper oversight. Look, if British boiler men were running the works, you wouldn't see smokestacks spouting that shit into the sky. How do we know this plant isn't put here to poison us all?" The last comment of Nelson elicited some grumbling from the men.

Dolly, keeping pace with Nelson, took out his pipe and packed it with tobacco, then lit it. "Now Nelson," Dolly spoke between puffing his pipe to a bright glow. "I will leave you in charge here," another puff, "so if things go awry, I'll make sure you're the first one hauled in and the last to go home."

"I cannot be held responsible for the actions of our countrymen when faced with injustice," replied Nelson.

"Nelson, let your fellas know that the Home Secretary has asked me to keep an eye out for seditious rabble rousers. Now you and I both know that all you want is to get each of your comrades work at a fair wage. But if you were to fall under the influence of foreign powers with plans to sabotage works vital to the crown and cause mayhem to disrupt those works, I would have to bring in my boys to crack all your fucking heads open to get those radical thoughts out of your brain. It would be the right thing to do to get the foreign poison out of your skulls."

Nelson and Dolly just stared at each other. Dolly puffed on his pipe.

Nelson broke the silence. "Wire-type received, Sergeant."

Dolly took out his watch to check the time. Everything was on schedule. He had just enough time to walk over to the aerodrome gate and check in for his appointment with the commander.

~

11:10 AM, Lloyd & Sons Aerodrome

Commander Penfold was at the gate waiting for the detective. "Let me welcome you to Lloyd's Mechwerks and Aerodrome, the home of the most technologically advanced airship in the world," said the sandy haired airman. Dolly estimated him to be eight to ten years older than him, yet young to be a commander. "Thank you, Commander. I wanted to discuss the security of the facility with you, and if possible, get a tour."

"Well, Detective, let me ask you a question. Do you have a fear of heights?" asked the jovial British officer.

"I would have to say I have not had an issue to date, but I surmise you're asking me before we go up there" said Dolly as he craned his neck to look up at the behemoth ship.

"Spot on, Detective. If you are amenable to great heights, I will show you Her Majesty's greatest achievement to date, and it is quite a good vantage point to reconnoiter this plant and even peak into the neighbor's yard," Penfold said with a wink and a click of his tongue.

"Well, let's give it a go," replied the detective, with a mix of excitement to get the tour and mild apprehension as to what he would be like at those heights.

"That's the spirit. Follow me." The two men made their way into the plant and to a verticulator. "Detective Williamson, today you will be exposed to many 'first of its kinds.' I hope you will not be jaded by the end of the tour. Here is the first of our wonders, the world's longest continuous verticulator."

The man inside the verticulator car opened the accordion door to give the two men access. "Cecil, please take us up to the engineering deck," said Penfold.

"Step on in, gents," said Cecil, a young boy who sat on a stool next to the controls for the verticulator.

The gate crashed closed. Cecil pushed a button, then threw a lever. Dolly could hear the dynamo whir under the car then the cables jerk up. The verticulator shaft for the first fifty feet had a wood casing that blocked the view. Once they cleared the casing, the car was completely exposed to the elements, except for the wire cage that made it structure. Dolly was in awe of the panorama of London the lift provided.

"Detective, the HMS Victoria will be the First Ship of the Line for the European fleet, with over two hundred guns and a crew of six hundred sixty airmen. Where the HMS Warrior had a length of five hundred and eighty feet, the structure of the Victoria would be eleven hundred feet bow to stern.

"To make this project possible, we are working closely in conjunction with the mechanists and have been commissioning mechanist engineers into the Air Service. I am an example. Before my coming into the Air Service I trained as an engineer in Birmingham, then chartered as a guild member after my apprenticeship. My specialty is pumping and compression, but here I am, more of a project manager than a tinkerer."

Soon, the view was obstructed again as the verticulator entered the scaffolding sections, and they whizzed by floor after floor of workers that were crawling all over the ship. The elevator stopped hard, and Cecil opened the cage. "Hard to imagine you are one hundred and eighty feet in the air," said Cecil.

Penfold continued his tour. "This is the heart of the ship, the compression room, and why we were able to leapfrog the Prussian zeppelin design. Rather than having gasbags housed within a cloth and metal frame, the HMS Victoria, like its smaller sister ship, the HMS Warrior, has pressurized spherical gas cells and the ship uses Mechanist Envenrude L. Pruflek's vapor compression ballast system. This innovation allows the ship to store a supply of LQ gas in a compressed state to function as ballast. Then the gas is pumped and put to a vapor state in the cells to cause flotation. The process makes the airship far more agile. Coal-powered steam-driven propellers provide propulsion, but the gas can be rebalanced between cells and ballast tanks to change pitch yaw and altitude. Follow me this way."

Penfold took Dolly up a set of stairs to the midline of the ship where he felt more like he was in a large production brewery than a ship. As far as he could see were giant brass domes. "Detective, here you see thirty-two brass cells. Each is twenty-two feet in diameter, distributed on a horizontal iron superstructure. With separate cells, the loss of integrity on up to ten cells would not ground the ship."

The two men walked along the midline gangways. Dozens of workers moved about on them, welding, riveting and sawing.

Now Dolly was feeling a little squeamish with the heights. He was the highest he had ever been, with only the rail of the midline walkways to stop him from falling hundreds of feet to his death. He could see the whole city, and more importantly, he could see the layout of the Baden works and the groupings of protesters clustered around the four gates.

"Commander, would it be possible for us to put some officers up here to watch those gates?" asked Dolly.

"That, Detective, is an interesting question. You see, I am here as the Air Service Liaison, a guest on the Lloyds property, while they build the ship. While they need to make me and my inspectors happy for us to accept the ship, this is their property, so you would need to ask the owners or do whatever you gents do through the court."

This would be an excellent place to watch from, but he would have to have Commissioner Mayne pursue the matter. At the very least, he needed to get Sargeant Aekins up here for the bird's eye view, and to assess how he saw the situation on the ground.

Penfold went back to his tour. "Now, armor runs from the top decks to the midline walkways. Then the lower armor runs from the bottom of the catwalk to the lower decks, creating a true ironclad airship. While upper and lower decks are traditional one-inch cold-rolled iron plate, the armor that spans the cells is Professor Honeysuckle's iron webbing. Touch it, Detective."

"It's flexible, not rigid," said Dolly.

"Exactly, Honeysuckle, an American inventor migrated to England by invitation of the guild, he has advanced a mechanical process to generate huge sheets of chain mail coated in hemp and vulcanized rubber to give added protection. Very light, and the flexibility dissipates impact," Penfold added.

"Of course, the discovery of Luminiferous Quintessence, the lightest of the eldritch elements, changed airship design and eliminates the risk of explosion that came with using earthly elements like hydrogen, and that plant is our only source. I have been up here watching the Huns, and it's clear as day to me that, just as I am spying on them, they are looking up at me."

"There will be no ship with more or superior ordnance. Holding over two hundred guns and thirty-two tubes for drop bombs, she can outmaneuver smaller ships and outgun any airship, but without that gas, this is just a junk pile on stilts." said the Commander. "Let me show you the wheelhouse and navigation." Dolly followed the Commander through bulkheads, hallways stairwells and gangways, a complex maze to the destination of the bridge of the ship.

"So here is another first. This ship has the latest version of the Trigonometric Solution Register, a mechanical calculator that develops firing solutions for the gun batteries, and this is mechanically linked to the Astronomical and Solar Gyrosynchronous Navigator. Two amazing mechanist inventions that facilitate the navigation of the airship and automatic resolution of gun targeting," explained Penfold.

Dolly looked about, but he couldn't make heads or tails of all the gauges and registers that made up the bridge.

Penfold now began to paint a picture as they looked out the large forward-facing window of the bridge with Dolly standing behind the ship's wheel. "Think about this, Detective Williamson. From a distance, her rifled top deck gun turrets hold steady on a target as the TrigSol adjusts the guns in synchrony with the rapid moves you make at this wheel. GyroNav and the gas compression flotation system allow you to outmaneuver, and the TrigSol to outgun, your enemies. After destroying an enemy air fleet, you then could rise high over a metropolis and annihilate the populace with drop bombs and mortars, while ground-based guns would never achieve the altitude she could obtain." There was a perverse pride in the commander's eyes as he painted the picture of the havoc the ship would wreak.

"Very impressive, Commander. I can see now the importance of your work, and the amazing job you're all doing. While I will talk with my superiors about the protesting at the works across the road, might I suggest that you reach out to your superiors to see about a detachment of Royal Marines to be quartered here or at a bare minimum to come up here and provide a tactical assessment for you?" suggested Dolly.

"Good idea, man! You know I am no warrior. I came into this service as an engineer, but I do know a good plan and smart execution will win the day."

Dolly thought how he would love to get shifts of constables up here with telescopes to watch the crowd for trouble.

2:00 PM, Gilchrist Manor

The steam coupe Sister Rose drove belonged to Weng Lo. It was the latest model fabricated by Swift Carriage Company, capable of a top speed of forty miles per hour. There were only a few places where you could let the carriage out at full throttle in the city, but there were many places on these country roads where Rose could let the red and electro-chrome speedster show its paces.

Rose needed Preston Gilchrist's guidance and the poet rarely left his home. When he did it was to go to the asylum. Rose was one of the few people Preston enjoyed seeing or at least let in the mansion. The manor house also contained the largest library of arcana in England, maybe even in the world. It contained shelves of texts that had not been together since the grand library of Alexandria and many more composed since then by eastern and western scholars, dissecting ancient works or striking out into other fields of study. She could access the millions of pages written in hundreds of tongues, some not utilized in millennia. The library's proprietor had dedicated his existence to exploring and interpreting what the tomes held.

The county road to the mansion was long and straight. Rose opened her up whilst keeping an eye on the boiler temperature and the water level, along with the speedometer. The first two held steady as the last one climbed. She rolled along at thirty-two miles per hour.

As she reached the manor, she engaged the clutch, throttled the steam exhaust, and administered the brake, bringing the car to a moderate speed and making the corner into the drive. She suddenly threw the throttle and let off the clutch. Gears engaged, and the coupe shot down the gravel drive, spitting a wake of gravel. The trees that flanked the driveway whizzed by as the cool air rushed over the windscreen and through her hair. Going this fast, Rose had no occasion to contemplate anything but driving the car—freedom.

As she neared the residence and the parkway in front, the clutch was pushed to the floor, the steam throttle released, and she dampered the burners. Once stopped, she flung open the door and skipped out. The scene was sight to see. The raven-haired lass in brown calf-high boots and airmen pants standing next to the sleek two-seater. She wore a sapphire-hued and brown brocade waistcoat over a navy silk and baleen bustier. Rose pulled her wind goggles down around her neck, then tussled the road dust out of her hair.

A harried footman jogged to greet her, falling tardy of his duty of opening the coupe door for the driver.

"M'lady, do you have any bags?" he asked.

"Just the one. Could you also fill the bin with pulverized coal and keep an eye on her while the boiler cools? Thank you,"

Her athletic strides took her across the parkway as she removed her driving gloves, tucking them in her belt.

The chief butler was at the front step. "Ms. Caldwell, it is a pleasure to have you back at Gilchrist. How long will you be staying?"

"Just today, William. Let me guess. Preston is in the library?" inquired Rose as she looked up at the large elderly man.

Willian Brentwood stepped sideways and signaled with his hand for Rose to enter. Once in the vestibule, she strolled past the stoic-looking footman waiting at attention, with his white-gloved hands remaining at his sides. She glanced at him and guessed he might be new at the house and unfamiliar with her demeanor at Gilchrist manor. This was one of the few places where the landowner was perhaps weirder than her.

Walking down the hall, past the drawing room and turning left to enter the library, Rose noted how spotless and desolate the chambers looked. Nothing out of place. When she reached the door, she twisted the handle, hoping it would be unlocked, but the door was latched. "Preston, it is Rose and we have work to do." She turned and leaned her back against the door, waiting.

Brentwood was standing at attention. "He has been in there for over a week."

"Have a hearty lunch prepared with some fresh orange juice and his laudanum. I will bring him back. Promise," She gave him a smile as she unbuttoned her tunic.

"Thank you, m'lady." Brentwood turned to leave as the library door unlatched. He proceeded downstairs to the kitchen.

She turned and slowly opened the door to the library. It was dark. Preston had blacked out all the windows with draperies and sat naked on the oriental carpet with an oil lamp, books, and papers surrounding him.

"Doesn't the wool of the rug make your bum itch?" Rose asked as she closed the door behind her, latching it. Rose looked around the chamber to get her bearings. She stepped closer into the aura of the oil lamp. Preston had the *Tome of Daemonology*, *Jaharudin's Verses of Other Domains*, and the *Third Grimoire of Ashrok* open along with undecipherable scrolls he was feverishly reading and cross-referencing from book to book. In the eyes of her beloved church, there were multiple acts of heresy and blasphemy occurring in front of her. She could not fathom how he could read so many languages, some being forgotten or other worldly.

"Preston, Preston," she called.

No response.

"Azul Hassan," Rose yelled.

Preston turned and peered at her. "Ah, how splendid to see you again, Sister," answered Preston in English with a heavy Arabic accent.

"Azul, you need to take a rest. You are wearing out this body," said Rose.

Preston stared at his hands then noticed he was naked in the presence of a lady. "Sister, my sincerest apologies. My condition is improper." He stood, covering his privates and made his way to an armchair, where he had dropped his dressing gown. Preston donned the robe then turned to greet Rose. "My dear Sister, you see how I get engrossed in my research."

"I do, Azul. But I need Preston back to consult. Can you get him back here?" Rose now held Preston's hands in hers, and looking down on them, they were covered in ink stains from writing and dust from the tomes.

"What is it? Maybe I can be of aid," said Azul.

"You may. But I was expecting to talk to Preston." It wouldn't be quite as easy to bring him back. She decided she would have to work with what she had and continued to talk with Azul.

"Azul Hassan, I presume you are familiarized with the practices of the Necromancer?"

"I am well-versed. I have read the texts of the necronist and the classic and ancient, such as the scrolls of Osiris."

"Have you seen this?" she pulled out an illustration she had drawn up from memory of the totem she saw at the Chilton town house.

Preston stared at the drawing. "Very curious." He was lost in thought, looking at the sketch and shuffling towards his book case.

Rose looked to the sill of the door and saw Brentwood's signal that he was ready and waiting outside: a simple sheet of writing paper under the transom. Rose walked to the exit and released the latch, peeking out. There stood the butler and two servants with trays. She opened the door. Brentwood hurried to get the first tray into her hands. She set it on the floor inside the office, then grabbed the second tray. Without saying a word, she spun around and used her backside to push the door closed. It shut loudly, and that startled Preston. "What are you up to?" challenged Azul with a belligerent tone laced with paranoia.

"Just lunch. I am ravenous," stated Rose.

"Very well," reacted the alter ego of Preston.

Rose put the tray down on the desk and lifted the plate covers. Potato soup and roast beef sandwich with pickled beet. She took a bite of the sandwich then placed it on the plate. She was famished. Her situation left her without means, and that meant she did not get regular meals, let alone veggies and fresh baked bread.

Preston shifted the bookcase ladder and then ascended the ladder, bringing down several volumes. He sat at the desk and turned on the desk arc lamp. This was an excellent sign. Her friend didn't seem to acknowledge his arbitrary action of turning on the electricity in the room, more intent on examining the book he had in front of him than consideration for Azul's fear of modernity. Rose sauntered over to the second tray and picked it up. This tray had the laudanum bottle on it. She palmed the vial before picking up the tray and setting it on the other side of the large desk.

Preston flipped through the pages, reading in some language that Rose could not identify. She lifted the lid off the other tray and ate, watching Preston page through the text. Certain he was absorbed in research, she put a dropper full of laudanum in the orange juice, a healthy dose.

"Azul Hassan, when did you eat last?"

Preston looked up, befuddled, then smiled "I don't recall."

"Here is some fresh juice." She handed him the glass. He accepted it and set it down on the desk, absorbed with his inquiry.

"Here it is. The—the—the totem is...used in the Pwen Hanan by a hougan in a Voodoo ritual of soul capture." He pointed in the book at an engraving of five different totems, one appearing very much like Rose's sketch.

"Ooh, where did you see this? What you drew here?" said Preston, wide-eyed and in his heavy accent, pounding his finger on Rose's drawing.

"In London. Along with a body stripped of life."

Preston picked up the orange juice and took a big gulp, followed by a thirst-quenching sigh. "Look right here, in Dr. Melbourne's *Journal of West Indies Pagan Practices and Incantations*, he interviewed a Voodoo hougan priest that claimed to use such an apparatus to absorb the spirit out of an individual and trap it in a gourd." He looked up. "Imagine your soul sputtering around in a gourd. How crude is that?" Preston said in an English inflection.

Rose picked up her glass of juice and said, "To keeping our souls out of gourds."

Preston clinked her glass and took another swig.

Rose followed suit. "What were you working on before I came in for your help?"

A befuddled Preston followed Rose's gaze to the tomes on the floor. "Oh, that I need to get free from an Iz Hauwl labyrinth on the fourteenth astral plane. I am researching how to construct the labyrinth, hoping that it leads to me finding weaknesses in an existing one." Preston smiled at his own ingenuity.

Rose directed him back to her pressing matter, the object that killed Chilton. "I see. Does the book there tell you what the priest does with the soul?"

He looked back to Melbourne's *Journal* and read, "Soul

witchery by a hougan can either enslave the target soul or imbue it unto another. You say you found this here in London?"

"I did. I was asked to consult on a case of a wealthy Englishman who was found dead. The body drained of all spiritual energy to the point the physical body withered and mummified," said Rose, reading over Preston's shoulder to see if she could pick anything up. For once it was a book written in English.

"Voodooism is interesting because it is influenced by Western religion, but the manipulation of the arcane is primal. Very primitive, a derivative of Azande witchcraft and like all witchcraft and shamanism, rudimentary in understanding the metaphysics, but powerful in manipulating the raw energy," said Preston.

Rose sensed Preston's intellect pushing through. "What could a witch doctor, or what did you call it a hou—"

"Hougan. It's a Voodoo term for a high-level practitioner. We can assume this person is proficient."

"Can you figure out what they are doing with the souls?"

"That may be a stretch to determine the purpose. What I can say is your essence, your soul is your being beyond the me and I of the material world. It attaches to a mortal form until death. Some of us learn how to detach and return; that is projection. If you can tap into the soul of another, you can control the mortal form, transfer the spectral form, or convert the soul essence to the raw energy of the aether. There is a good description in the *Hygromanteia*, or *The Magical Treatise of Solomon*." Preston spun in his swiveled chair and grabbed a book from the shelf immediately behind where he sat. "I keep a copy close at hand as it's such a fine reference guide." He set the book down and flipped through the pages then stopped as if he had lost his train of thought. Preston looked up from the book with a bewildered look.

"Rose, what are you doing here?"

"Preston?"

"Yes… Oh dear, have I been away again?"

WEDNESDAY, THE 9TH OF JUNE

9:00 AM, CHILTON HOUSE

Mr. Sims had wire-typed Dolly that items were missing from the vault.

Dolly returned to Chilton House with the local London sergeant. It was agreed that Dolly would take the lead on the inquiry.

Dolly found himself in the Board Room at Chilton House again, this time interviewing each of the partners.

At this moment, attending were Mr. Sims, and the partners Owens and Lester Chilton, Sir Francis's eldest heir. It would be one of many interviews that day to gather statements and substantiate claims.

"In the wire-type Mr. Sims sent on June 8th, it was noted that an inventory was taken of the vault and contents were missing," began Dolly.

"I had each partner review what contents they had in storage along with items that were in trust to the firm and kept in the partner strong room. While I could not be certain what else may be missing there was—"

Lester interrupted Sims. "Get to the point man. The detective does not require your foppery. He demands answers," Dolly was thinking what the new baronet said out loud.

Lester took over from Sims. "Twenty thousand pounds' sterling of gold guineas are gone. My father raised funds for the Duke of Wellington's expedition into the Pyrenees in 1812. The Crown floated bonds to pay the troops, and we managed the syndication of the bonds. Our fee was five thousand pounds' sterling, and a condition was that payment be in the same way as payment for the troops: gold coins. The value of the gold has increased to be worth twenty thousand pounds at current gold prices. That is what was plundered."

Dolly was struggling to imagine how much gold that was. "Is it common practice to hold that much currency?"

Lester smirked while taking the folder from Sims and pushing to the side of the table Dolly sat. "Detective, Chilton House is the preeminent merchant bank in the world. That is what we keep in the partner's vault. Our other strong room is four times the capacity and holds much more cash and gold."

Dolly opened the binder and thumbed through the accounts. Some of the items he did not recognize, but some of them he knew and could postulate the value. He was gob-smacked by the fortune in that room. "What was lifted from the smaller lock box?"

"The gun," replied Lester. "My dad kept the pepper box in there in the event he was forced to open the vault and could turn the pistol on his assailants."

"Who knew about the pistol?" Dolly asked.

Lester, Owens and Sims looked at each other. Owens spoke up "I would think he told every partner. It was your admission into the inner circle of the partnership when you were granted space in the partner's strong room. Sir Francis and I did the honors of teaching a new partner the combination. Francis would go to that drawer and show them the gun and proclaim that he would go down shooting before he would let burglars steal from Chilton House."

"How much would all the gold weigh?" Dolly finally asked.

"Around four hundred pounds. The gold was packed in ten canvas coin bags," answered Lester.

"So, several trips or several men," Dolly pondered aloud. "And nothing else was missing?"

"That is what was shared with me, Detective," replied Sims. Dolly stared at Lester first then made eye contact with Owens and Sims. "If there was anything else that went amiss, either intimate or something that you or a client may have that was incriminating or humiliating, I need to know. Let all the partners know, and if there is something, they can come in confidence."

Lester queried, "Detective, are you suggesting any of our partners are blackmailers?"

"Mr. Chilton, I have your father's murder to solve. I will collect the evidence to convict the murderer and send them to the gallows. Nine other detectives and I must deal with the whole of London. You're fortunate to have powerful associates that will keep this case a priority, because I can tell you from experience, there will be ten more murders on my desk before this one is closed.

"Now. I suspect that your father was murdered to cover up

who took the gold. It is a substantial fortune and gold can be melted and struck as bullion and moved to the continent or abroad. If it's that simple, fine, but I never seem to get the simple ones, and I have questions that are hounding me. Things just are not adding up.

"For example, who knows about this gold? It's been in your custody for what—forty-seven years? Has it always been in those strong boxes and in those bags, or did Sir Francis move it or have an occasion to talk about his bags of gold in the safe?

"The thieves knew which boxes to open and had no intent in any of the other boxes." Dolly leaned back to read the paper in front of him. "Such as box 116 with two hundred 500-pound banknotes. I bet that could fit in just one of those canvas bags. Why this vault and not the other one that you say has more cash in it? Could the robbers have forced your father to open that vault?"

"No, he only has one combination. The vault managers also have to enter a combination," replied Sims.

Dolly nodded. "Interesting. So they either knew that, or they were specifically looking to only access the partners' vault, and that brings me back to how I may have impugned your character. I need to know if there were compromising documents to be certain that the gold isn't a red herring for me to chase. If there were documents that were held in there of the type I mentioned, then that is the motive, not the gold.

"So I get to spend all day going through your employment rolls and interviewing your staff, meaning I'll be here for quite some time and if you think of anything, please come back and let me know," said Dolly.

"Are you done with us, Detective?" asked Owens.

"Thank you for your cooperation. Can I see the vault managers next?"

Sims answered, I will have him come up."

The three men got up and left.

As Lester and Sims left the board room, Sims followed Lester into his office.

"What is it Sims?"

Sims closed the door and spoke in a hushed tone. "Sir, I suggest you go out to the manor for a few days of rest and contemplation."

"What are you talking about, man? I have made arrangements for my father's service here and must pick up his portfolio of business before the Rothchilds or Peabody Morgan stick their noses in the trough."

"The floor safe in the shooting lodge, sir. That is where your father kept the black files. I was not entrusted with the combination, but he directed me when you took over that you should know about those files."

Lester sat down, exhaling. "Black files? What are you on about, Sims? He never told me of the strong box. I don't know the combination or its whereabouts."

"Maybe something will come to you, something he shared so you could open the safe. Sir, I hope that you are not so naive to think that, given the influence of this firm, we wouldn't have access to other's secrets."

"Sims, I'm not a fool," returned Lester. He recognized that his enterprise had influence and exposure to state and personal secrets. He certainly couldn't imagine that his father would use someone's secrets to extort them.

Sims left the office. He wanted to see what was in the black files and how he might employ them. More so he now realized from Lester's reaction that he was not party to his father's treachery.

~

10:00 AM, Gilchrist Manor

Preston lay in the tub. Rose sponged his back. She remained overnight to nurse Preston back to this world.

Preston didn't talk much after these episodes; it took all his faculties to stay focused and present, or he would drift off and Azul would be return. He fixed on his breathing, the sensation of the sponge on his neck and the water streaking down his back.

Preston's thoughts strayed again until he realized Rose caught him gazing at the looking-glass on the wall above the sink.

"What are you staring at?" Rose inquired. He had been gazing at her image in the mirror. She was in a chiffon nightgown, and he could see the silhouette of her athletic body and the black markings of glyphs she had tattooed on her skin as wards.

"The mirror. Sometimes when I go away, when I accept his power and knowledge, I no longer see light reflected in this world but the reflection of the spectral from other planes of reality on the surface of mirrors." Preston finished and had a thought. Just before it flew into his conscious mind, he had to act. Preston twisted to look at Rose, accidentally splashing her with water and making the night gown see through. It clung to her breasts.

"Rose, sanctuary."

She had only moments to act as everything Preston experienced, or thought would likely be perceived by Azul and potentially used against them. Rose rushed out of the lavatory.

Preston focused his mind on the process of astral projection and the use of a gemulet as an astral sanctuary. By thinking through the theory and practice, he would push out the thoughts he had to share with Rose and keep them from his dark passenger, Azul.

He worked through the steps to create an aetherial sanctuary. First, you required a gemulet struck in a precious metal enclosing an aether stone or crystal containing eldritch gas. This would create a tiny bubble of the aether to structure the sanctuary, for the users meet in, away from the mortal world but paradoxically still here. Rose had created one under Preston's instruction a few years ago. Next, you needed a pool of water. The gemulet would be submerged in the water, and the travelers would then immerse a part of themselves as well. Tinctures would be added to improve conductivity of the spirit through the water to the gemulet. Then you would need to recite the incantation.

The words were available in several tomes, *Liber Loagaeth*, *The Book of Soyga*, the fourth book of *Occult Philosophy*, or the *Hygromanteia*. The incantation was fairly pedestrian the final piece was to make a secondary connection outside of the fluid. The ritual would allow the practitioners to project their spiritual forms into the aether to slip between the threads of this material world to another dimension. Variations of this were used for hundreds of years, by just about every metaphysical sect as a way to commune across time and space.

What Preston and Rose were about to do was entry level astral projection, where their spiritual essence, the true beings they were beyond the concepts of the I, would go to a secure location. A place where Preston could speak freely to Rose without Azul reading his mind.

Rose scrambled back to the tub. Preston was gesturing her to go quicker with his hands.

Rose dropped her equipment belt to the floor to have two hands to open the box. It was a mitered puzzle box and required multiple movements to twist, turn, and open sides before the locked chamber opened to free the gemulet. The circular metal object was five inches in diameter with glyphs on both sides and a crystal in the center. That crystal was an interdimensional safe room. Rose threw the object in the tub where it sank to the bottom.

Unclasping the latches on her roll, she drew out two tinctures, confirmed the substances of the vials, then dumped both in the tub. It was a lot of water; more tincture was better.

Preston reached into the water to blend the eldritch soup while Rose stepped into the tub with him. Standing in the water that went up about mid-shin on Preston, they embraced to make the secondary connection and murmured the enchantment into each other's ear.

Preston was in the library at Cambridge standing in front of Rose. Rose was in the garden of her childhood home with Preston since neither had gone to the trouble of building a construct within the gemulet, they would both perceive the space in their own way. Most practitioners craft a room or private space where they would reside during the projection. Both were physically still in Preston's home standing in tepid bath water, but they had projected into the astral nexus point in the crystal and through the nexus point to another dimension. Now what they discussed would not be available to Azul Hassan.

Preston spoke. "You delivered the missing piece last night. The Mumbo priest has a ritual to slave a soul to an object. We can use that to help me,"

"Whoever this person is, they are a murderer and being pursued by me and the metropolitan police," said Rose.

"The cops will never find the witch doctor without your help," replied Preston. "Find the hougan and see if a bargain can be struck. You're a clever girl, Rose. See if you can barter services or pinch the ritual. Then, next time, Ol' Hasan sneaks out, you can suck him out."

"I must get back to London," said Rose as she thought about how she might find the Voodooist and negotiate a deal to learn a sacred ritual.

Preston stepped away, reflecting on his plan. "This will mean betrayal of Azul and cost us some of my capacity to decipher and understand the works of Arcana," mused Preston.

"How is stopping a dead Sufi Mystic from occupying your body treachery? He deceived you, if you have forgotten?" said Rose.

It was in the library at Cambridge where Preston found the journals of Azul bin Hassan Tazziz Faroq al Jani Djin. He translated the works, captivated by the mystic's accounts of traveling to new planes of reality through astral projection. Preston thought the book to be imagination, a work of fiction, but shortly after reading it, he became conscious of a spirit guide. Azul himself. It began as a thought, then a voice. Preston now had him in his mind. He was certain he was going mad, not that he hallucinated, but he heard the voice. Then there was a trickling in of wisdom from beyond his conscious and vivid dreams of an ancient occultist's life over six hundred years ago.

The more time he devoted with the tome, the sharper this other worldly spirit was within him. He could now comprehend ancient tongues dead for centuries. This knowledge led to unlocking more secrets and details of the mystic's adventures. Preston became obsessed and roamed the world, solving Azul's puzzles. Each riddle revealed more of the mystic's code. What remained was the last of Azul's puzzle, requiring Preston to go to Serapeum, the daughter library to the great library of Alexandria. There he decoded the final chapter of Azul's tome. It offered an incantation that Preston was deceived into thinking would allow him to project astrally like Azul, but instead, it released Azul's spirit from the book and bound it to Preston.

"While he deceived me into sharing my body, he instructed me how to examine other worlds and gave me the awareness of the true nature of the universe. I found a reasonable arrangement in his educating me while he looks for a way to free himself. What I cannot endure is the wreckage he has left behind. My entire family thinks I'm bonkers, and when I'm back, my body is left like a used dish towel. I've had enough, and we can use this priest to trap him," said Preston.

"What if you perish and become trapped in his prison?"

"It's not like that, Rose. I am constantly in here a little, but he shoves me into his maze. That is how it works. Little by little, as I draw on our common pool of learning, he gets stronger until I feel like I am in a dream I can't wake up from,"

They both knew the field was weakening. It was time to go back.

"Scarlet cherub," said Rose.

"What?" replied Preston.

"If I learn and can conduct the ritual, that will be my cue to you. When I say it you need to be ready to come back and grab hold of this body."

"Agreed. You always make me smile, Rose. I surmise, though, that when the best time comes to extract Azul, I will be too far gone to communicate with. Lost in the darkest recesses of the maze where I dwell during the possessions."

When the embrace broke, both opened their eyes, and they were back in the United Kingdom, standing in a tub of water.

Preston stared at her and held her face gently.

"You two are up to your silly games again," Preston said in his Arab dialect.

FRIDAY, THE 11TH OF JUNE

9:00 PM, ALBIE'S SUPPER CLUB

Dolly loved their payday custom. Keane and Williamson would draw their salary and head to the bathhouse for a proper soaking, then drop off their dirty clothes at the laundry. Freshly bathed Dolly had on a new twill suit, a blue shirt with a rounded collar and a ribbon cravat that the tailor told him was the fashionable trend. From there, the two continued to supper at Albie's on chops and roast veggies with a brown gravy, washed down with a frothy ale. They talked about life and sometimes shop.

They were an odd pair; Williamson, a Scot and Protestant, and Keane, an Irishman and ardent Catholic, but they were Metropolitan police detectives first.

"I received a letter from my brother today," mentioned Keane.

"The one in Minnesota?"

"He is officially now in the United States. Minnesota became a state."

"And you're still planning on moving there?"

"Fucking right, I am. No little cottage in this wicked city for me. I live light, and I've been saving for my stake in a business in America."

"Callum, you're a city dweller, mate. You can't live out in the wilderness. There are savages and wolves out there."

"We don't have those here? It's the mathematics of risk and reward, mate. Here I get paid eight pound a week as a detective in the most cosmopolitan city in history, and all I deal with are thieves and murderers. Now James is already there, and see, he's a geologist and looking through the territory for iron and copper deposits. You see that ship over at the yard? That's pig iron, mate, or some type of fancy iron alloy, and there will be more and more of that needed. So me and James are going to buy up land in this Minnesota where he finds the minerals. Because over in America, a fella can own land and everything on it and under it. So the risk I see is calculated. Me little brother is smart as a whip, and I have a packet saved up, so I'll go over there and risk wolves and Indians for an iron mine. That seems a lot easier and less risky than getting eight pound a week to mill through an endless line of murders."

As drunk as he was, Keane, made some sense. "I can't argue with that."

"Take your rich fella, who left his big estate in the country to flee back to the city, informing nobody. Then he ends up burnt to a crisp," said Keane.

"Ahh, but no traces of a fuel to start a fire and nothing burned," replied Dolly as he polished off his plate of chops.

"Well, it might be one of those spontaneous combustions I read about," Keane argued back.

"His clothes were as fresh as yours," exclaimed Dolly.

"Will you quit fuckin' interrupting my presentation to the Bailey? And take off that silly tie. What are you, some plantation owner in America?" replied Keane as he moved to untie Dolly's tie. "So, I was sayin'. You have the crispy rich dead fella, then twelve hours later, you discover two blokes dead in the very bank vault he owns. Locked up in a Yale combination safe that only six, well now five, of the wealthiest men in the empire have the combination to open," Keane presented. He slammed his meaty fist down on the table, sending plates and silverware dancing.

Dolly had to lunge forward to catch his pint.

"Crime solved! Your rich fella was kidnapped to get into the safe. The blokes that grabbed him ran into the guards, blasted them, and took off. Did I miss anything?" Keane said, grinning and droopy-eyed from drink but certain in his inebriated state he had just solved the crime.

"How is it you have resolved more cases than me?" asked Dolly. Then he leaned forward to offer what Keane had missed. "The strong boxes had been opened and two of the three emptied before they were slain. Blood spatter inside the boxes shows the course of those events. The guards were in the safe when they were killed. The direction of the shot came from outside the safe, not from inside as you would expect if you surprised robbers. Then the weapon was dropped inside the strong room without further disruption to the other strong boxes—"

"You also missed the part where a Voodoo priest removed the soul from the rich fella." It was Rose Caldwell, and she had been listening to the small talk.

Keane looked up. "Jesus Mary and Joseph—Dolly, could you

show respect for my everlasting soul and not bring that witch around me? Her soul is already damned."

Rose took a chair from another table, twirled it backwards, and sat down, resting her arms on the back of the chair. "My researcher identified the totem as a spirit siphon. The object functions as a conduit for the spiritual ritual called Pwen Hanan, where the soul is transferred to another vessel. My guess is that Chilton crossed a Voodoo priest, and now revenge has been exacted."

"Let me ask you something, Sister. When you burned down that rectory, did a Voodoo priest make you do that?" asked Keane.

"If you would like, I could exorcise the mongoloid demon that controls your mouth?" retorted Sister Rose.

Keane put on his serious face and reached across the table, grabbing Dolly's wrists. "Mate, we've known each other a long time. You're the smart one here. You have the chance to move up the ranks, but you got to get rid of this heretic. You make us all look bad, Fredrick."

Dolly knew Keane was saying what he felt. He embraced Keane's wrists. "Callum, you have seen what people do to each other. Do you believe all that evil is manmade? I don't, and neither does Rose. Just as you and I have seen horrors together, I have seen worse with her."

"Well, you both can fucking burn in hell. I am sure there is room for one more heretic and Protestant, but there will be no guilt by association for Detective Callum Keane." Keane pushed back from the table and walked out of the pub.

Dolly moved to go after Keane but needed to find out what

Rose had learned. "Could this be fabricated to cover up for a heist?" asked Dolly.

"You mean the soul stealing? No. Your fat drunk colleague may have it right, but Chilton was under the direction of another through Pwen Hanan, not a kidnapping."

Dolly shot her a baffled look.

She continued. "I am just learning about this arcana. It is primordial and works along the courses of necronist seance and spirit manipulation. From the condition of the body, I think Chilton was tortured spiritually until he succumbed to the wishes of the persecutor. Maybe he was tortured to get the combination, or he could have been enslaved and made to open the safe himself only to be killed later."

Rose reached into her handbag and pulled something out. Without showing it to him, she shifted it across the dinner table and into his hand. "Fredrick, place that charm on your watch fob."

"What is it?" He studied the weird talisman of silver. In its center was a glass vial with a brilliant blue gas circulating about. He slid it on to the ring that held a small pen knife at the end of his silver watch chain, then stuffed it into his waistcoat pocket.

"That is something I crafted. An apotropaic amulet." She pointed to the stone on the choker she wore around her neck. It had a comparable stone. "It's a ward. If we are hunting for a Voodooist that can control life force, that trinket will provide a defense. If a Mumbo were to beguile you, the enchantment will be limited as it confuses the ward for your spirit energy," said Rose.

"A decoy for my soul?"

Rose continued. "Yes, the Voodoo call the spirit energy Ju Ju. The manipulation of Ju Ju is where the power of the Mumbo lies. They have a primal knowledge and have learned to tap into and exploit this spiritual energy. There are descriptions of the capability to direct the living and the dead. While you still seek the motive and the identity of the fugitive, what I know is that this individual understands and controls the necromantic arts differently than how the necronists tap into the spirit worlds. If this person could control Chilton while alive or dead, they are a dangerous adversary. I don't want you or I to get close and become enthralled. That eldritch talisman is my best attempt at a shield."

SUNDAY, THE 13TH JUNE

8:00 AM THE CARLTON HOTEL

Dolly was called to the Carlton Hotel. A request for a sergeant in the detective branch meant either a serious crime or a matter of discretion with someone in high social circles. In the past, his superiors requested his skillful touch to deal with the affairs of the rich and powerful, always considerate of station and reputation while making certain that the Crown's law applied to all. Too bad it wasn't something simple like a lord getting held up by a tramp and her pimp. Instead, it was another homicide, and from the sound of it, Dolly now had a repeat murderer to capture. The constable who had summoned him mentioned on the ride over that it was another burned up person with no sign of fire. While never one to jump to conclusions, Dolly could not help but assume it was the same person.

He sent the policeman to fetch Sister Rose to the crime scene after he dropped Dolly at the fashionable hotel. He was greeted by the hotel manager, a portly Frenchman nervously moving around the hotel lobby and agitated by the law enforcement presence. A lobby and hallways with cops drew unwanted attention. He brought Dolly to the suites on the eighth floor via the verticulator. Dolly doubted the chubby Franc ever took the stairs. At the double doors of the apartment stood a patrolman. This was standard practice for protecting crime scenes until a detective attended to the scene.

The spacious saloon included a sitting area, a work desk and a large table for dining. The table, unused for dining, was instead buried in packages and bags from the emporiums of Saville Row. Adjoining was the bedchamber and the scene of the crime.

The body lay near the center of the disheveled bed. The man's dressing gown was open, exposing his bare body, the back arched, pelvis thrust upward and arms sprawled out. What was stranger than the agonized contortion his shape was frozen in was the state of the body. It was another desiccated, gray and wrinkled corpse, looking like it was stolen from a crypt. While shocking to the others, Dolly was less shocked by the dead man's condition and far more concerned that his occult killer was on a spree of murder.

The manager stood to the right of Dolly and stared at the scene as he spoke. "The accommodations are rented by Señor Emilio Moya. He has leased this suite for the last four months."

Detective Williamson began his investigation. While inspecting the room, he asked questions of the manager.

"Who discovered the body?"

"The valet," replied the manager.

"I will need to speak with him," said Dolly.

"Of course. He is down the hall in the staff room," replied the manager.

"What can you tell me about your guest?" asked Dolly. He assumed the body was Moya but still had drawn no conclusions.

The French manager spoke in a pompous tone about the patron as if it were an advertisement of his hotel. "Señor Emilio Moya can trace his lineage to the most serene house of Braganza, a distant cousin to the King of Portugal. He was not involved in affairs of state but rather was living here in London as a gentleman."

"Is he a man of means or inheritance?" asked Dolly. Any guest of this hotel had access to a fortune. It was where it came from that might help shed light on the case.

"His family had shipping interests then moved into land and sugar cane in the colonies," replied the manager, with hands folded. Dolly thought, *I wager you have more to tell.*

"Was he seen returning last night with any other persons?" asked Dolly.

"I wouldn't know. I came in at eight in the morning. The night staff had left," responded the manager.

"Can you get me a list of the staff on duty?" asked the detective as he continued surveying the bedroom before stepping in. He paid attention to the floor to ensure there was no evidence he could disturb by entering the chamber.

"Yes," the manager replied. Dolly stepped in and moved toward the body. "I will need to interview them. When do they start shift?"

The manager did not follow Dolly into the bedroom. He stood outside as if he would be infected by whatever killed the man. "The night staff starts at eleven p.m. and finishes at seven the next morning."

At closer scrutiny of the body, the right fist of the corpse was distorted and clenched, as if it had suffered a hundred years of debilitating arthritis. On the ring finger was the signet ring of the Moya Family. Dolly assumed the body was Señor Moya but would need further confirmation.

The suite had no signs of a struggle, no blood stains or any of the common signs of foul play. Although Williamson knew the item was occult, he used his handkerchief to shield himself from residual poison or magic that may have laced the totem. Dolly pulled slowly to ascertain the depth it penetrated the body. It held fast and required effort to dislodge. Dolly and the manager were given a shock as the corpse expired a moan and lost all rigor when the object was removed from the wound. It startled the detective so much he dropped the spirit siphon. After Dolly gained his composure, he pulled out a small mirror and held it over the mouth of the deceased to confirm that the subject was expired.

Putting the mirror away, the detective walked to the writing desk to get an envelope for the totem. On the blotter was a note on the hotel stationary. It was a man's handwriting.

Those that profited have paid.

E.M.

He retrieved an envelope from the center drawer in the writing desk and placed the totem in the envelope.

At that moment, Rose entered the room with her arms full of equipment. Her skin glowed with exertion. "Thank the heavens this place has a verticulator. I can't imagine huffing all this gear up a stairwell." Behind her was a constable carrying more cases.

"My experiment is ready for debut," She presented the large black box fixed to a wooden tripod with a flourish, taking a bow. "What you see here is a camera obscura I modified with my scrying lenses. These plates are treated with my tinctures. I bake them into the gelatin. Now step back as I need to vapor the room." She began to set up the equipment. "You might want to get the manager and the others out of here."

"Ms. Rose Caldwell. Might I remind you that you are here as an observer and your presence is at the whim of the Metropolitan Police Department, where you have only one supporter? Me."

She gave him a square look.

"You don't boss me," said the detective.

Rose lifted her brow and rolled her eyes "Okay. Long one last night?" She went back to opening cases and assembling her contraption.

"No, Rose, it was not. It was a pleasant evening, but today isn't. I have two society types killed mysteriously, and you come in here with all this—this hooey-palooley marching me about. I am the Detective Sergeant, and you are the crazy lady who sees ghosts through a bottle glass."

And you're also my only lead on this case.

"Detective Sergeant Frederick Williamson, I beg your pardon. May I please have your permission to examine your crime scene?"

Dolly turned to his men in the drawing room. "Alright. The lot of you get out to the hall,"

The room had cleared. After briefing the constable in the hall, Dolly came back firing questions. "Rose, what do you make of this note?"

Rose walked over to the writing desk. "I'll capture images to see what I can scry, but it looks like our culprit is still sending messages,"

"Oh, you might want to look at this." Dolly took the envelope out of his coat pocket and handed it to Rose. "It is one of those spirit siphons. I had quite the shock when I removed it from his chest. Poor fella let out a gasp and collapsed. I thought for a minute he was still alive."

"A death knell," said Rose.

"A what?" he said.

"A death knell. There was a lingering spirit essence still affixed to the body, and when you tugged out the siphon, he exhausted his dying breath."

"So, he was dead?"

"He might not be dead but trapped or banished. I can't tell, but I know this body had its life force extracted like Chilton." She turned and smiled. "That death knell is a good sign there is residual energy here," mentioned Rose before placing the amber lensed goggles that hung about her neck over her eyes. She set three of her incense burners in the room then waved a hand fan to create circulation. Dolly stood out of the way wondering if he should breathe normally when she was vaporing the room. It must have been alright because Rose never wore a mask.

Rose reached into a case, pulled out a glass slide and placed it in the top of the camera. She stood to the side of the camera. "Dolly, does your pocket watch have a second hand?"

"It does."

"Fantastic. Would you be a dear and let me know when fifteen seconds has passed? Start timing once I remove the lens cap."

Dolly reached into his waistcoat, pulled out his watch and popped open the cover. "Ready."

"Go," said Rose as she lifted the cap off the lens to expose the plate to the light and eldritch energy.

"There's fifteen," said Dolly.

She replaced the cap and switched the photo plate.

"Rose, what do you make of it when folks like Keane call you..."

"A witch?" Rose completed his sentence.

"He is a good bloke. Devout, you know, and a great cop. He's cleared more murders than me."

Rose set down the plate. "Fredrick, I have never broken my vows and plan to never do so. When I joined the sisterhood, I joined to seek out the truth and understand the spiritual. I learned that the unseen is far beyond any one dogma, and many times, that dogma and the arcane become subordinate to the will of a single man, and that's when ill comes to be."

The two took over ten imprints of the desk area where the note was placed and the bed where the body lay. As Rose packed up her equipment, and the mortuary removed the remains from the room, Dolly questioned the valet in the hall.

"Mr. Yardley, how long have you been working for Mr. Moya?" asked the detective.

"I don't work for Señor Moya. I am a hotel employee and

serve several of the gentlemen on this floor prepared to pay for service."

"Did Mr. Moya happen to share with you where he was going last night?" Dolly followed up.

"Yes, he did. He was meeting Mr. Randall Strathmore and a Mr. Owens at Whites for drinks and whist," replied the valet.

"Is that the Strathmore and Owens of Chilton, Chilton, Owens and Strathmore?"

"Why, yes, it is. Señor Moya's a client of the firm, and my understanding is that his family and the Chiltons have socialized for generations," added the valet.

Dolly now had two dead bodies within a week, with identical ends that only an excommunicated nun could explain. Now it appeared there were social connections, if not face-to-face meetings of the two dead men.

As he finished up his questions with the valet, he watched Rose make her way out of the suite with her kit. "What happened to the cases where a fella shot his old lady for running around?" mumbled Dolly.

"What was that, Detective?" asked the valet.

"Nothing. Just reminiscing about the good old days."

MONDAY, THE 14TH OF JUNE

7:00 AM SCOTLAND YARD

Monday morning, the detectives were back in the pen with the commissioner for case updates.

Dolly arrived early, having managed only a few hours sleep between the Carlton crime scene investigation and his need to prepare for the weekly case review starting any minute. As rough as Dolly felt from a deficit of sleep, Keane reflected it physically in the manner he showed up at the branch office.

"What's the steam lorry driver's name that drove over you?" questioned Dolly.

Keane was pale and looked flu-ridden. The tall detective sat down at the adjoining desk that faced Dolly. "Dolly, I ain't been right all weekend. I guess I ate bad mutton or something foul at Albies. Me head is throbbing, and I been all woozy."

Dolly stared at him with no outward expression. "It's called a hangover." Then he went back to organizing his notes.

"I felt like this since Saturday morning, and I haven't had a drop since I was with you," replied Keane.

Commissioner Mayne walked into the pen. There was no formal command in the branch. Younger detectives were subordinate to detective sergeants, but no superior officer existed so all the detectives reported to Commissioner Mayne. To keep the office on task, Mayne held a weekly meeting where he listened to the comments of each police officer and could administer direction to the group. "Alright, gentleman. Let's have it. You start, Keane."

"I have a wash-up on the Thames, awaiting affirmation from the mortuary, but it looked like a stabbing before they deposited her in the river.

"I closed the Clove Row murder. It was Ginger Kelly, another member of Sweeney's gang. Apparently, Sweeney and Ginger were both rolling the same music hall singer, and it came to blows. After Ginger beat Sweeney to death, he passed it off like the Green Street boys, to protect his arse and stir up the strife between the gangs.

"I have also been putting in time down at the gaswerks helping Dolly with keeping an eye out for trouble," Keane finished.

"Detective Keane, you seem out of sorts," stated Mayne.

"I feel out of sorts. I guess I got bad mutton on Friday."

"Dolly, do you have anything further to introduce on the case at the gaswerks?" Mayne asked.

Dolly looked up from his papers. "I looked around and made it known I was watching. Talked to one organizer named Nelson Bruce,"

Several of the detectives called out, "Brucie," then the entire group chuckled.

"As you can tell, Commissioner, comrade Brucie is an admitted Marxist, with numerous arrests for disrupting the peace and one conviction. He served a year of hard labor. I put him on notice," said Dolly.

"Thank you for the update, Detective Sergeant. Why don't you continue with your case load?" suggested the commissioner.

"I have the Chilton case. Sir Chilton found dead in his Belgravia office on Sunday morning, June 6th. Further investigation turned up a burglary of about five thousand gold guineas, worth twenty-thousand in pounds' sterling from his offices in the city of London."

One of the detectives in the pen let out a whistle when he heard the huge sum. Dolly was seasoned enough to talk over the rabble. "I am working with Sergeant Jones of London Police who is lead on the robbery. I opened another homicide case last night. Emilio Moya, a national of Portugal with connections to nobility. His corpse turned up in the same condition as Chilton. I will consider these incidents together as my conclusion is that the cause of death was the same. Thus, the culprit is also the same.

"I propose to make queries of the staff regarding the actions of Señor Moya at White's gentlemen's club. He was a guest there the preceding night." Dolly knew he would have his best results if he gave the private club for gentleman of royalty and society advanced warning. This could be achieved through Spencer Walpole, a club member. "Could you reach out to Home Secretary Walpole to let the club manager know of my plans and determine if an invitation will be extended?" suggested Dolly.

"I'll wire-type the secretary and see. You be discreet. Those are the true halls of power. You pull any of your shenanigans, like deciding to bring that witch of yours near there, and I'll have your badge and pension," stated Mayne.

"Yes, sir," replied Dolly.

The group of detectives consumed the next hour with the reports of the six other agents. Each rattled out opening, pending and closed cases of homicides and thefts throughout London.

Dolly had a full day arranged. Next stop was the flat of Sister Rose and then late night interviews with the staff at the Carlton. He would see if he could squeeze in a nap between Rose's and the Carlton.

11:00 AM, Rose Caldwell's Rooms

There was a banging on the door. Rose was in the midst of fixing the image in the bath of chemical. Timing, chemistry, art, science and magic all had to align to develop the image.

"Wait a bleeding minute," Rose said. She watched the clock on the wall to see how much longer she needed. "I can't open the door," she yelled, so the Scotsman could hear her through the thick metal barrier.

"Any trouble in there?" came a man's voice through the door. *Dolly, Mr. Punctual.*

"I am fine. The door must remain closed until I fix these photo plates, or the light will spoil the image," she emphatically responded.

She withdrew the plate out of the fixing solution, set it on the drying rack, then made her way to the door, pulling off her rubberized gloves and throwing them on the bench.

Rose wiped her hands on her canvas apron and unlatched the multiple locks, bars and the warding hex-box to open the door.

Dolly was yelling down the alley. "Hey, off with you two... You bugger off, or you'll be in the boys ward tonight." He turned back to the open door, giving one more quick glance down the street to make sure the boys were away from his carriage.

"This is my place of trade. Could you please come here with less ruckus?" asserted Rose.

"Good morning to you too, Sister Rose Caldwell," Dolly greeted her with his melodic tone, a modest Scottish intonation weaved into his English accent. He seemed bigger and clumsier as he maneuvered the steps down to the underground flat and the cellar's low beams supporting the floor above. "Have there always been so many street Arabs in this neighborhood?" Dolly asked, removing his tall hat and smoothing out the beard he was letting grow in.

"Ever since the dye mills have opened, there have been more and more," responded Rose. She lit oil lamps as she strode the flat. It was an old basement with no windows. The open door produced the only natural light into the flat.

"Secure and bolt the door," said Rose, lighting a lamp as she spoke. Once the door closed, the whale oil lamps would serve a hazy yellow illumination.

"When are they going to run current to this part of town?" Dolly asked.

"Come back this way." Rose led Dolly out of the small area

with a coal stove vented through the wall and two threadbare wing chairs with a small table and heaps of books. Across from the entry door was her writing desk. A folding partition divided the cramped space of Rose's bed and dresser from the larger section that made up where she worked. The rest of the basement was part storage area, part workshop. She led Dolly by lamplight through a row of homemade wooden racks. A variety of jars and glass vessels held fluids and exotic substances, a cross between an apothecary, a sideshow curiosity and a winter pickle storeroom. "My landlord wouldn't pay for gas lighting let alone arc lights. You know they dropped a gas line just on the other side of that wall under the avenue. All she has to do is fit out the apartment with pipe and this could be gas-lit," added Rose, pointing to the street side wall of her basement dwelling. *Of course, I would need to be up to date on rents too.*

As Dolly followed her, he chimed in, "Rose, your place usually has a pleasant smell of candles and incense. What is with the vinegar smell?"

It was lost on Rose. She had been breathing the chemical for hours and lost the ability to sense the aroma. "Oh, that is just the chemicals for fixing the images for what I wanted to show you. Follow me."

Rose's cellar floor was unfinished and made of hard packed clay and stone. She had placed carpet runners in between racks and shelves to keep the dust down and the floor warmer. Rose led the detective down the main aisle to the workspace and strode over to her latest gadget. "This, Detective, is the phantasma graph. I have married the latest in the photographic sciences with arcane scrying to facilitate the uninitiated: to see the world as it is, was and can be." Her right arm was outstretched and waving at a glass cylinder about eighteen inches in diameter set on a brass base with a brass crown. Her contraption looked like a cross between a fishbowl and a Russian samovar with copper tubing joining the top to the bottom of the chamber. On the opposite side of this recirculation tube was a bellows. Within the glass tube, in the bottom half of the container, hung a heavy cerulean gas with phosphors glimmering in the vapor.

An armature secured to the base incorporated a lens system, a photo plate holder and an oil lamp. "This ended up being more complicated than I thought, but you'll like the results," Rose pronounced as she took one of the glass sheets and placed it into the holder. She took a matchstick and ignited the lamp attached to the phantasma graph. Rose then pumped the bellows, causing the gas to recirculate in the chamber. "When you have seen me scrye a location, I use incense and potions that cause an ethereal reaction, which helps me to see the images. To see what the camera has caught, I must project the image back upon an eldritch element. For this, I use a refractive gas. I found a specialist apothecary that can source alchemical materials. I finally settled on seureleum mestificatos, or SM gas, but it is heavier than air, so it settles out over time. To get the gases in the tube to disperse, I recirculate them with the bellows."

Rose could see Dolly's eyes glazing over as she peppered him with her lecture on her innovations until his eyes caught the figures appearing in the mist. In the chamber was a vignette of a gentleman garbed in a nightgown sitting at a desk writing. It was room 8A at the Carlton, and the man was Moya. Behind and to his left stood a handsome young woman adorned in an elaborate bustled gown with a lace veiled hat peering over his shoulder. Through the swirling image, Rose could see Dolly frozen with astonishment, fixated on the picture. Dolly finally spoke, "Rose, this has got me absolutely knackered. You're telling me that this is an image from Moya's suite the night of the murder, and this is actually Moya sitting there?"

"You can see what I see when I use my vapors and lens while conducting a scrying ritual. What I have done is imbued the incantations into my construction. That is to say, yes, you're seeing an astral imprint of a moment from the past."

"Rose, we could settle every case that is outstanding," Dolly said as he clapped his hands together.

"Unfortunately, no, my friend. If the latent energies have dissipated, I can't capture them, and if the homicide had no arcane influence, then there would be no imprint made."

The smile left Dolly's face.

"This next one is good," Rose said as she switched glass plates. The next slide illuminated as Rose produced a steady stream of the gases through the tube. The picture was more vivid and resolved. The image was what looked like a negro woman. Rose could confirm it was the same woman from her height and clothing, but she had removed the veil. The genesis of the light for the exposure appeared to be generated from the man's chest. He reclined on the bed. A streak of light weaved its way to a glowing sphere the lady bore in her left hand. "There it is. The transgression in progress, your mumbo priestess taking Emilio Moya's soul. The image is so clear because the soul transferal is a violent discharge of metaphysical vitality."

Rose observed Dolly. He went from a cop conducting an objective analysis of the scene, searching for clues, to a human disgusted and horrified by what the tableau presented. It was hard to fathom what Moya went through, but here you could see agony and fear on Moya's face. Moya still looked human, not like the mummified shell left in the hotel. This was the moment where the priestess used her power to rip his eternal essence, that which is beyond the mortal realm, and stole it or destroyed it. Rose wondered if the detective understood what he was observing. If Moya's soul were destroyed, this would be beyond murder in wickedness. The survivors, family and friends of a murder victim can take solace that the victim is somewhere, maybe even a place better than here, but no longer with them physically. In this case, the victim's unique essence, that being that is you beyond the voices in your head, is obliterated. No longer eternal or universal; no chance of an encounter on some other plane at some other time. Obliterated!

The Sister felt a strange joy and sense of accomplishment watching Dolly looking at her contraption. He was like a schoolboy staring in the window of a toy shop. Rose also felt sorrow as she focused on the image within her invention, the murderess conducting black magic. Ironically the priestess' face was also a mix of exaltation and sorrow. It was then while looking at the predator and the prey that Rose saw something similar and familiar in the faces of the victim and the murderess. Rose wondered if Dolly saw the same.

"How is this possible?" Dolly asked watching the vision fade as the smoke stopped blowing.

"It's science, Detective. Have you read the works of John Dalton?" Rose took out the slide and stored it in a protective holder.

"No, I'm just a dumb cop, Rose."

"Dalton advanced the theory that the whole universe is comprised of atoms. The simplest of elements. All the elements are made of the same aether and the number of aether particles makes up the difference between lead and gold. Preston taught me that the universe is of the aether, and it's all connected. By understanding its properties, we can manipulate matter, electricity and in this instance, I can detect the old aether imprint left from a moment in time," Rose declared.

"So this is science, not spiritualism?" asked Dolly.

"It's both. I say they are the same, just different ways of looking at the universe."

"Well, like I told Keane the other day, I never thought a man could fly, and now we are building airships the size of buildings."

"Keep that mind open as possible, Fredrick. If you don't, that is when you are damned," Rose replied.

Rose knew Dolly took that in as a philosophical metaphor, but she meant it. She had seen souls sent to other planes of reality. She had been to other planes herself. It was when you grappled with the concepts of the eternal and universal that your limiting beliefs drove you mad.

"Dolly, when we find this woman, I need to learn how this arcana works."

"Well, she can teach you while she waits for the gallows."

"That is my point. She can control the forces of life and death itself. She won't be afraid of your gallows," said Rose.

"I am a simple fella, Rose, responsible for detecting the work of criminals in this city and bringing them before the Crown for justice to be served," Dolly said as he looked over her contraption. There were many similar contraptions in various states in her shop. "Any of these other things work?"

"Some do, some are in progress, others are parts to tinker with," answered Rose as she organized items on a counter, almost an attempt to clean up the mess. "What if the priestess has killed no one? She could just have trapped them in that orb she was holding. She could be holding them hostage," Rose followed up.

Dolly gave her a look of disdain, "Well, here is my small mind closing. I signed off this morning to hand Sir Francis Chilton's body back to his family. So seeing as most folks bury the dead, am I supposed to instruct them to hold off until we catch a Voodoo sorcerer that may or may not have their loved one's soul in a box; or do we dig him up after I get Miss Mumbo here in irons and have her funnel Sir Francis back into his rotting corpse?"

Rose hated this part of Dolly. The less he understood, the more his hackles were raised. "Dolly, that's not the point. I want you to work on catching her so I can learn from her. This could be a powerful weapon for Her Majesty."

"Nice try, Caldwell. Use my allegiance to the Crown. Just walk me through that conversation with the home secretary. Your Honor, I have it on good authority from an ex-nun that we will soon have the ability to trap the souls of our enemies. After I apprehend the person who damned the souls of one of your mates, not to worry. I am hot on her trail because I know what she looks like from a ghost picture I saw in a tenement basement. I would ask that we not hang her until she teaches the ex-nun how to steal souls. What did I miss? Oh yes, and could I please have a pension and a knighthood?" He walked down one of the aisles to leave.

"Dolly, there is a bigger game here. You and I are fighting this war together. This is about the light and the dark, and we need any advantage to win," Rose implored, grabbing his arm to halt his exit.

"Rosie, dear, I thank you. This contraption of yours is plum. We got something here to go on, but this is a murder investigation and a robbery. I need to identify your mystery woman and catch her before she kills someone else or gets away. Let's say I get somewhere on this lead and we find her. What should we expect with this magic Is it like firing a gun, or does she need to get prepared?" asked Dolly.

"It's ritualistic. She has to establish a contact with the victim and enthrall him. Preston told me that some of the most potent work requires multiple hougans or very powerful ones. I expect she has a natural talent and is getting more experience with the most complex of the Voodoo rituals. The amulet I gave you will afford protection."

"This might sound stupid, but do you think she has the power to stop a bullet?" asked Dolly.

"I doubt it," replied Rose.

"Well, there's a bright spot. This thing of yours on my watch fob should give me enough time to put a shot on her." Dolly looked Rose in the eyes. "This won't be another case where I shoot someone and they don't die."

~

11:30 PM, The Carlton Hotel

At half past eleven, Dolly arrived at the Carlton. The hotel was frenetic with horse-drawn and steam carriages pulling up and departing. A society event in the ballroom recently concluded, and couples in tuxedos and ball gowns lined up waiting, for livery to retire home.

The detective sergeant made his way to the lobby counter and requested to speak to the night supervisor. Hodges was his name. The day manager informed Hodges that Detective Williamson would need to talk with the night staff. Hodges was a man who prepared.

"I would be delighted to call on the staff and have them sent to you for interview," said Hodges as he handed the handwritten list to Dolly. "I also have arranged an office, my office, for you, Detective Williamson. To get you out of all the hustle and bustle of the hotel."

Dolly knew it was to keep him out of the sight of guests. What hotel wanted an active homicide inquiry in plain view of its patrons, even late at night?

"I don't wish to be problematic, but it would be best for me to just visit with the staff on the floor," suggested Dolly.

"Very well, but my office is yours if you should need it. Who would you like to chat with first?"

"Let's begin with the doorman. Is this Winters on duty tonight?" said Dolly.

"Yes, that is him at the door." The manager pointed to an average-looking man in a top hat and overcoat.

The doorman was frenzied with the commotion of guests exiting, and Dolly had to make sure he was standing out of the way of the traffic. Winters was sweating between working the door and being overdressed for the balmy night. "Good evening, sir," announced the doorman.

"I'm Detective Sergeant Williamson of the Metropolitan Police Service. I understand that you were on duty Saturday night and Sunday morning."

"Yes, I was."

"I would like to ask you some questions," voiced Dolly.

"And I would be delighted to answer them. Tell you what, I have a break in a 'alf hour and I go over to that alleyway to have a smoke in peace. Meet me there," replied the doorman.

Dolly made his way to the register to discuss the events of the evening with the bell staff and concierge, four young bell hops and an elderly gentleman.

"Good evening, gentleman. I'm Detective Sergeant Williamson of the Metropolitan Police Service, and I would like to speak with you if you worked the night of the eleventh."

"This is my first night in a week," pointed out the Concierge without glancing up. "I was off that night," one of the four bell hops said.

Dolly looked at the remaining three. "Would you mind if I had a chat with you three in Mr. Hodges' office?" The three acknowledged yes with looks, shrugs and head nods. "Then let's make our way there. You can take the lead as I don't know my way around here."

The door to the manager's office was open. This was the shared workspace of both the day and night manager. It was small berth with a roll-top desk and two wooden chairs to its side, not much more than a closet. Hodges was seated at the desk. Dolly took the rear, following the group into the office. Seated at the desk, Hodges voiced, "Can I help you gentlemen?"

The lead bell hop replied, "The detective told us to come in here to have a chat."

Dolly pushed through the trio "Sorry about the change of plans, but I felt it best to speak with the boys in private."

"Oh, yes. Alright, let me get my things, and you can have the office. We are short on chairs. Adams, go down the hall to the accounts office and pinch a chair from them," said Hodges.

"Yes, Mr Hodges," shot back the young Adams as he scurried down the hall to fetch a chair.

The three lads and Dolly settled into the cramped office. The boys sat on wooden chairs facing the desk, and Dolly perched on the corner of the desk to make the situation more casual yet still assert his authority. He started the questioning with a simple query. "You hear about what transpired last Saturday in room 8A?"

"Slaughter, I heard," declared a bell hop.

"Blazed up in his bed was what I was told," said Adams.

"I would appreciate if you fellas help me catch the criminal," said Dolly.

"How can we help, mate?" asked Adams.

"All of you think about that night and if you witnessed anything unusual. If perhaps you spoke with Señor Moya, or knew about his whereabouts or associations with others that evening," instructed Dolly.

The taller bellman spoke up. "I was on the eighth floor collectin' shoes to shine and saw a fella enter that suite."

"What time was this?" Dolly asked, pulling out his journal and pencil.

"I'd say round two in the morning, gov," the boy said.

"Your name?" questioned the detective.

"It's Tim Walter, sir."

"What else did you see, Tim?"

"None to speak of. I was going about my business collecting boots and shoes to shine,"

"Do you remember what the man looked like?"

"No, I was a ways down the hall. He was a gentleman, smartly dressed with a fancy walking stick. He was at the door talking to who I assume was Señor Moya, then he went in," said Tim.

Dolly thought this could be helpful but needed more. "When you say he was smartly dressed, you mean like a dandy, as some of Señor Moya's associates may dress?"

"No, more like a gentleman, you know—a business man, but there was something a touch flash about him," answered Tim.

"Did you see the man leave?"

"No, I didn't think much of it, so I went about my rounds and finished the floor before he left the room."

"Did any of you other fellas see the gentleman with the walking stick?"

The group looked to each other for an answer. None came.

"Did any of you observe an African woman in the hotel?" asked the detective.

Again the three exchanged silent befuddled looks.

"Thank you for your time. If any of you recollect anything further, please come see me at the Yard." Dolly pulled out his silver card case and handed each of the men one of his cards.

It was just about time to meet the doorman. Dolly made his way to the alley. He packed a pipe with tobacco and lit it. The doorman finally took a break and walked up the alley to Dolly. "I can talk now," said the doorman.

"So you were on duty last Saturday night?"

"Yes sir. I rolled in about ten to get on me livery and have a cup of tea," the doorman answered as he rolled a cigarette.

"Did you see Señor Moya leave the hotel?" asked Dolly. He knew from the valet he left earlier, but he was looking for conflicts.

"No, I didn't see him leave,"

"Do you remember Señor Moya returning?"

"Yes, sir. Well, sir, he returned by a cab around twelve-thirty, I'd say," answered the doorman.

"Was he with anyone?" followed on Dolly.

"No. Just himself."

"Did he say anything to you?"

"Just the usual pleasantries."

"Did you happen to see a man, a smartly dressed business man with a walking cane that night?"

"Quite a few at this place, sir."

"This would have been later, around the time Señor Moya returned, or even later?"

"Well, there is Mr. Strathmore. If I recall, he came in about one-thirty that evening," the doorman said as he finished up his smoke.

"Why would he be coming in that late?" Dolly asked.

"Well, I don't know the specifics, but he is a regular guest here.

When he is in town from America, he stays with us." The doorman blew out smoke with a puzzled look and stamped out his cigarette butt on the pavement.

"He is staying with you now at the Carlton?"

"Yes, sir."

"Did you happen to see a negro woman come into or leave the hotel?"

"Now that, sir, I would have noticed, and I did not," said the doorman.

"Thank you for your help. Here is one of my cards. If anything crosses your mind, you can reach me by wire-type at Scotland Yard," recited Dolly.

The detective made his way back into the hotel and found the manager. He waited by the lobby counter until the manager had completed some task. When he finished, he looked up over his glasses and presented Dolly with a pleasant smile. "So, Detective Williamson, were we of any help?"

"I have a few questions for you."

"By all means, should we step into my office?" asked Hodges. Dolly followed Hodges behind the reception desk to his office. Once ensconced Hodges settled into his chair behind the desk. Dolly stood in the doorway.

"Did you see anyone here that seemed suspicious that night?" asked Dolly.

"I did not."

Did you see either Señor Moya or Mr. Strathmore come into the hotel?

"I did not, but Mr. Strathmore has the penthouse, and that

suite has a private verticulator and entrance on the east lane. He uses it from time to time."

Dolly made notes. "Is Mr. Strathmore in tonight? I would like to ask him some questions. Could we have Walter run a message up to him?" asked Dolly, thinking this would be a quick way to qualify if the man the bell boy saw in the hall was Strathmore.

"No need to have him do that. I can call up to the penthouse butler and ask if he is available. We recently installed a telecom system of Mr. Bell. What a time-saver. Rather than have a bell boy run up, now I can just call up to that floor." Hodges went to a walnut box on the wall with a brass cone on the front. "This won't take a moment." He selected an input hole to plug in the connecting cable. "This is Hodges. I have a Detective Williamson who would like to speak with Mr. Strathmore. I see. I will let him know."

Hodges placed the earpiece back in the holder and unplugged the cable. "Detective, you will need to call on him tomorrow. He has already retired for the evening."

"Thank you very much, Mr. Hodges, and if you would please leave a message for Mr. Strathmore that I would like to have a word with him at his convenience."

"I will pass on the message," replied Hodges.

Dolly got up and made his way out to the front of the hotel to catch a cab.

It had been a good day. Rose and the bell boy had given him solid leads to follow. He had identified two murder suspects, a negro woman with supernatural abilities and a society gentleman. A gentleman that just may be in this hotel.

TUESDAY THE 15TH OF JUNE

1:00 PM, WHITE'S GENTLEMAN CLUB

This was not Detective Williamson's first time at White's, He had been there in the past to report to the Home Secretary on the status of a case. Sir Walpole was a member of London's most exclusive club. Located at 37–38 St. James's Street in the city of Westminster, the building was famous for its bow window, where the table directly in front was reserved for the throne of the most socially influential men in the club. They called them the arbiter elegantiarum. First Beau Brummell held the honor, then Lord Alvanley. It was that very window that Alvanley bet a friend £3,000 as to which of two raindrops would first reach the bottom of a pane of glass. It had been remodeled since then to include the latest technology from the UK and abroad mainly for members to brag about since few were comfortable with all the newfangled mechanisms coming of age. Rather than cause a stir, he took a soft approach and asked the permission of his superiors to provide access to the club. Less chance of ruffling the feathers of the secretary or a powerful club member and setting his investigation back days or weeks. The club had a member list that included the royal house, ministers of Parliament, lords, dukes, and barons.

The manager allowed the detective to interview the staff that worked the front desk and in service at the club. It had to be discreetly done, so Dolly spoke with the staff behind the closed door of the manager's office. He determined from the interviews that, as the guest of Lester Chilton, Señor Moya dined with Sir Rory Birch and Mr. Strathmore, Chilton's American partner. Following supper, the gentleman retired to the game room to play billiards. The party broke up at 11:30 PM. with Lester Chilton leaving in his steam coach and Moya catching a cab.

Dolly asked if any of the party were present at the club and would take the time to speak with him about Señor Moya. The manager returned and advised that Mr. Strathmore was currently at the club and would meet with him in the smoking lounge.

The Detective was escorted by the manager to the smoking lounge. Floor to ceiling windows illuminated the entire room. It was a voluminous space for an older building. The walls were paneled in exotic wood with ornate cornice work. Eight separate seating areas encouraged members to gather and socialize with enough space between to deliver privacy. Each cluster comprised overstuffed leather sofas, wing-backed lounge chairs with end tables, pedestal ashtray, and floor standing phosphor lamps. Dolly contemplated the wealth that built this esteemed building as he took out his notebook and reviewed his questions.

The ceiling had a network of belts and pulleys to operate a fan system to keep the air moving in the room.

Randall Wells Strathmore stood near the teletype clacker,

reading the strip to get the latest stock quotes and news. The clacker was in a prominent position in the lounge behind the sofa that faced the massive fireplace. Most members considered themselves too elite to look at a stock tape but wanted to show off the status of instantaneous worldwide communication. Strathmore was different. He needed to stay on top of world finances. Many of the club members' inheritances were invested with Chilton House, and Strathmore was a steward of that wealth.

A striking man, Strathmore towered over his companions; seeming even taller with his long neck. He wore a standard banker's dress of gray pants with spats, white round-collared shirt, black tie, his pinstriped waistcoat and a black overcoat with tails. He had a black mourning armband. Dolly wondered if he might mourn his own victims. Strathmore, by Dolly's guess, had to be in his forties given what he knew of his financial exploits but looked much younger, almost boyish.

The manager handled introductions. There was a level of formality that all endured at these prestigious clubs. "Mr. Strathmore, may I introduce Detective Sergeant Fredrick Adolphus Williamson of the Metropolitan Police. Detective Williamson, may I introduce Mr. Randall Wells Strathmore of New York."

"Thank you, Milton," said Strathmore, acknowledging the introduction and dismissing the manager.

"I wasn't aware that White's had any American members," said the detective.

"I am a guest of the late Sir Chilton and his son. While I hail from New England and now live in New York, I spend an inordinate amount of time in London and need a place to unwind," said Strathmore in a Yankee accent. He let go of the ticker tape. It dropped in the waste bin set to collect old tape and put out his hand.

Dolly returned the outstretched hand with a firm grip and a shake.

Upon release of the clasp, Randall's hand went to a walking stick that rested against the pedestal holding the ticker. It was made of ivory and a lacquered wood. "Let us have a drink and talk." He used the cane to steady his gait as he walked around the sofa, his left leg suffering a handicap. "The irony is, as managing partner of the New York office, I spend more time in London than I do in New York."

Dolly asked another question. "Did you recently hurt your leg?"

"Aren't you Brits supposed to put social decorum above all? Not mention the elephant in the room, even if you're waist high in elephant dung." Randall tapped his leg with his cane and gave Dolly a smile. "No, this was a hunting accident some years ago."

"I'm a Scotsman and a cop. People expect me to ask uncomfortable questions and lack social propriety," retorted Dolly.

The two men sat down.

Strathmore was the American managing partner of the investment banking partners of Chilton, Chilton, Owens and Strathmore. Randall had become only named partner ever to not be a citizen of the United Kingdom. The firm had international interests that included naval shipping, plantations, railroads and industrial investments, and was aligned with the mechanists. They financed the guild's projects. This banking house was so powerful that wars could not be waged without their funding. The rumor was during the Napoleonic wars that Chilton was financing both sides.

Randall amassed a fortune with his financial wizardry and insight into the new world markets. He was an early backer of Cornelius Vanderbilt, enabling the commodore to finance the Vanderbilt Air Transit Company. Vanderbilt proposed that air rather than sea or rail would win the race for transcontinental travel and that he could build an airship line crossing the wilderness between the east and west coast of America. The prize was a lucrative postal contract with the government between New York and San Francisco. At the time, LQ airships were only operating out of Prussia and were experimental. It was worldwide news when Vanderbilt struck the first deal to export LQ gas from the Europe to America. He built a special steam tanker to bring the gas by sea from the Baltic then across the Atlantic Ocean. When the first mail was delivered to San Francisco by air in only eleven days, the stock for the company shot up and Strathmore and his investors made a packet.

"Now, Detective, before you ask about my whereabouts and movements with Mr. Moya and where I was at when he died, I would appreciate if you would share with me what exactly happened to Moya."

Dolly wondered if this was his way of throwing him off kilter before he answered, "Señor Moya was murdered in his rooms at the Carlton. I cannot share the specifics, but it was not a pleasant sight, and we are still finding out the exact cause of death."

Randall looked over to one of the staff standing near the wall. With only his gaze and a small wave of his hand, he signaled for service.

A server approached the gentlemen. "Can I get you something, sir?"

"Why, yes. What is your name, son?" The waiter was at least twenty years older than Randall.

"Arthur, sir."

"Yes, Arthur. You can fetch me a glass of whiskey and a Partagas. Mr. Williamson will have?" Randall's tone dropped off as he shifted Arthur's attention to the detective.

"I will have the same."

"Excellent! Thank you, Arthur," said Randall, unbuttoning his coat and the lower buttons on his vest to get comfortable.

"What can you tell me about Señor Moya?" asked Dolly.

"Well, Detective, what would you like to know?"

"I would like to know who murdered Señor Moya and Sir Francis. That would make my day. In light of that, I need as much as you can share about Moya, beginning with his visit to this club," stated Dolly, looking at Randall to assess body language and tone.

Randall smiled, sitting both hands on the top of his walking stick, arms outstretched in front of him. He then leaned in closely and quietly said. "I can't answer that question, but I will let you know all about what Señor Moya and I were up to on Saturday night." Randall leaned into Dolly. "I would like your professional opinion on something," Randall said in a quiet and serious tone.

Men like Strathmore, smart privileged men, would play this game. The game where they presumed Dolly was a dumb Scot, that he was too stupid to find out what they were hiding. Dolly relished that game because he had so much practice. *So, let's play* thought Dolly before declaring, "What might that be, Mr. Strathmore?"

"How many murders have you investigated?"

Dolly thought for a moment. "I have closed seventy-eight cases as a detective. Some of those cases had multiple victims."

"Impressive. What would you say was the most common cause? Lust? Greed? Envy?" Randall said, bouncing his eyebrow as he pronounced each sin.

Dolly thought for a moment. "There are four other deadly sins, but given the ones you listed, I would say greed."

"Greed. I was unsure, and I do appreciate a professional's opinion. Now, with Señor Moya there is the potential for either greed or envy."

"Please elaborate," interjected Dolly.

"The Moyas, while related to the throne of Portugal, are self-made. Emilio's grandfather captained slave ships. Señor Ernesto Moya, Emilio's father, produced an exceptional amount of coin for Chilton's bond syndicates in the slave trade then onto the harvest and sale of West Indies cotton and tobacco on the return passage. Don't look so shocked, Detective. The city of London was built on the flesh trade. If not in financing the ships or insuring the cargo, they did so on the return of cheap goods made in the colonies. Frankly, it's the beloved mechanists and their engines that got the empire out of financing the slavers."

Dolly fancied the blunt talk of the Yank, and he settled in for Randall's lecture. "First Chilton financed his ships then he helped diversify investments across the trade. When the Commonwealth outlawed the slave trade, Moya needed to change businesses. Those that made money insuring his cargo and financing his fleet followed Moya's transition into other colonial ventures. Emilio's father, always one step ahead, moved into the sugar business in the West Indies.

"Now, Ernesto had two sons, Hernando and Emilio. Both were sent to the best schools in England. His father thought with an English education his heirs would become captains of finance with a foot in the New World and one in the Old … Ah, here we go." Arthur had returned to them pushing a serving cart.

He poured and handed them each a crystal tumbler of scotch whiskey then displayed a box of Cuban Partagas cigars to Dolly. Dolly selected a cigar.

"Thank you, Arthur," Williamson said.

Arthur nodded while Randall kept talking. "Hernando was cut from the same cloth as his father, a man of action. But he is the younger son, and his inheritance is far smaller than Emilio. Hernando went to Brazil to make his fortune in the sugar business. He has plantations in Brazilia and Haiti. We have co-invested in his enterprises and done well.

"The older Emilio learned something else in England. How to be a man of leisure. He stayed in London after he finished school to carouse with the group of English dandies rather than join the family business. With each success, Hernando makes Emilio richer and finds it disagreeable that his brother has a say in company affairs and receives a large allowance. I know Hernando will be the master of his fortune, but he lets his family situation and the privilege of his brother fuel resentment. With Emilio dead, the Moya fortune of nearly seven million pounds goes to Hernando."

"Is Hernando in London?"

"Not that I know of," said Randall.

Arthur then turned to offer Randall a cigar. Randall took one. "I would like a flat cut, not a V cut, please." He handed the cigar to Arthur, who cut the cigar then handed it back to Randall.

"May I cut your cigar, Detective," said Arthur.

"Please."

Arthur made the cut then handed the cigar back to Dolly. As Dolly wetted the end of the cigar, he then removed loose tobacco from his mouth. When he looked up, Arthur was igniting a lighter.

"Arthur, get us matchsticks to light the cigar. You'll ruin the flavor with that filthy lighting fluid."

"Yes, sir."

"You see some things should not change, like lighting a fine cigar with a flame of a match after the sulfur is burned off." He leaned back in his chair to draw on the cigar as Arthur held out the match.

Dolly noticed now the top of the man's walking stick was a carved wolf head with gold filigree and the collar around the wolf's head had a pattern of circles, with a smaller circle or dot in the center of each larger circle.

"This is a fine cigar, Mr. Strathmore."

"I am personal friends with Don Jaime Partagas. He has an amazing plantation. You know, they say these cigars are rolled on the thighs of virgin girls. Can you believe that?" asked Strathmore.

"Smoking a cigar that is this smooth, I believe it," replied

Dolly as he held out the cigar sideways, gazed at it and gave Randall a smile of satisfaction.

"We became friends after I looked at his property to assess the collateral for a loan he has with Chilton. He took me on a tour to see the assets. First, he showed me the tobacco fields. Not worth much. Next, he showed me his inventory of tobacco that is curing. Now there is a value that can be priced to market right in Havana. He could tell I was struggling to see how I could approve the size of this loan he sought with what he had shown me, so he said he was prepared to secure the loan with his prize chattel, a group of slaves. Forty in number he had roll his cigars.

"After lunch, Don Jaime and I rode in his surrey to the building, and to my surprise, when I enter, it's not forty vestal virgins rolling cigars, but forty old men. Toothless scrawny, not a one looks like he would live another day or could work an hour in the field without keeling over." Randall took a sip.

Dolly laughed. "So much for the loan, I'd say."

"Well, funny you say because that was what I was thinking. Forty young slave girls that can roll cigars. That is stock, and if the cigar market falls, they're still breeding stock or trainable for the house or field but how do I give him 20,000 pounds' sterling for some tobacco and forty men with one foot in the grave?" Randall stretched out his bum leg and rubbed it while he spoke.

"Well, one thing I have learned is that I can always learn just one more thing, and I needed to learn about the cigar business, but I also can't look a fool in front of Don Jaime.

"I wired Don Moya, Emilio's father, who was still alive at the time in Haiti. I requested to know if he had knowledge of the tobacco business and the matter of the value of a cigar roller.

He introduced me to Don Jose Hoya de Monterey, who agreed to meet with me the next day. So the next day, I had a meeting with Don Jose at his plantation and asked him what he would pay for five of Don Jaime's top cigar rollers. He told me that if they could roll a pyramid like these, he would pay one thousand pounds each. I asked him if I could go to see his rolling rooms and you know what he said? 'Amigo, you will not find any virgins there either.'"

The two men laughed. Dolly needed to get Randall off his stories and onto the subject of Saturday night.

"What was Mr. Lester Chilton's disposition on Saturday?"

"Reasonable for an English man who just lost his father to a heinous murder and had his bank robbed. If I know Lester, he will try to lose himself in the work and pick up as much of his father's clientele that he can," said Randall.

"Was there a reason you all convened Saturday night?" asked Dolly.

"Emilio wanted Chilton to loan money against his inheritance to invest in Babbage's manufacture of difference machines. He touted that the next advances in mechanical automation would require his methods in computation."

"And?" pressed Dolly.

"Lester said Babbage hadn't a chance without support from the guild and was resistant to investing with Babbage."

"Would Lester Chilton have a reason to kill his Father and Moya?"

"Detective, Don Moya left an estate of over seven million pounds. While that is a fantastic sum of money for most, it is nothing to the Chiltons. Lester and Francis were close as a father and son could be and business partners as well. Lester had more than enough money to wait out Sir Francis' last day on earth, when he would inherit another fortune he could not spend." Randall finished as he dropped ash in the ashtray on a corner table.

Dolly felt the time was right. "So why did you meet with Emilio at his hotel room the night of his death?"

Randall smiled and paused before he answered. "I won't ask how you knew I met with him nor will I deny that I did." Randall adjusted his position to get closer to the policeman. "I met with Emilio because I wanted to hear more about his scheme with Babbage. It intrigued me, and there are interested pools of capital that the mechanists have no influence over. I am not interested in missing out on a good deal because some guild cronies of Chilton would get upset."

"Was there anyone there that can corroborate your story?"

"Maybe your witness? Other than that, no. It was brief. I was also staying at the Carlton. I dropped in to make a date with him for lunch," answered Randall.

"At one-thirty in the morning?" Dolly queried.

"Detective, that may seem strange to you, but we had just been carousing and gambling not a few hours before. I imagined he would either be up and ready for more, or passed out and not able to answer his door."

"So you were the last one to see him alive?" said Dolly.

"No, Detective. That would be whoever killed him," answered Randall.

"And you think that is Hernando?"

"The brothers never did see eye to eye. They were too

different, and Hernando's good stewardship enriched Emilio, who gambled, drank and whored. You said it yourself. Greed is a primary motivator. I would have Arthur get the betting book and wager that this boils down to family and money, Detective."

Dolly thought this would go in circles unless he could find evidence beyond what he had to connect Randall, but his gut was telling him that Randall knew more than he was letting on. "Here is my card. If you think of anything, please wire me. I would be indebted."

"Sir, I will, if I recall anything. There is nothing more that I want than to help you find the culprit and bring him to the gallows. As far as being indebted, never say that to a banker, my friend."

WEDNESDAY, THE 16TH OF JUNE

9:30 AM, SCOTLAND YARD

When Dolly entered Commissioner Mayne's office, two gentlemen were already sitting in the two seats in front of the commissioner's desk.

The two men stood upon his entrance. Mayne remained seated with a sour look.

"Detective Sergeant Frederick Williamson, I would like to introduce you to French consul, Dr. Felix Anou," Anou was a slight man with a bald head and a goatee, although he was an English-educated physician and had been in the United Kingdom for decades as an attaché to the consulate; his face, his clothes, his tone, accent, and demeanor all reeked of France.

"And this is Special Envoy of the French government, Guild Master Gerrard Saint-Yves," said Commissioner Mayne. Dolly struggled to understand what a necronist was doing here. The guild's close relationship with Emperor Napoleon made them a foe of the Queen. Many thought they used their scrying powers to give the Emperor an advantage on the battlefield. Other rumors were that the necronists negotiated a covenant between the Devil and Napoleon for his protracted life. Between the government's concerns of the guild being saturated with enemies of the Crown and both the Catholic and Anglican Church considering their practices unholy, Parliament had never ratified the guild in the commonwealth.

"Good morning, sirs," replied Dolly, shaking both men's hands.

Dr. Anou, the smaller of the two, wore a light gray suit with a matching waistcoat, his dark goatee waxed to a point and his mustache tips curled.

The guild master presented himself; dressed in the classic garb of the necronist guild. Other than the edge of his white shirt cuffs showing, the ominous character was cloaked entirely in black. His long black silk brocade coat practically brushed the floor, with two rows of pewter buttons closing the front. On his high collar was the gold insignia denoting his rank as a Grand Master of the Wyrding, he was upper echelon necronist. Only six had that rank.

The commissioner continued. "Detective, it appears that the coroner's inquiries to reach the next of kin of Emilio Moya raised eyebrows in Haiti, and they wired the French Republic."

Dr. Anou interjected, "The French government requests the Crown to support their pursuit of a fugitive that may be on UK soil. The Emperor's ministry will share all the pertinent facts with your department to assist in this matter."

The commissioner could see the consternation on Dolly's face and intervened to get him up to speed. "Dolly, this came from the home office. Walpole agreed to cooperate and offered the

Metropolitan Police Service a sharing of intelligence and the arrest of the suspect."

Dolly took the cue. *Take your medicine.* "Who will be my liaison?"

"Mr. Saint-Yves," responded Dr. Anou.

"Not a Gendarme, or at the very least, one of the Emperor's secret police," suggested Dolly.

Saint-Yves spoke. "Detective, the Emperor chose me because I am an authority in the arcane and have investigated the techniques of the fugitive. I can be of considerable service to your department and can help you to catch her."

"You are seeking a woman?" Dolly replied. His interest was aroused.

"Yes, an ex-slave who instigated a rebellion in the protectorate of Haiti," replied Anou.

"A colored girl?" Dolly followed.

"Most slaves in Haiti are negroes," stated Dr. Anou.

"Why is this of concern to the guild?" asked Dolly.

"This is a matter of interest to the Republic of France and the security of its citizens. This woman is engaged in unwholesome practices; his Holiness Cardinal Almont, the See of the Catholic Church, as well as the guild have deemed these to be unnatural and heretical acts," declared Dr. Anou.

"Now the Church and the necronists are making joint proclamations. My, how times have changed," taunted Dolly. Fifty years ago, when the necronists appeared in France as a cult, the pontiff declared them heretics. If it were not for the support of Emperor Napoleon, it is feasible that the

Holy See would have sought to purge Europe of the necronists.

Dolly took another tack. "What makes you think the fugitive is here?"

"The plantation where the revolt started was a Moya-owned estate. Señor Hernando Moya was murdered. The Colonial Police advised the government when your coroner sent a cable to Hernando Moya to inform him as next of kin to Emilio Moya. I am not a police officer like you, Mr. Williamson, but it is logical that if both Moyas were slaughtered the same way, that it is the same murderer out to seek vengeance on the Moyas. You attempt to associate a natural cause to supernatural incidents of Señor Moya's death and that has bewildered you. I can explain how he perished," said Guild Master Saint-Yves.

Dolly crossed his arms. "Well, let's have it."

The necronist met his stare.

"You found the bodies in a state of dehydration, as if all the body's fluids had been removed or as if the body had been burned, yet there was no sign or source of a fire. The guild consulted with the spirit world, and we have learned that the fugitive has tormented the souls of the living by invoking the fires of hell to appear here on earth."

"So, you're saying you have talked with Señor Moya's ghost? You fellas are going to put me out of work if you can start having spirits point out their killers," retorted Dolly.

Saint-Yves's face never showed a variation of emotion. "Detective, I did not partake in the seance, nor do I know if those that did were contacted by Señor Moya or some other spirit guide. I can guarantee you that if the woman is practicing heretical arts in London, you will need our cooperation with her capture."

"So, you're the guild expert on Voodoo?" asked Dolly.

"What makes you ask that, Detective" replied Saint-Yves. Dolly got the rise he was looking for out of the Frenchman. Not even a necronist could stay stone-faced forever.

Dolly pressed. "Let's be clear. From this point on, if you answer my questions with a question to evade giving me the information I desire, we're finished. Come calls from the Earl of Derby or the Queen herself." The detective turned to Mayne. "Take me off the case and give it to someone that has time for this farce."

Before Mayne could answer, Gerrard spoke. "Very well. It appears you know something of the arcane and therefore know our fugitive, and likely the suspect you seek, is a practitioner of Voodoo. I have been to Haiti and understand the nature of the practices and the capabilities of the practitioner. The woman we seek is a high-level Hougan witch doctor. She can twist the will of the living and raise the dead."

"If we can keep it straight that I am the detective in charge, and you are a liaison with no jurisdiction and under no circumstances are you to act on your own, then I'll give this a go. We will apprehend her, lock her up and leave it up to our two governments to determine how justice will be meted out. If you agree, I will make sure I share my knowledge to date and continue to uncover during the investigation. Fair enough?"

"Detective, I agree to your offer. I only suggest that when the hour arrives to capture the Hougan, that my qualifications and services will be required to guarantee no further deaths at the hands of this enchantress," replied Saint-Yves.

"We will cross that bridge when you hand over some evidence to where we can find your witch. Where do I reach you when I need your help?"

"I will be staying at the French consulate and can be type-wired there," responded the guild master.

Dolly smiled. "Thank you, gentlemen. I will be in touch, and I will look forward to seeing your notes on the incident in Haiti." With that, Dolly left the office and returned to his desk.

He sat down and gave his desk a visual survey, letting out a heavy sigh. He noticed at the top of the incoming mail bin an envelope addressed to Detective Sergeant F.A. Williamson in elegant calligraphy.

He flipped it over. The envelope was sealed with wax, but he could not make out the imprint. He opened the note with his penknife, noticing Rose's ward dangling next to it.

The message read:

Dear Mr. Williamson,

You are invited to dine with Mr. Lester Chilton at the Meadhurst Manor on 24th June 1858.

Given the distance, the Chilton home will be open for you to stay as a guest on the noted evening. Please advise us of your acceptance of the invitation and intended arrival at Meadhurst so that our driver can meet you at the station.

Cordially,

Lester Chilton. Barronett

P.S. Dinner attire is respectfully requested.

He threw the letter on his desk and mumbled to himself. "Now I need to get my hands on a dinner jacket." When he looked up, Mayne was there.

"I don't like French men in my office any more than you, Williamson, but don't be making a scene because of your pride as a detective. You have four bodies and you're no closer to finding the killer or building a case, so get your nose on the grindstone and let them help."

"Yes, sir," replied Dolly.

"Detective, save the tone. What's the difference between these blokes and when you call on your witch?"

"She's English."

Mayne noticed the other detectives watching. He turned and left before they started a pissing match.

Meanwhile, Dolly knew there was no need to argue with the boss. Mayne didn't ask for cultists to help, and he didn't approve of Rose. If the Home Secretary was prepared to let necronists help on this case while crying that the French were trying to start a riot at the gaswerks, then pressure to solve the case was coming from someone directly on Walpole and it was mounting.

9:00 PM, WENG LO'S TIEN GOW PARLOR

Rose passed through the raucous smokey Tien Gow parlor. The area was packed with Chinese migrants; it was loud. Maybe Rose perceived it louder since she didn't speak the language. The illegal gambling den was a contrast to Lo's attempt at a high-class environment with his dealers and staff clad in tuxedos and gowns and the bulk of the working-class patrons looking like they walked in right off the street; many had done just that.

Even here she got looks as she followed Weng Lo's lieutenant, Jimmy Lin to visit Master Weng. Rose and Weng developed an unusual relationship based on their history before she turned into a demon hunter and Weng the chief of the Lucky Three Triad in London. Rose administered to the Saint Luke's Children's Home, where he was a benefactor. He had lived there for a time when he first arrived in England. His tenure was well before Rose began her ministry there. Rose figured they were about the same age. When she fell into her troubles, Weng made certain she was taken care of when others, including the church, abandoned her.

Outside his office door was an imposing Chinese man in a tuxedo. He never broke his stare, continuing to observe the gambling parlor.

Jimmy knocked. Another guard peered through the view slot then opened the door, admitting them into the narrow corridor leading to Weng Lo's office.

"Miss Rose, how good of you to visit. Did you enjoy the fleetster?" asked Weng as she and Jimmy Lin entered the office. The gangster lord was reviewing his books and did not get up. Jimmy moved to the side of the room, standing at attention until his master directed him to sit, leave or speak.

"What a thrill. It was like flying," answered Rose.

"How was our friend, Preston?" asked Weng. Weng was one of the few individuals who unconditionally accepted the metaphysical, and Rose could share with him what she experienced in her practice. She knew little about his history, but he had alluded to having a relative engaged in the mystic arts.

"Weng, the possessions take such a toll on him, but we have a strategy to liberate him of his unwanted house guest."

He chuckled. "So why do you call? Are you in need of the coupe again?"

"No, it is the matter of Preston's condition. I require your professional help to find someone. Someone who doesn't want to be found," said Rose.

"Tell me more," coaxed Weng.

Rose continued. "You've heard about the Chilton and Carlton murders?"

"Yes," he replied.

"It is the work of a Voodoo priestess. I was able to divine a vision of her. She is African and possesses a powerful command of the arcane. The same methods she has used to kill can, in my estimation, be used to rescue Preston."

Weng looked at his long-braided ponytail and played with the end of it, giving his black hair all of his thought. "And?"

Just spit it out. "And I need your help to find her."

"Like you said, Sister, she does not wish to be found. This wizard that murders powerful white men in London. You now ask the Chinese gangster to help you catch her? Why would I be interested in getting on the bad side of a wicked Voodoo priestess?"

"It would help me and more so Preston. I need to learn from her. I need to talk to her and see if she will help."

"Rose, the only reason you know of such things is because of the burly Scotsman you help over at the police department. What do you expect he would say about you consorting with the Lo brothers and the Lucky Three Triad?"

Rose grinned and sat down on the couch away from Weng's desk. "Weng, the detective knows my work has me traverse many diverse worlds, and while I have never mentioned our friendship, I doubt it would shock him."

"I assume the policeman would not approve of the company you keep," countered the triad leader.

"It's common practice for law enforcement to reach out to the criminal element when trying to solve a crime. If Dolly were to take issue with our helping each other, it would likely be from resentment that my underworld contacts are of a higher pedigree than his." Rose looked to see if he bit on her backhanded compliment.

"Let him reach out to his contacts. This is too messy, a mysterious witch killing wealthy society types with an ongoing police investigation. Sounds like a tar pit to stay away from." Weng shook his head and looked at her sternly.

"I don't understand, Weng. All I need is your help locating her. After that, I'll deal with the priestess. You won't be connected."

"You look outside that door at what I have going on. Do you think the police don't know there is a gambling hall underneath the noodle shop? We have an understanding. I need not get mixed up in this. Too many big names, too much newspaper attention, and that's not good for trade," Weng said while he walked over to the couch to sit by Rose.

"She has gold," declared Rose.

"My dear, Sister. You barter with the possessions of others. That is not particularly Christian." Weng rose from the lounge. "I have made my decision, Rose Caldwell. Did you have other matters to discuss?"

"No," Rose returned. She had gone too far.

"Then we are done." Weng went back to his desk and spoke in Mandarin after completing his sentence in English.

She heard the office door open and shifted to see Weng's bodyguard waiting for her to depart while he held the door.

Rose stood and looked back at Weng, who had already gone back to reading his book. She pondered pushing further but appreciated that Weng's decisions were definite when in front of lower ranking members.

She stepped out and was again escorted by Jimmy Lin. Jimmy smiled as he ushered her through the gambling hall. An elderly man at one table turned and wailed at her as she walked by.

"He says you are bad luck and you should go away" translated Jimmy.

"He would be right," she said as the pair exited through the metal door that hid the illegal hall from the eyes of the public.

Rose climbed the dirty old staircase up to street level and the alley entrance of the club. The rhythmic shuffling of her and Jimmy's footfall up the wooden steps were broken when Jimmy stopped and asked a question. "How much gold does this woman have?"

She smiled to herself but wiped the smirk off her face before she turned to him. "I have it on excellent authority that she took over twenty thousand pounds' sterling of gold from the Chilton House."

"Who is this excellent authority, witch lady?"

"The detective on the case," she explained.

"If I help you find this person, how will you help me?"

She thought quickly, "I can provide wards to protect you from her powers."

"Yes, you can do that, and you can be a diversion to her if she is there when we grab the gold. If I can find her, and I can secure this gold, I will tell you where she is," responded Jimmy.

Rose thought, *Now I will become part of Jimmy's heist.* "Jimmy, Weng said no."

"He said no to you. I am not you. What can you tell me of this woman?"

"I can show you what she looks like if you come by my flat," said Rose.

"What else?"

"The culprit left a note at the crime scene. That makes me think she has completed her business in London. I expect she will attempt to leave the city. She has over four hundred pounds of gold. That won't be simple to tote around, and she's black. so even in this cesspool called London she will stand out in a crowd. The woman will go someplace where she can fit in and have flexibility, so I would say she will travel to the continent or to America. I'd say the Northern States or the West Indies."

"That is helpful. I will get a search started. Don't seek me or talk to anyone about this matter. If I have something I will find you." Jimmy shook her hand. "Weng's chauffeur is in the alley. He will take you back to Bethnal Green." Jimmy checked his cuffs and made sure his coat was buttoned, a sure sign he was done with business. "Good evening, witch lady."

FRIDAY, THE 18TH OF JUNE

9:15 AM, PELTON'S BOOKSTORE

The bell sounded when Jimmy Lin and Allen Chen walked into Pelton's bookstore, a shabby little-used bookshop in Hay Market. The store was devoid of customers.

Jimmy followed Allen as walked he around the cashier counter. Next to the register, Jimmy noticed a racing form for the weekend and an empty teacup. Chen shoved aside the ratty curtain stretching across the doorway that served as a privacy screen from the store to the rear rooms. "Trevor, it's Friday," Allen Chen called out melodically.

Collecting weekly interest payments was grunt work, but Jimmy's occasional unplanned involvement made certain his underlings were not skimming. Every so often, like today, he would escort his men on the weekly shakedown of debtors. He also needed to be on the streets to ferret out leads on the gold. The owner of Pelton's was one of a dozen or so blokes he thought might have a lead on the thieves. Trevor was a degenerate gambler that owed money to all the bookies and to loan sharks like Jimmy. The gambler didn't make money from his crappy bookstore or his horse handicapping. He earned a living as a document forger, and he was one of the better ones that Lin knew. Trevor could know who was looking to fake some paper for stolen gold.

Around the corner, Trevor Conroy poked his head and peeped over his glasses. "Friday already? Oh, what a surprise, Jimmy. Did you come along today? No problems, I hope."

"Don't act surprised its fucking Friday, Trevor. I am like the racing form. I turn up every Friday," said Allen.

Trevor got up from his desk and scurried to meet Allen.

"Well, of course/ I realize I have a debt to repay and —"

Jimmy pushed by Trevor to discover what he was working on. Trevor's office space was cramped but neat. Trevor was an artist, but had equipment for what he couldn't create by hand. He had several types of printing machines, from clacker printers to variable stampautotrons to replicate government documents, and it appeared he was in full operation with multiple machines whirring and clicking. His specialty was documentation for smugglers and fences to get illegal goods into the continental markets.

"Looks like you have a job?" asked Jimmy.

"Yes, I've got some work. Just came in, a rush job," answered the forger.

"You better have not spent the down payment. That's money you owe Mr. Lo." Allen was playing extra tough with his boss around. "How about you save your stories for your mates at the paddock and bring me my cash?" Allen finished.

"So the interest for this week is eight shillings—" calculated Trevor.

"Chen, rip this place apart and uncover my money," said

Jimmy as he tightened his ascot. Trevor's interest calculation was correct, but Jimmy needed to learn how much the forger had been paid. He couldn't leave Trevor with too much money as it would just go to betting on horses.

"Mr. Chen, no need to get physical. These are delicate apparatus. Let me get the payment." Trevor went over to his coat to get his pocketbook.

Jimmy stared at the document descending from the stampautotron as it slowly lurched out of the rollers. The machine selected the correct letter template, inked them and pressed the page with the stamp. He cocked his head to read the upside-down type. The document was a bill of sale for 1450 one hundred-gram bars of bullion purchased in Amsterdam in 1842 from a metals dealer to a Venetian banker.

Chin grabbed the billfold from Trevor. The intimidating goon brought the wallet to Jimmy, who looked inside and pulled out thirty-three pounds. Jimmy exclaimed. "Holy fuck, Trevor. This job was a big payday." The thirty pounds would take care of Trever Owens' gambling obligations. "Trevor, you are having a lucky streak."

"I'll have you know I have plum picks for the courses. There is this trifecta that is an absolute lock—"

Jimmy interrupted. He didn't give a shit about horses. "Trevor, tell me about this assignment you're working on." Jimmy looked at the sheets on the line drying, a waybill for a steamer line moving the gold from Venice to Liverpool. A bill of sale from a Venetian merchant bank to a trust in the United States.

Lin did the math in his head, converting grams to pounds, figuring the losses in paying for smelting, recasting and paying a document forger; this looked like just the right sum of gold to be left over after losses and costs for the witch's gold.

He held out the wallet to Trevor. "This is how lucky you are. You tell me about who employed you and when they are returning to pick up the paper, and you might get me to cover this week's interest myself and leave you with all of these banknotes for that trifecta."

"Jimmy, honor among thieves, mate. If it were to get out about town that Trevor Owens spills the beans, I would never get work."

Lin put the billfold into the inner breast pocket of his coat. "No worries, Gov. I understand. Looks like I found the last honest criminal in London. Good luck at the track tomorrow."

"Ah. Mister Lin, how about leaving a bloke with a fiver to see him through the week?"

Jimmy made his way out of the back room. "Come on, Chen. We got a schedule to keep."

"Let's say I was to provide this information. You and I would be good for let's say two weeks of interest, I could get that deposit back and be sure that my name would never come up."

Jimmy stopped short with his back to Trevor. He had to admit that was a ballsy move on the forger's part to up the ante. \ This certainly was Jimmy's lucky day. It had been less than twenty-four hours, and he had a solid line on thousands in gold. This could save him days of running around town, listening to the stuttering shit birds that provided underworld information. All this would cost is a few weeks' interest, and Trevor was a degenerate who would lose the thirty pounds in the wallet and then come to him for another loan.

Jimmy plucked out the wallet and held it up for Trevor to grab. "You tell me everything about what you're putting together, who and how they are getting the paper from you, and we can keep this lucky streak going for you."

~

8:00 PM, Canterbury Music Hall

The meeting place was Canterbury Music Hall. Keane had a table where he could keep an eye on Nelson Bruce and his associate Allister "Red" McKenney. The nickname was from his hair color, not his political affiliation. Both parties had a stake in the meet-up and wanted to make certain the encounter took place without witnesses.

The Canterbury was brightly illuminated, with sodium arc lamps ensconced in the walls and the most magnificent chandeliers. Each fixture had over one hundred arc reflectors that cut through the haze of soot and smoke that hung in the theater from countless cigars, pipes, and cigarettes. The house band played an interlude between acts, and many of the patrons sang along while a charming girl held up cue cards with the lyrics to the ditty.

Dolly approached the table with two whiskeys. He was singing along, reveling in the atmosphere of the hall. Setting one glass down in front of Keane, he held his up for a toast as he sat down. "To a night out on Her Majesty," said Dolly in an acknowledgment that the Metropolitan Police Service would be picking up the tab.

Keane said nothing.

"Callum?"

Keane turned to Dolly.

"Sorry, mate. I was daydreaming," Keane replied.

"Are you alright, Keane?"

"Brilliant. Just have a lot on my mind, casework and such," Keane replied, still a bit distant and dissociated.

"Well, here's to the Queen," Dolly motioned.

"To the Queen!" replied Keane.

"What is the latest with the Chilton murders?" asked Keane.

"Are you going to take another stab at clearing up the case with your alcohol-sodden deductive powers?" replied Dolly.

"I only share my logic to show you how to close cases. If you're ever going to have a career, you need to close a case once in a while."

"Thanks for the career guidance," said Dolly "Will you get all shitty when I tell you that Rose established what the killer looks like?"

"How the hell did she manage that?" Keane asked, setting down his drink.

"She built this contraption. It is like a camera, but it captures spiritual remnants. I couldn't believe my eyes."

"What was the picture of?" asked Keane.

"I saw two pictures, one of a black woman standing over a white man at a writing desk. The second was the same woman and man, but she was gripping a sphere and penetrating his heart with a wand while he writhed in torment. Between the orb and the stab wound was a streak like lightening going across the night sky," explained Dolly.

"Rose Caldwell has these pictures?"

"Who else in London would construct a camera that takes pictures of spirits but the good Sister?"

"Anything else I should know?" asked Keane.

"I have corroboration that the suspect is a negro from Haiti, a runaway slave. Monday I have luncheon at the French embassy to learn more."

"Who are you meeting with?" asked Keane.

Nelson Bruce arose abruptly from his chair and crossed to the side of the auditorium, making his way to the rear stairs of the hall that served the balcony.

"Looks like it's time," Dolly said before slamming back his glass of whiskey. The detective went to the opposite side of the music hall then zig-zagged his way through the revelers to the back stairwell that led to the balcony. The lighting was poor in the upper balcony, and there were no tables, just rows of seats. These were the cheap seats, but the theater chairs were nice with velour cushions, compared to the wooden benches of lower class halls.

Upon reaching the balcony, Dolly worked his way to where Nelson Bruce sat in the rear row. From this spot, they could see anyone approach and were deep in the shadows of the rear balcony. There were only a few patrons in the mezzanine on a Thursday night, and they were close to the railing where the view of the stage was better.

The two others in the row with Nelson were embracing each

other and were too engrossed with their affection to hear what transpired between Nelson and Williamson.

"How you doing, Brucie?" asked Dolly. He had passed the bar and picked up two ales. He handed one to Nelson.

"Thanks, mate. I'm still struggling for the worker."

"You called for a meeting. What do you have to share?" asked the detective.

"You are correct. There are forces at play to instigate a panic," responded Nelson. He handed Dolly a pamphlet.

Dolly unfolded it and read.

Citizens of London, Beware

The Baden Gaswerks is building the Royal Fleet at the expense of your children!

We have it on good authority from prominent doctors and scientists that the construction of the plant and the sub-street sewerage is part of a complex system for the Baden Gaswerks to defuse insidious gases through the city. Its dark purpose is not to fill airships with LQ gas but to sterilize the immigrants flooding the city's ghettos.

Unite! Resist! Revolt!

"Where did you get this?" Dolly frowned. Now he had two cases about to boil over where he was the lead detective.

"Near the works. Some bill posters were gluing them up, and

there have been a few laborers passing them out. When I asked who hired them to pass and post the bills, they had no notion where they came from, but they had been paid for the work." Nelson said, never taking his eyes off the stage.

"This reads like what you were spouting to rile up your comrades the day I was down at the works. I would say verbatim." Dolly put the handbill in his inside coat pocket.

"Well, it isn't the Commonwealth Communist Union. I made sure of that, mate. I got your message clear as glass and told the committee you drew the line, and it was my reputation if it was crossed." Nelson's speech was harried.

"Then who's the organizer, if it's not you?" asked Dolly.

"None of the trade unions I know. I inquired around, and none claimed the bills," added Nelson.

"You pull off the picket line. I don't want one of your guys down there even walking their dog. The PM will call in the fusiliers to clear the crowds if there is any violence."

"I moved my lads yesterday, but the crowds have doubled. The migrants are paranoid that the aristocracy will poison their children to keep them downtrodden. I'm steering clear of that site now, Detective, so as far as I am concerned, this is the last we need to talk."

"If something goes down, expect to be carted in for appearances, but I'll make certain that your aid is recognized," said Dolly.

"Much appreciated." Nelson looked at him with a sarcastic sneer then went back to watching the stage.

Dolly walked away and toward Keane. On the way back, he stopped at the bar again to pick up two beers. When he returned to the table, Detective Burton was sitting with Keane, and there were already drinks on the table.

"Adam, good to see you," said Dolly, then he noted the third beer. "Someone sitting there?"

"No, that's for you. I noticed you two registered in the logbook. Thought I would come over after my shift to grab a drink with you fellas," answered Burton.

Dolly placed the pints down and pulled the chair around. "Well, it looks like we have a few ales to drink here, Keane." Dolly then reached into his coat pocket and pulled out the handbill and gave it to Keane.

"Fuck me," Keane said.

"A few more beers before I'll be doing that," said Burton smiling at his own joke and reading the bill over Keane's shoulder. "Oh, those are glued all over the walls of the gaswerks," Adam related.

"The leaflet isn't as significant as what Nelson declared. He asserts that he nor the other trade unionist are behind this. In fact, he already pulled his brothers out of there before I proposed it."

"That means he expects something is going to happen, even if he doesn't know who is behind it or what they are planning," Keane added.

"Righto, mate. We have some work to accomplish on Monday, but right now, I'm just going to get drunk at the Queen's expense, and you fellas are welcome to join me."

The detective's briefing had concluded and Dolly was now in the constables' briefing room listening to the upcoming police operation to break up the crowds at Baden Gaswerks.

Sergeant Eakins was chosen to command the operation. A uniformed officer with military experience, he was highly qualified in procedures where crowds were involved, from the planning of a parade or the smashing of a riot. Dolly, Keane and Burton were all in attendance as they had spent the most time gathering intelligence on the case at the gaswerks.

Once the operation was initiated, Eakins would be in charge. Today he was laying out his strategy. He stood in front of a chalkboard with a map of the neighborhood around the gas and iron works drawn out.

"As you see, there is a natural flow of the avenues to the plant. Three streets east, west and south with a gate at each end. The northern gate sits opposite the south gate of the Lloyds Works with the perimeter road between the two fences. There will be three muster points. Here, here and here." Eakins pointed to the spots on the map marked A, B and C.

"Muster point A will have two waves. The initial squad will go down Northern Docks Road and secure the north gate. At the same time, squad two will secure the western gate. Squads three and four will move on to the east and south gates.

"We will send in horse-mounted constables to separate groups and then police on foot behind them to disperse and guide people away. Those that won't disperse, or resist will be rounded up. Each muster point will have police wagons staged to move in and pluck up those that we arrest."

After a pause, Eakins continued, "I have spoken with Commissioner Mayne and have the 10th Fusiliers on ready if mass resistance ensues. Our preference is first to get everyone off the right of way to the gaswerks premises then to disperse and move the crowd out in an orderly fashion. Questions?" declared Eakins.

A constable raised his hand.

"Yes?" Eakins acknowledged the constable.

"Why are we breaking this up if there has been no violence?" the boyish constable asked.

Mayne interrupted before Eakins could answer. "Detectives Keane and Williamson have evidence that the common trade associations have fled and that there is a nameless group seeking to incite a riot at the location."

"Do we know who?" asked another constable.

Dolly spoke up this time, sitting on the edge of a desk with his jacket off. The room was steamy from the June heat and the large congregation in the small space. "The gaswerks are pivotal to our national interests. We know the throngs are not the usual trade unions causing trouble, and we can't put a finger on who is behind it. They are getting the migrants fired up, and we need to break it up before a bunch of ignorant buggers get hurt for no reason."

The group began asking specific questions about tactics and strategy. Dolly lost interest and started his way out of the briefing room.

As he stepped out, Mayne signaled to him to come over. "Dolly, I need you and Keane down there tomorrow to keep an eye on things. We still have no idea what the caper might be, and once the crowd is under control there, we may lose the opportunity to find out who has been stirring things up at the plant."

~

12:00 PM, French Embassy, London

Guild Master Saint-Yves had extended the invitation to Detective Williamson to meet for lunch at the French Embassy. He sat alone in the bright and spacious dining room, an island of black in a sea of white linen covered tables. The guild master sat in a contemplative trance, watching his thumb and forefinger slide up and down the stem of his water goblet. The condensation caused the motion to make a high-pitched squeak each time he did it. He stopped when the detective was escorted into the dining room.

The maitre'd approached the table with the detective following. The detective was nearly a foot taller than the maitre'd, and he walked with a confident gait.

"Guild Master, your guest is here to lunch with you," pronounced the maitre'd.

Saint-Yves was stood up and greeted his guest.

"Detective Sergeant Williamson, I appreciate you accepting my invitation. I assure you that you will enjoy one of the finest lunches in London and come away with information pertinent to the Moya Case," said the guild master.

"Thank you, Guild Master."

"Call me Gerard. Since we will be working together, I would like us to be on a first name basis."

"Then thank you, Gerard. You can call me Dolly."

"Please sit. Dolly, pardon me, but is this not a woman's name?"

"It's short for Adolphus. That's my middle name, and it has been my moniker since I joined the police service."

"I meant no offense, but it just sounded strange to my ear."

"None taken," said Dolly.

The guild master turned to the maitre'd "you can bring a menu for the Detective, si vous plait"

"So, you're looking to nab this Voodoo priestess and bring her to justice?" asked Dolly.

"Our intentions align, Detective. You need to catch a murderer. I need to keep this primitivism from getting out of the jungle," said the guild master.

"What can you share with me to apprehend the killer?" asked Dolly.

"Her name," said Gerard as he drank his tea.

"You know the name of the person who killed Moya?" Dolly reiterated as he took out his notebook.

"Her name is Angelica Du Haiti, and I have met her."

"If you don't mind, I will take some notes," said Dolly while he wrote the name in his book.

"The guild has been aware of the Voodoo practices in the New World for some time. Your Doctor Melbourne wrote a treatise on some of the pagan rituals, but it was more anthropologic than spiritual. To gain understanding, we had emissaries meet with the Voodooists and study the arcana. Ten years ago, I was part of the necronist mission to Haiti, and that is where I met the woman in question.

"France had just abolished slavery in the colonies, and plantation owners were concerned that practice of Voodoo would lead to the organization of the recently freed slaves and eventual revolt. We French know how ugly a revolution can be, and the Minister of Colonial Affairs contacted the guild to help assess the situation. We were intrigued, of course, to see if the tales were true of the ability to control and raise the dead. On the tour, we determined that there was a population of slaves that believed in the religion of Voodoo, but they were not practicing any arcana. It was a religion with no control or understanding of metaphysics," said Gerard as the memories of his past came back to him.

Ten years had passed since Saint-Yves, a young silver seer, had the privilege to be part of a delegation to investigate the threat of Voodoo to the French colony or the Emperor. The guild was happy to have the government of France fund the expedition to evaluate Voodoo. This primitivism intrigued the necronists as it appeared to engage death magic in ways like what necronists were experimenting with in clandestine research.

His mind drifted back to the expedition under Guild Master Huey.

They tramped through the hot jungle of Haiti for six days. His urban upbringing in Paris left him unprepared for the long slog through the humid insect infested tropics. The trek was grueling even with the troop of porters and guides. His feet became blistered from walking and cracked from waterlogged shoes. Mud clung to his legs and made his steps heavier. His robes that he was so proud to wear absorbed the sun and held the sweat and humidity. Eventually, they found the secluded village. They had followed an estuary that led to the awe-inspiring waterfall, where the village had developed at its foot. Gerard was physically uncomfortable, sweating in his black necronist robes and morally unsettled observing a village filled with nearly naked men and women.

They were not greeted with open arms. Many of the inhabitants were escaped slaves and those that had grown up in the village had heard the stories of the cruel life on a plantation and had a genuine dread of the white man. As they closed in on the village, it became clear that they were being followed and were surrounded and outnumbered. At the edge of the river, just before where the village started, they were met by the Voodoo king and his retinue. His name was Papa Lafayette, a wiry old man with only a loin cloth for clothing and coated in a sheen of sweat and musky from the unwashed life of the jungle. He stood with his Ju Ju staff, the mantle of his power. The staff was horrifying. The tall warped and petrified wood had four human skulls attached to it. These were the heads of the past Voodoo kings, who imbued the staff and the present king with all of their power. The Frenchmen could speak with the king through Lafayette's interpreter, a mixed-race girl. A true vision, the type of person you will always remember the first time you saw. Remarkable in her natural beauty and the glimmer of her aura. Even with his limited training, Gerard could detect the shimmer of her mortal and metaphysical charm.

Gerard came back to the present and chose carefully what to share. "There was, however, a village that was folklore to the slaves, where runaways who reached it settled in paradise under the safeguard of the gods of Voodoo. It was there I met Angelica. She was likewise an initiate at the time to a powerful Voodoo witch doctor. She was his protégé and interpreter."

"You saw her conduct rituals that killed men by removing their soul?" asked Dolly.

Gerard thought back. His mind raced with the memories from a decade ago, back to the initial contact. He recalled in his mind's eye Lafayette and the vitality and raw power he exuded, how his ebony skin glistened from the humidity. Papa boldly told the mission that they were not welcome and they were to leave. As Guild Master Huey attempted to parley with the Voodoo king, Lafayette began working a thralling incantation; the guides and porters quickly fell under his influence, and they broke and ran in fear. Huey was impressed at the strength of the invocation the king was fabricating and the king equally impressed with the necronist's defenses against it. Huey and Gerard saw through the Voodoo illusion and stood their ground.

The acknowledgment of each other's capacity to wield such power became the thread of common respect that the two parties could build on. The necronists were the first outsiders allowed in the sanctuary. The two parties learned from each other. The necronists could articulate the science of the metaphysical, and Papa Lafayette could help them to find a way to a primal connection with the arcane. That was the weakness of the necronist way: their connection to the supernatural was an intellectual one, not visceral. The necronist path to the metaphysical was books, learning and experimentation; the Voodooist path was spit, sweat and blood.

Huey understood the tremendous opportunity the necronist had after the group witnessed a Voodoo ritual where Papa Lafayette summoned the spirits of past Voodoo kings back to earth to possess the dead. It began more like a frenzied bacchanal with naked practitioners dancing themselves into a trance, so contrary to the puritanical dress and demeanor of the guild. Gerard, a talented necronist, was adept at scrying messages from the afterworld and beginning to hone his skills at controlling the wills of others, but what he saw that evening was raw and pure necromancy.

The village was located at the waterfall for a purpose. The falls were a rift point into the afterworld, a doorway for Ju Ju spirits to move from one plane to another. Papa Lafayette was in the center of the ritual, directing the ceremony. Four corpses were brought into the circle. Lafayette recited his incantations, and the dead rose. They became the mortal vessels of spirits that had passed. The savage could do what the necronists could not, reanimate the dead and do so by bringing spiritual energy from the afterworld.

"No. She did not have those powers then, but Papa Lafayette did, and I saw primal necromantic arts being performed. They were ignorant of the metaphysics behind what they were doing, but he still could wield the power of life and death."

A few nights later, the necronists were invited to Papa's hut. He had the three necronists sit with him on the floor around a small clay pot. He was brewing some concoction. Angelica was there, but she was standing on the outside acting as the interpreter. The Voodoo king said that he had decided that he would train the necronists on the condition that the necronists guaranteed the safety of his people. Huey wholeheartedly agreed to the pact. Lafayette said to seal this pact the four of them would drink from his pot. He ladled the foul-smelling soup into wooden bowls and each man drank. He smiled and gestured for them to drink it all. When done, he laughed and talked to Angelica. Her face lost color. The old man kept repeating to her the same words. She then told Gerard and the others their fate.

She explained how all four of them had just consumed soul worm eggs. Their flesh and eternal Ju Ju would be consumed by the Great Devourer when the worms hatched and grew. They were all bound by a death pact. In six months' time, the worms would hatch, and in a year from that day, those that were not cleansed would be dead. Gerard and the other young Seer Hume would stay in the village and train alongside Angelica. Guild Master Huey would return to France to secure the written agreement of sanctuary. Upon his return, the four men would again sit in this hut, and he would brew the potion to cleanse them of the eggs or larva.

Huey left the next day. Gerard and Hume became pupils of Papa Lafayette alongside Angelica. Saint-Yves and Hume's learning became fundamental to the most important of the necronists metaphysical discoveries. Ten months later, Huey returned with the compact signed by the Emperor himself.

"In the end, we learned what we could, and we gave the witch doctor and his tribe sanctuary. It was a worthwhile tradeoff for the guild, and now we know the true extent of the Voodoo power," said the necronist.

"How are you sure it is this woman that is our murderer?" Dolly followed up.

He remembered the stories she and Gerard shared about their pasts and dreams of their future together. He remembered the times they laughed as he fumbled incantations and how disappointed he was that she chose not to return with him to Paris to join the guild. His younger self wanted so much to share Paris and the guild with her. He knew her natural spiritual manipulation would bring her to the rank of guild master and they could continue to be together, but that was not what he would share with the Englishman.

"First, I know the innate talent she had, and if she continued to progress at the speed she was learning, she would now be capable of these acts. Further, there is a connection to the murdered. She was a runaway slave before she joined Papa Lafayette. She shared with me that it was a Moya Plantation where she was born. The older Moya's cause of death was impossible to determine and the state of his body was attributed to the house being burnt to the ground. When I heard about the younger Moya being killed and the condition of the body, I was certain that it is her."

"Do you know if she has any family or associates in London?" asked the detective.

"No. She had never been off the island, and she would not leave until she learned everything from Papa Lafayette."

Gerard observed the patience of the detective. This man would sit in silence and wait for him to divulge more. He needed to see the detective's commitment to stopping the threat.

"Detective, have you ever heard of Nicolas Fouquet?"

"No, I haven't."

"Nicolas Fouquet was the minister of finance for the Sun King. Louis the XIV. He was a trusted advisor and very influential in the court. The Prime Minister, Jules Mazarin, passed to the aether, and Nicolas very much wanted the job. He decided to throw a magnificent party in honor of the King in hope of impressing his allegiance on him.

"He opened his Chateau to all the court, he invited the greatest minds, he even had a special play written and directed by Molière in honor of the King. There were endless courses of food, some never seen before in Europe. After dinner, Fouquet invited the crowds to walk his garden, where he held a fireworks display as grand as there could be. Can you guess what happened the next day?" asked Gerard.

"He got the job," said Dolly.

"No. He was arrested for embezzlement of taxes. It's true. He did embezzle, but the King was complicit in the misuse of the taxes. Fouquet was sent to solitary confinement for the rest of his years. You see, the King did not see his actions as adulation, but as a rivalry to his own greatness. Now do you see where Angelica Du Haiti and Nicolas Fouquet made their mistake?" asked the guild master.

"You don't want some primitive occult to diminish your spiritual science," said Dolly.

The guild master's shoulders relaxed, and he smiled "Yes, Nicolas and Angelica outshine the master. That is why we are aligned in our purpose. You cannot let a murderer run around freely, and the guild cannot have some primitive witchcraft look more powerful than what we wield. So, I can help you make sure that she does not leave this island alive."

Dolly put his notebook in his jacket and stood up. "Guild Master, that is where you and I are not aligned. My purpose is to find the criminals and bring them to the Queen's justice. What is fitting of the crime is not my business. I leave that to the judge and the barristers. I bring the criminal, the evidence, and the witnesses. It appears to me you have already passed judgment."

Gerard had misjudged the Englishman. He was more committed to the principles of his profession than to what it would take to keep people safe. "Please have a seat, Detective. I am sorry if I misspoke. My command of English may have led to misusing of words. What I mean is that you have my commitment to capturing Angelica, but you also have my commitment to do everything in my power to stop her from killing more English. Now, please sit down. I did promise you the best lunch in London, and they have not even taken our order," said Saint-Yves.

The Detective returned to his seat, and that was enough of a sign to the guild master that the door was still open to get the cooperation he would need from the English police to act against the murderer of the Moyas and Sir Chilton.

TUESDAY THE 22ND OF JUNE

9:30 AM, MUSTER POINT A, NEAR THE BADEN GASWERKS

Dolly was slow to arrive at the scene. Upon finding Keane, he quickly got up to speed on the situation. The operation would go ahead in thirty minutes. He met his fellow detective east of the plant at the Woolwich Road muster point. Here, squads one and two would divide up and seize the north and west gates, while squads from the two other muster points would take the south and east gates. The police were setting up a cordon to limit traffic into the neighborhood of the works. Unseasonably hot, the city was nearly unbearable as the humidity caused the coal ash and soot to hang heavy. This weather would only pump more pressure into an already over-pressured boiler. Dolly hoped they could methodically release that pressure before the proverbial boiler blew up and hurt someone.

Two duty sergeants discussed the present situation. The area was occupied with police loitering and talking idly, but the momentum was picking up as Sergeant Eakins issued orders for last-minute alterations to the positioning of equipment and men. At least twenty constables stood at the ready as mounted patrols drew up the horses and formed up to take the front line.

Dolly was in good spirits until he heard protestors had blocked all the entry gates to resist and impede the right of way. That meant arrests and possible bloodshed.

"Morning, Callum Keane. What have you been up to this fine day?" asked Dolly when he met Detective Keane.

"I've been working with Wells here to prepare. In another twenty minutes, we will have groups ready. I'm aiming to remain with the force for the west and observe the crowd," replied Keane.

"Sorry for my delay. I have been down at the docks and to the train stations circulating pictures of my suspect," added Dolly.

"What picture? Let me see it," requested Keane.

Dolly pulled out one of the few remaining bills he had in his coat and passed it to Keane. In the process, he felt his pipe. He resolved if they had a half hour before the operation he would enjoy a smoke.

Keane studied the poster bill. It showed a hand sketch of an African woman's face, including the title:

Wanted for questioning at Scotland Yard

Ms. Angelica Du Haiti

Aged 28-34

Notify a constable immediately

Keane looked at Dolly with a peculiar look of shock and apprehension. "How did you come to know this name?"

"I'm a detective, Keane. It's my business is to identify criminals. I'm certain that's my girl."

"How did you come to know her name, her likeness?"

Dolly's buoyant mood washed away at Keane's strange interest in his case. "I obtained intelligence from sources, multiple confidential sources."

"It was that witch, wasn't it?"

"Oh, it is a legitimate corroborated lead, I assure you."

"I am asking you, who? If corroborated, who are the two sources? Tell me," demanded Keane.

Dolly had never seen Keane act like this and was reticent in sharing too much. "By the Foreign Office. What is up with you Keane?"

Keane continued to deliver a cold stare, remaining silent as if he was pondering about what to do next.

Dolly ripped the bill from Keane's grip. "Don't you mind who I work with. Rose's methods are as reliable as yours."

Annoyed, Dolly stalked over to the side street, where a row of steam-powered paddy wagons lined up to transport prisoners and one of the new command wagons, the latest in mobile communication technology. It was grander than a paddy wagon about the size of a mover's truck with a wire type and tape clacker. The wagon was capable of splicing into the telegraph wire system and providing up-to-the-minute communication. Two police clerks were in the back sending messages back to Scotland Yard and to the other muster points.

The detective strode up the wooden steps to take a glance at the latest in police communication machinery. "Hey, gents," he said to the two young constables that were clerking the wire-types.

"Good morning, Detective Sergeant," replied the youthful clerk holding the clacker tape.

"Do you mind not smoking in the van sergeant? It's a little stuffy in here, and this is all sensitive gear."

"No worries, mate."

As Dolly turned to step down, Keane was right on his heels, glaring at him. "What the fuck, Keane? You're on me like a case of the crabs," barked Dolly.

Keane just glared at him.

"Are you alright? You look like you need a lie down." said Dolly.

An ear-shattering blast snapped the two men out of the conversation. More than just a sound came. The shock wave reached everyne's bones, and it was accompanied by debris showering down across the muster site.

Dolly instinctively pulled himself into the communications truck. Lying on the floor, he could hear the constant patter of dirt and gravel raining down on the top of the communications van.

"What the hell was that?" declared the clerk.

"Wire-type for ambulances and order them to form up at this rally point," Dolly commanded.

Sergeant Eakins ran up to the communications van. "Wire the other squads to move in immediately, then request updates."

"Yes, sir." The two clerks banged away at the piano keys of the wire-type machines.

Williamson had plenty of experience with explosions and bombs back when he was handling the Irish troubles. This one was bigger than anything he had experienced. He searched for Keane, but he was gone, likely towards the blast to discover what had transpired. He desired to do the same and followed suit.

Dolly could see smoke billowing above the metropolis. It had a greenish purple tint in contrast to the familiar grey smog generated by the hundreds of London's smokestacks. Somewhere there was an LQ gas discharge.

Dolly went to the duty sergeant, who under Eakins' orders had earlier committed the squads towards the plant. He was coaxing his men forward. "Alright, alright, move up, lads. Keep it orderly. Keep yourself calm, and let's enforce the peace." Twenty coppers with truncheons drawn moved in lockstep down the lane behind a line of ten horses.

Dolly grabbed Eakins' arm to get his attention. "I need a driver and a carriage."

"Over there. O'Neil is running the motor pool," answered the sergeant.

The police officer in charge of vehicles was yelling over the commotion to get steam carriages in position behind the police line. "You two saddle up and follow the line in the event they need to toss in prisoners," he yelled.

Dolly jumped on the runner board of the steam lorry and

clutched the sill to steady himself on the car. Not that he didn't wish to walk, but it gave him a view over the patrolmen to observe what was up ahead. "Just keep moving. I'll let you know if I see anything," Dolly said through the passenger window to the two constables inside.

As they closed in on the Works, the air was becoming thick and heavy with soot and smoke from the explosion and ensuing fires. Out of the haze, screams and shrieks were bursting through, then citizens followed. Some people running, some shuffling, others helping the injured away from the disaster within the fog. The line of constables broke as they were rushed and overcome, not by rioters but by the injured and dismayed.

Dolly hopped off the wagon and grabbed a young man walking on his own but visibly wounded. "What happened? What did you see?" asked Dolly.

"There was a blast at the gaswerks. Absolutely horrible. People blown to bits," said the man through tears of hysteria. The detective looked the youth over for severe wounds. It was hard to tell with all the dirt-caked blood what wounds the man had. Dolly guided him towards the muster point. Dolly assumed he must be in reasonable health that he could walk and talk. "Keep walking this way. There is help ahead."

Another victim was wandering towards Dolly, clearly looking bewildered, "Sir, continue moving forward toward the aid station." The man just stared at him. That is when dolly noticed the blood running from both of his ears. He wrapped his arm around the man and walked him back to the muster point and handed him off to a constable.

Dolly jogged over to the line of paddy wagons and called out to the sergeant in charge of the pool. "You need to send more wagons up to help move the wounded."

The sergeant turned, blew his whistle and waved the steam lorries forward. Dolly jumped on the first one and leaned into the passenger window to speak to the driver and his partner. "Drive right up to the explosion so we can see what is going on. I don't want you stopping for injured. We must assess the situation, then steam back and let the blokes in the communication truck know the status."

"Yes, sir," hollered the driver.

It was slow-going, as debris and bodies lay upon the road. Although the dust from the explosion was clearing, it was replaced by an eerie green haze clinging to the ground as they moved closer to the blast site. This jade mist was not LQ gas; LQ was purple and lighter than air. That alchemical element was streaking up high into the atmosphere, mixing with the smog that over hung the city, giving it a strange beautiful lavender glow.

Dolly stepped off the steam lorry and climbed over rubble blocking the way. Visibility was about eight to ten feet in the green dusty smog. Dolly began to make out shapes of people, horses, wagons and wounded on the streets. Throughout the soupy fog, the moans and cries of the wounded came through clear. The initial squad of police was now overwhelmed helping the victims, and the police whistles and yells of frantic officers trying to help came from all directions. The emerald haze thickened as he closed in on the gaswerks. Reaching the outer wall, he began to use it as a guide through the haze to the explosion. Every step of his path was littered with rubble or gore, but being able to feel the rough stone wall grounded him and helped to fix his location.

The detective reached the end of the wall where it turned to go east at the corner of the perimeter road that passed between the Lloyd Works and the Baden Gaswerks. Dolly looked up and saw the hulk of the HMS Victoria sitting in its berth. Men scurried on the scaffolding and open decks. From what he could tell, the ship looked undamaged, but the same could not be said for the plant. He could see the damage illuminated by the fires in the crater and both plants. A mere twenty feet down the road ahead, the edge of the blast crater started. At the bottom of the crater was the exposed underground pipe that transmitted LQ from the gas works to the aerodrome. It had ripped open and was spewing purple fumes into the sky. It was a monumental disaster. Having no knowledge of machinery or alchemy, he speculated what it would take to stop such a sizable leak. What he did have some knowledge in was the evaluation of a bomber's work. A crater this size and the damage done to the gaswerks and the aerodrome facilities looked to his eye to be kegs and kegs of powder, and it had to have been under the street. The explosion had damaged both work sites, obliterating buildings, damaging tanks and breaching the walls.

Through the gaping hole in the gaswerks perimeter wall, Dolly could see that the emerald gas was emanating not from the transfer pipe but from damaged tanks on the gaswerks property. The green gas had a sickly-sweet smell and taste, like having a mouth and nose full of licorice. For the first time, he thought if he should breathe in these vapors and what the effect would be on himself and his colleagues.

As Dolly peered through the fog to the other side of the crater, there appeared to be more wounded, but there was no way to cross to help. The north and west squad were cut off by the crater and he could not cross. His stomach sank as he finally oriented to where the crater was. Anyone picketing at the north gate had been standing on top of the explosion. Earlier estimates were there were a hundred protesters at that gate. If so, then there was a guarantee of one hundred casualties. By his assessment, they would need a lot more help. He had observed at least twenty dead and similar number wounded and unable to move.

He yelled to the paddy wagon driver. "Go back and get them to send up more help. Medical help. Have them wire the east road muster to move up and get help over to the other side of that crater. Have them wire the home office. We need the army here to secure a perimeter, and get the fire brigades up here."

"On it, sir." The steam lorry let out a big chuff of steam as he ratcheted the gearing into reverse and backed out. Dolly couldn't recall all the orders he just shouted and figured the driver wouldn't remember either by the time he got back, but Eakins was a professional on how to get resources in place to regain control of a situation.

As the steam engine faded, he heard another sound approaching from above. A dull hum that grew in intensity. He looked up to see the HMS Warrior break through the smog overhang to take up station at the gaswerks.

That was a good sign for Dolly. It meant that the Army and Air Service would exert an overwhelming force to quell any further rioting.

The air destroyer shone bright arc lights down at the ground. Dolly could make out sharpshooters on the midline walkways.

A loud but tiny voice came from the audiophone of the Warrior. "This is Captain Archer of Her Majesty's Air Service. You are to peaceably disperse and allow the police and fire brigades to assist the wounded. Any rioters or looters will be shot."

The detective surveyed the area as the ship moved from over his head around to the other side of the gaswerks. The spotlights from the Warrior helped to burn through the dense fog, aiding Dolly in his appraisal of the area. Several passes of the spotlights helped him make out the edges of the shops and buildings across from the plant. Two buildings were destroyed, and the rest looked like a strong wind could knock them down.

As the din of the ironclad faded, Dolly heard the cries of a woman from one of the buildings across the street from the gaswerks. It sounded to him to be coming from the luncheonette with all the windows blasted out.

It was difficult to see through the jade fog now that the airship had circled, and its beams of light were focused elsewhere. He stepped over the window sill into the café, watching not to cut himself on the jagged remnants of glass. He heard the crunch of the shattered glass on the floor under his boot when he placed it inside the shop. Along the wall were the coin-operated server chambers. The dining area was strewn with tables, chairs, bodies and body parts. None were alive. He heard the woman's cry again and thought he saw a female form move past a doorway in the back behind the cashier's counter.

Dolly drew his Colt Navy revolver, pulled back the hammer and brought the pistol up close to his eye. Rotating the cylinder, he made sure that there were caps in place on all the chambers, and then he clicked a chamber into place.

He edged around the doorway, looking down the sights of his pistol. No one was there. This was the luncheonette kitchen. It did not appear to have any damage, but those that had worked there had abandoned their posts and fled to safety.

The chiller was open. On the counter were chopped vegetables, and pots were still boiling on the cooktops. At the far end of the room, the door was ajar and moved.

The detective made his way to the end of the kitchen to check the door, his breathing shallow and irregular. This time he pushed the door open with his shoulder and raised his pistol. He saw someone that resembled Angelica Du Haiti move through the back of the storeroom and out the alley door. It was like looking at the phantasmagraph in Rose's apartment, a translucent apparition in the green fog. Was this gas making him hallucinate?

Cautiously moving through the aisle between the shelves of the storeroom, he reached the door, turned the handle and threw it open, stepping to the side as the door opened inward.

He peered around the doorjamb before stepping out in the alley. All he saw was the man's fist point blank as it smashed into his face.

∼

10:15 AM, Hildy's Luncheonette, near the Baden Gaswerks

Dolly went down hard on his back.

Struck square in the nose, the Scotsman was blinded by the potent blow, his eyes wet from the sharp pain across his whole face. He wasn't certain if it was blood or tears in his eyes. He could taste and smell his own blood, a dreadful change from the taste and smell of the gas from the plant. The iron taste was on his lips and running in the back of his throat.

He tried to get up but was quickly slammed down onto the ground with the entire weight of his assailant on his chest, and now he felt hands around his throat. The grip was crushing.

Dolly panicked. He could sense the attacker driving his thumbs under and around his windpipe to crush it. His eyes cleared, and to his horror, he recognized who his assailant was: Cullam Keane. He struggled to cry out his name, but nothing came.

Like any choking victim, he naturally struggled to get Keane's hands off his throat. He was not strong enough to break his grasp. He stared at Keane.

"She's in me head, Dolly" Keane struggled through his clenched teeth.

Dolly let go of Keane's thick wrists, moving his hands to Keane's face, gouging both of Keane's eyes with his thumbs. He thrust deep and hard, pushing his nails in between the eyeballs and the nose bridge.

Cullam yelled and released Dolly's neck. Williamson gasped in precious air. Keane's arms went straight up, breaking Dolly's grasp of his face, then Cullam came down with both fists on Dolly's nose one more time, the blast of pain paralyzing him once again. Keane leapt off Dolly, allowing him to roll left and use the shelving to help himself to a seated position, clearing the second round of runny eyes.

Soon enough, he learned the reason for the reprieve of Keane's assault. Cullam had found Dolly's pistol, and Dolly was staring down the business end of his own gun. Keane was just outside the doorway, standing in the alley, and Dolly sat on the storeroom floor.

Williamson could see Angelica's vague outline in the gloom

behind Keane. Was she there or not? "Has Angelica got you under a spell?" Dolly asked in between taking breaths into his burning chest.

"Why couldn't you leave her be, Dolly? No one else will get hurt," Keane said as he sobbed.

"She is hurting you," said Dolly, trying to get through to Keane. Williamson could see Keane had slipped back into his trance and was aiming to take a shot.

Dolly swept his leg to catch the corner of the open door and kick it shut. As it slammed Cullam, a shot flew and lodged in the door. Williamson stood and clambered back towards the kitchen. He struggled to tug on the shelving to see if he could force the racks over to create an obstruction, but they were fixed to the floor.

His chest burned from the deep breaths he was drawing, faltering as he dashed into the kitchen. He flung the door behind him closed, searching for a lock, but there was nothing to secure the door. His eye spotted the knife next to the chopping block and minced onions. He seized it instinctively for protection. His racing mind and darting eyes assessed the area. He grabbed an empty pot and ducked into the open chiller, then threw the pot out of the kitchen through the door, out into the luncheonette hoping his assailant would follow the noise.

Keane burst through the door and surveyed the kitchen. He didn't fall for the racket of the pot landing in the other room. The detective was pressed up against the racks in the chiller with the knife ready.

"Come out, Dolly. I know you're in there. I can see your breathing in the cold," said Keane.

Shit. He heard Keane step up to the cooler, loitering just outside the door. Dolly took a deep breath, looked at the knife and thought, *What am I going to do? Stab Cullam to death?* He could see Keane's shadow on the floor of the cold room. Dolly was cornered. His only move was to kill Keane. "Alright. Tell her I will drop the case. I will let her go." Dolly was out of choices, and he couldn't kill Keane. He strode out in front of Cullam Keane and dropped the blade.

Behind Keane stood Angelica Du Haiti, near the exit to the storeroom.

Keane didn't move. He stood frozen, staring at him pointing the handgun at Dolly's heart.

"Detective, I am not a savage and have no quarrel with you." The woman said in a lyrical West Indies accent. She was wearing a striking maroon crinoline dress, looking more like a lady strolling the park than a murdering witch, that is until you saw the tall staff decorated with skulls and feathers in her hand rather than a parasol.

"Let him go," Dolly begged.

"I cannot. He is my only guarantee you will leave me to my business. Your colleague will remain with me until I escape. If you or others follow me, they will die by his hand. Forget me, and I will return him safely," asserted the enchantress.

Dolly heard Keane mutter, "No."

His eyes flashed from Angelica to Keane. Keane was back. Dolly could see recognition in his gaze just before the gun went off and a shower of blood covered Dolly's face. Dolly looked into Keane's eyes as the life left them. The top of Keane's skull was missing. Smoke curled out of the barrel

Keane had stuck under his own chin. The pistol dropped to the floor just before Keane's lifeless body did the same.

Dolly bellowed, "No! No!"

As he realized what Keane had done, he reached for the firearm and drew up on the witch to fire. She wielded her staff and howled something undecipherable, a conjuration. Keane's dead hand grabbed Dolly's leg. He looked down to see the deceased body moving, trying to seize his other leg. Dolly let out a scream and bolted away from Keane's moving corpse, his mind swirling in a soup of horror and disbelief.

The detective kicked at the arm that held him to escape the dead man's grip then suddenly the body ceased its supernatural animation. He glanced back for Angelica, but she was gone. He had to take a second glance at Keane to be positive he didn't move again. Then he rushed after her back through the storeroom then out to the alley. When he got there, Dolly heard a young voice yell, "Drop the pistol, mister!"

At the end of the alley were three British infantrymen with rifles trained on him.

Williamson dropped the gun and raised his hands. "I'm a detective in the Metropolitan Police Department. I can show you my badge," pleaded Dolly.

"Okay, real slow," said one trooper.

Dolly reached into his jacket and pulled out his billfold, opening it to show the infantrymen.

"Bloody hell, mate. I had no idea," said a soldier. They all lowered their carbines and relaxed.

"Did you see a woman come out here? A negro woman with a staff?"

"No, Detective, and we moved up here quickly when we heard shooting."

At that moment, Dolly looked down, and just outside of the alley lay a primitive, handmade doll. Upon closer examination, he observed it was a man-shaped fetish with symbols and pins stuck into it. Dolly picked up the doll and began to sob.

The front page of the Guardian showed a lithoprint of the HMS Warrior passing over the billowing smokestacks of the alchemical works.

The caption read:

Airship struck awe in the gaswerks rabble as its enormous hull blotted out the sun; 60 guns trained on the dispersing crowd.

Dolly read the main story that detailed one hundred and sixty-eight dead and fifty-seven wounded in the blas,t including three shot in the subsequent looting. He thought about the shooting of a certain police detective. That was left out of the papers.

The first three pages were all stories related to the disaster at the Baden Gaswerks. One article was on the LQ gas leak being contained by the alchemists shutting safety valves and reducing gas production and how there were no hazards to the public from the gas being breathed.

Another story opined that, with LQ production not damaged, the transfer line would need to be a priority repair to get the HMS Victoria's flotation cells supplied with lift gas. She was grounded until the repairs on the line were completed, adding to the British authorities' suspicion about the nature and intention of the explosion.

Dolly set the daily paper down on the small cafe table. Seated at a sidewalk table, he was enjoying his tea and a poached egg and toast. Passersby did not avert their gaze from the man with a broken nose and two swollen black eyes. What they could not see were the bruises on his throat under his collar.

Guild Master Gerard took a seat at his table. "Very unfortunate," he said as his finger tapped the front-page story. "I assume from your condition you were on the front line breaking up the riot.

"It was..." Dolly's voice was faint and hoarse. It hurt his throat to breathe, even more to talk. "It was sabotage, not a riot. We will look at your government as the obvious instigators, but that is not why I wanted to meet. What do you make of this?" He put the man-shaped effigy on the table. The guild master picked it up and studied the front and back of the doll.

"This is what is commonly referred to as a Voodoo doll. It is a talisman used to influence the spirit of the living. It can be used to cure ills, bring good fortune or bad," said Gerard.

"Or to control a person?" asked Dolly.

Gerard knew of this practice, recalling Papa Lafayette creating a similar doll and the using it to dominate a wayward villager. "Oui. In the hands of a powerful witch doctor, this can be used to inflict excruciating pain or control a subject as if they were a puppet."

"I found this near the gaswerks" whispered the detective.

"Do you believe she controlled the saboteurs with this fetish?" asked the guild master.

"No. She used it to manipulate Detective Keane. He tried to kill me in a possessed state," answered Dolly.

Gerard picked up the figurine again and studied it. "You see these markings where the eyes and ears are?" the Frenchman said as he pointed them out to the detective. "This indicates she was also using him as a spy. Angelica could channel what your detective saw and heard. Did this Keane know of my existence in London?" The seer looked concerned at this development.

Dolly thought for a moment. "No, he knew that I had identified Angelica and was working on her whereabouts and capture. I mentioned the identity was confirmed by a foreign source, but he assumed he learned about her through an occult specialist I confer with from time to time." Dolly stopped to drink some warm tea to sooth his throat.

"You mean the angel summoner, Caldwell?" asked the necronist, knowing the Englishman's answer.

"Yes," replied Dolly. He had heard Rose called a lot of things but never an angel summoner.

"You would be wise to assume there are others under her spell," said the guild master while he played with the salt shaker on the table.

Dolly thought for a moment. *Shit, she could have half the city under her control.* "How do I know you're not one of her minions?" asked Dolly.

"I can divine that you are not one of her thralls. As to me, you don't know. All you have is my word that I possess powerful wards that protect me from her charms and incantations," answered Gerard.

Dolly accepted the answer and thought about the ward Rose gave him. "She tried to kill me, and in the process, got a friend of mine killed. I need to stop her from doing any more damage."

"Dolly, you were close to this Keane?"

"I was. We both started as constables. Our beats were near each other. We both moved into the detective branch around the same time. I'll admit I was always envious of his eye for detail. He was a natural detective and a good friend."

"You see now that your police force is not equipped to deal with someone like Angelica. To be frank, I would not attempt to confront her on my own, and I am a master seer."

Dolly swallowed hard as he drank his tea, wincing with each gulp. "How do you propose I apprehend her if even you're not strong enough to defend against her?"

"Our affiliation with Emperor Napoleon has made the Crown and the mechanists suspicious and prevented our guild from growing our membership or establishing a guild house on your soil. However I am traveling with two other guild members who can assist, and I can reach out to members of the Lodge here in London for additional help," answered Gerard.

Dolly said nothing. He had heard of the Lodge but thought of the organization as quacks and charlatans, not real metaphysicists, and certainly not as well-organized as the guild.

"For complete safety, I would need to go after Angelica with a full wyrding of twenty necronist seers," said Saint-Yves, but he knew that the police and the government would never stand for that many of his guild in London. "But without that, I am thinking some from the guild at the embassy and some patriotic Englishman with have spiritual insight could find her and rid London of her treachery."

"When you say rid her you mean kill her?" Dolly said bluntly.

"I truly hope it does not come to that," said Gerard.

Dolly couldn't breathe through his nose, and every breath he took through his mouth made his throat throb. He wanted Angelica dead, but it had to be at his hands or at the end of a hangman's rope. "Well that would be murder under English law, and I would haul you in along with your pack of spiritualists as vigilantes," said Dolly making an effort to raise his voice.

"I know Angelica. We have a past, That may be just what will get her off this path of death she is on. The group I can put together will be better equipped to defend against her sorcery and minimize any additional loss of life. The incident yesterday was not a failure on your part. I am surprised that you're still alive. You should be proud of that fact."

It sure felt like failure yesterday. The thought of almost dying at the hands of Keane or later when he washed Keane's blood and brains of his face were fresh in his mind and a reminder of his failing his friend. "If you know her, maybe you can answer this question. Why didn't she kill me yesterday? She had the chance. She reanimated my dead partner, and rather than sticking around to have him finish me off, she ran."

The Guild Master paused, as if thinking about Dolly's question. "I lived with her for two years in the jungle. She was happy studying the arts. She had a true devotion to them.

Now, as an outsider, you may assume that her, and even me are bad or touched by evil because we study the metaphysics of the afterlife. Making that gross assumption may make it easier to justify your actions towards her, but assuming she is evil because she practices Voodoo is as naive as assuming everything you do is good because you are an officer of the law. She has always been determined. Perhaps part of that devotion was to get the means of her revenge for her mistreatment as a slave. That she has gone to this extent to exact her revenge does not mean she wants us all dead. I believe that Angelica sparing you is a sign that she still can be redeemed."

The waiter came by the table. "Would you like to see a menu, sir?"

"No, I ate earlier." The guild master replied.

The waiter looked to Dolly. "Just the check when you get a chance," he said in his hoarse voice. After the waiter left, Dolly continued. "It sure seems like you want her dead."

"That's where you're confused, Detective. Your way is the way of more death. I see three paths. One, you capture her, and she will be tried, convicted and hanged. Two, she fights and dies during her apprehension, or three, she kills you and others in her escape. All paths have death at the end. You are the guide on her pathway to death. I, on the other hand ,only want her to stop practicing her craft where she detracts from our mastery of the metaphysical. I can be a guide to life. English justice may not be served, but others need not die and she could live in cloister with the necronists," answered Saint -Yves.

The guild master's words sunk into Dolly. He wanted the Voodooist in the Old Bailey, not for Moya and Chilton, but for

Keane and himself. At the same tim,e he didn't want to be back in that situation again of being powerless to the mystical. "You put me in a shitty spot, guild master. Get your team together and find Angelica Du Haiti, and make sure when you do, that you tell me so I can be there."

"I will, Detective," answered Gerard.

"I just can't have some sorcerer turning us on each other," replied Dolly.

"Rest assured, Detective. The decision to involve us is a sound one. You're a fine officer of the law, but this woman works outside the bounds of earthly laws and physics. We are better equipped to stop her before another person is killed."

"Guild master, just make sure you stay within the earthly bounds of commonwealth law, and we will be fine. If you find her, wire-type me and I will act immediately," said Dolly.

~

6:30 PM, across the street from Silkwood & Company

The only way this would go well for Jimmy Lin was if the first time that Weng Lo heard about the heist was standing in front of his cut of the gold. That meant he had to keep his knowledge of his plans to a minimum until he was ready to act. Therefore, he was back to the boring low-level job of casing a joint. Jimmy needed the luster of a pile of gold on Weng Lo's desk to cloud his boss's memory of denying help to Sister Rose.

Jimmy would have eventually ended up at Silkwood & Company. Silkwood & Company was a nondescript building in the Hatton Garden area at the end of a T-intersection and not like the other jewelers with a storefront and display windows; it had no windows and a solid iron door. Silkwood was a jeweler's jeweler. They dealt in wholesale and did setting and work for the shops in the area. It was owned by the widow Silkwood, an old crone, but she had nothing to do with the business after her husband's death and left the shop to be managed by Simon Biel, a mild-mannered Hasidic gentleman that Jimmy and his ilk called Simon the Jew. He didn't move stolen property but would rework stones and precious metals for a fee. That made Silkwood one of three places that Jimmy would have gone to, as they would take under the table work. Along with re-cutting stones and breaking down jewelry, they had a smelter for the melting of precious metals, and for a jeweler, it was a good-sized one. Jimmy didn't need to run around looking because Trevor laid out how he was hired to paper the job to look like the gold was minted in Antwerp years ago then sat in a Venetian bank until sold to a trust, a trust managed by Chilton, Chilton, Owens and Strathmore. The re-struck gold would move back into the Chilton House vaults. Brilliant! Who would look for stolen gold in the place it was stolen from? The cops would be up and down the wharf looking for the bullion, and it would be home and hosed with a clean title right back where it was nicked from. That told Jimmy there was a partner or someone high up involved in the burglary. He liked this job. Nothing better than robbing a robber since they couldn't call the cops, and in this case, the criminals were blue bloods. They had been amateurs in how they have been getting work done, not that they were stupid. On the contrary, this caper showed ingenuity. The difference was he was a professional outlaw, and they were not. They were making simple procedural errors that left bread crumbs for someone of his ilk to follow.

Jimmy pondered how events played out; someone at the

Chilton bank knew about the gold and likely kidnapped old man Chilton to open the safe. They had to be a manager or some higher-up that understood what was required to deal with that amount of gold. This person also knew the likes of Trevor Conroy and Simon the Jew, not the type of folks you meet shooting quail with your high society friends. The part that puzzled Jimmy and made him a little worried was that the old man was killed by some kind of witch and Rose the witch lady wanted to get her.

He had met Rose's negro sorcerer. Walked right up to her door and knocked. Him being able to do this was another reason to think he was dealing with amateurs. They had hired Trevor to create travel papers for a Swiss national named Bertha Helstrom, rather than splitting the job between Trevor and another forger. Next upon completion, the travel papers were to be delivered to a certain address. Jimmy took it upon himself to be the delivery boy and chase down this lead. He brought the completed documents to the location, expecting it to be a drop and he would have to follow that person to the final destination. He almost shit himself when the door opened and an African woman answered the door. He played his charade as the Chinese delivery man. He even waited for a tip.

Jimmy snapped out of his daydreaming when a man walked up to the door of Silkwood's. He had two loaves of bread, a pail of beer and some packages. He knocked on the door and was let in. The same guy had left about a half hour before. Jimmy surmised he was sent out for dinner as the crew was working round the clock to get the job done.

The job was a big one. They had four hundred pounds of gold to melt down and recast as 100-gram gold ingots. The equipment they had was some of the biggest in London, but it was meant for mainly doing fine jewelry work so they faced a capacity issue. Melting the gold guineas in the crucibles, casting the ingots and cooling time meant it had to be a twenty-four-hour operation with multiple men to get the job done as quickly as possible. Simon would want to turn this job around fast so he didn't get nabbed with the stolen property.

Now Jimmy needed to get a guy inside.

FRIDAY THE 25TH OF JUNE

8:00 PM, ROSE CALDWELL'S ROOMS

Rose was at her desk with notes Preston had written to help with translation of the Chronicles of Ulric and the Liber Loagaeth, both borrowed from Preston's extensive collection. She mouthed the words of the Enochian language while staring at a looking glass and attempting to get the pronunciation of the angelic language correct.

The was a knock at the door.

Rose walked over to it, still practicing a word's pronunciation as she unlocked the door to let in the visitor.

It was Jimmy Lin.

"Come in, Jimmy."

Jimmy was alone, and that was rare. He was usually accompanied by at least one enforcer.

The thin Chinese native was smartly dressed, only the finest for Jimmy Lin. His attire was striking high-end business man, not the dandy fashion.

"To what do I owe the pleasure to, Jimmy?"

Jimmy alighted his narrow frame down onto a threadbare overstuffed chair. "To repay my debt. You are not going to believe this shit, witch lady. Well, maybe you will. Your life is a circus sideshow after all. I got a line on the gold and your Voodoo princess. I wanted to provide you with the address and let you know that she is traveling as Bertha Helstrom to Halifax Nova Scotia on Sunday afternoon." He took out a slip of paper from inside his glove and held it out for Rose to come get.

She snatched the slip of paper from his grasp and looked at it.

"You know where that is, witch lady?"

"Yes, I do," she answered while thinking about the address.

"Bet you don't get over there much?" Jimmy said.

"You would be surprised, Jimmy. Hey, I have a lot going on. Is there anything else?"

"What's all this shit for?"

"Well, Jimmy, this is what you would call an Eldritch laboratory and workshop. I do research and figure out how to use arcana to stop bad stuff from happening to good people. For example, right now I'm working on a spell to dispose of sarcastic gangsters," said Rose, arms crossed with all of her weight on her back foot.

Jimmy looked around. "You're funny, witch lady. You able to open locks, things like that?"

"Why, did you lose your keys?"

"Not exactly. See I was just wondering. Let's say that I needed to unbolt a door. Maybe you could use some of this hocus pocus to open up a lock." Jimmy stood up and started wandering around, looking at her menagerie of equipment and touching things.

"Jimmy, Thanks for the address. Is there anything else?"

"No, just looks like you could use more income, and you did tip me off on the gold, so you are already an accessory, you know... If you could make this easier, you could, I don't know maybe upgrade to a flat with windows and gaslight," said Jimmy.

"Thanks for the offer, but I already have enough enemies. I don't need to acquire more," she said, looking to the door.

He picked up a relic, a silver object in the shape of a skull featuring a glass top so you could see inside. Jimmy saw when he looked inside it that it was an actual skull that had been gilded in silver and in the skull cavity were glyphs and loose items, a feather and what looked like a finger bone. "What the fuck is this? Some guy's noggin?"

Rose grabbed it from him. "That is an ancient relic, the skull of a saint. When I learn the summoning, I can use this to call upon the angel Ariel, the lion of God, to assist me."

"Looks like it's worth a bob or two?" said the gangster.

"It's priceless." Rose placed it back in its wooden case and closed the box.

"You're not worried about people nicking your priceless items, are you? This dismal neighborhood is full of criminals," Jimmy asked.

"Most people are scared of me, think I'm devil-sent. They don't know what I have and worry that I'll curse them if they cross me," answered Rose.

Jimmy smiled. "Yeah, that's good. Real good. Nothing scarier than the fears people make up all on their own." Jimmy walked to the door and turned before he left. "You aren't planning on seeing Weng Lo in the next few days, are you?"

"No," said Rose. "Good, I don't need him knowing what I am up to until it's done," answered Jimmy.

"Your secret's safe with me."

"I know. Anyway, you had best get moving. Your girlfriend Bertha is going to Nova Scotia on Sunday. You better get on her social calendar real quick." He laughed at his own joke as he left the flat. "Ta ta, witch lady."

∼

7:55 PM, Meadhurst Manor

Detective Williamson had arrived in the late afternoon at Holbrook, the closest train station to Meadhurst, a four-hour train ride from London. At the station, the Meadhurst chauffeur was on the platform to collect Dolly and his bags for the long drive to the manor house. Upon his arrival, his host was unavailable. He took some time to walk the gardens near the house and take in a short nap.

Anytime he closed his eyes, he risked reliving the ordeal with Keane. Initially, he replayed the scene to see if he could have forced an alternative outcome where Keane survived. Other times, he would doze off and his nightmares would return, mingling events from his past. Rather than Keane, it was now Father Milton strangling him or Keane being burned alive, looming and laughing at him with the top of his head missing.

Now Dolly was awake and preparing for a dinner with one of the richest men in England. He looked at himself in the mirror. His nose felt like it was finally healing, but both eyes had turned a deep purple. The valet handed him his pocket watch. He examined the pen knife and amulet he had attached to the fob. He tucked them in his waistcoat pocket. Out of habit, he popped open the worn case of his watch, gave the knob a twist to keep tension on the watch spring and glanced at the time. When he read the time of 7:55 PM, it hurt more than his nose or his throat, for around this time on a Friday he and Keane would be out on the town sharing tales and drinks. This was his first Friday night without his friend.

What a difference from two days ago, when Dolly was covered in soot and fighting for his life. Now he was a guest of Sir Lester Chilton at the family manor, Meadhurst. He stood in front of a full-length mirror having another man help him dress. He was happy for the help from the valet. He didn't want to stuff anything up and peppered the valet with questions regarding social formality and manners.

"Mr. Williamson, you will do fine. Sir Lester and his family are the salt of the earth, and they take no benefit in making you feel foolish," said the valet. "I appreciate it very much, Mr. Walker," said Dolly.

"I will mention it to Helmsley, the butler, to keep an eye on you so you don't pick up the wrong spoon." Both men chuckled at Walker's joke.

"I need all the help I can get. I'm just a common Scot earning a wage, not used to all this ceremony," said Dolly.

"You can repay me by catching the villain that murdered Sir Francis. There, you are all ready," Walker said as he finished brushing lint off the jacket. "You can make your way down the stairs, where Helmsley will get you a drink. Most of the family will congregate in the parlor with the other guests just before dinner," said the valet.

Dolly thought he could use a drink and made his way downstairs to meet his host.

Helmsley was at the bottom of the stairs. "Mr. Williamson, Sir Lester would like you to join him in the parlor," said Helmsley.

"Excellent. Show me the way." The butler led Dolly down a long hall that echoed with the two men's footsteps. At the end, he knocked then opened the door, stepping in ahead of Dolly to announce his arrival. "Sir Lester Chilton, your guest has arrived, Detective Sergeant Williamson."

"Thank you, Helmsley. That will be all," said the young baronet. "Detective, can I fix you a whiskey?"

"I'd love one, Sir Lester," replied the detective.

Sir Lester made his way over to the drink cart and filled two glasses from a crystal decanter. "I'd love one also, but don't tell anyone. This will be my second." Lester's levity lightened Dolly and made him feel a little less like a fish out of water. "Do you know the purpose of the butler's introduction when you enter the room?" Lester asked as he handed Dolly the glass.

"Thank you. I guess so everyone knows the importance of each man in the room?"

Lester let out a belly laugh. "It's a courtesy to help everyone remember names in these social occasions,"

"Here's to better days."

"Cheers," said Dolly, taking a drink. "Mm... This is very smooth."

"It's the peat. They filter the whiskey through," said Lester as he held up the tumbler to the light and looked through the amber liquor.

"Your home is splendid." Dolly was at a loss as to what else to say.

"Thank you. Meadhurst has been in the family for two hundred years. It was just two years ago that I persuaded my father to update the place. We have our own steam engine and generate electricity through a dynamo attached to it. That powers all the arc lights on the property. We have a type-wire line and voice lines within the house." Sir Lester sat down on a sofa perpendicular to the massive hearth and signaled with his hand to the opposite sofa. "Please have a seat." Dolly sat across from Chilton and set his glass on the low table between them.

"I so do appreciate you coming up here to meet with me. I wanted to talk with you about—"

Helmsley opened the door again. "Sir Lester, Mr. Randall Strathmore and Lady Anne Chilton and Lady Margret Chilton."

As the trio entered, Sir Lester whispered to Dolly, "After dinner, I would like us to meet in my study. I have something I would like to share with you in private." He then changed the volume of his speech. "Detective Williamson, this is my wife, Lady Anne, and my sister, Lady Margret."

"And we have already met. Good to see you again, Detective," said Randall.

"A pleasure to see you again, Mr. Strathmore," replied Williamson. He was unaware of Strathmore's attendance.

"As the rude Yankee, I will ask what the ladies are thinking. What happened to your face, sir?"

Dolly laughed. "I hope it won't put you off your meal."

"Oh no, sir, but it looks so very painful," said Lady Anne.

"What really hurts, and you will have to excuse the hoarse voice, is my throat," shared Dolly.

"I was on the scene at the Baden Gaswerks explosion, and there was an altercation between myself and another man. I would rather not share the gory details in mixed company."

Lady Anne implored. "Don't spare us. We sneak into the penny dreadfuls when in London. It's quite a rush to hear it from the front lines"

Dolly was not going to share what happened. It was too gruesome and fresh. "Ladies, I came out a little worse for wear, but let me say the whole scene was horrific. with hundreds killed in the blast and more injured. Rest assured that we will find the perpetrators and bring them to justice."

"I hope that it won't take you away from finding our father's killer," interjected Lady Margret.

A bell rang.

"Ah, dinner is ready for us," said Sir Lester.

A footman opened the pocket doors, and the group followed Sir Lester to the dining room.

Sir Lester sat at the head of the table. His left was reserved for Detective Williamson. To Dolly's left was Lester's sister, Margret, and across from Lester, at the foot of the table. was Lady Anne. Between Anne and Lester and directly across from Dolly, Randall Strathmore took his seat.

"Randall, what is this I hear of you leaving?" asked Lady Anne.

"Yes, catching the train up to Birmingham for some business then to Sweden. I plan to take the Swedish royal air cruise to New York next week after my business is concluded," said Randall.

"I hear that ship is mad with amenities," replied Lady Anne.

Randall was pleased to share what he knew about the ship. "Yes, it is the finest airship running. Prussian built, the absolute finest appointments, but I am taking it for the speed. It will berth in New Jersey in four days."

"We must try travel by airship, darling," Anne said to her husband.

Lady Margret changed the topic." We were interrupted by the dinner bell, Detective. I think you were just about to tell us about our father's case." There was silence while Lady Margret waited for a response, and Dolly did the mental calculus on how he should answer.

Sir Chilton interrupted. "Margie, this really isn't the place for that conversation."

The detective had two doors to choose from now, the first to politely follow-on to Sir Chilton's comment and stay on the civil and banal or take advantage of the situation and press the two men in mixed company. Dolly still had no idea why Chilton had invited him, but he was certain the likelihood of a second invite was low, so he had little to lose if the questions became too intense for the other guests. He slid off the napkin ring, placing the fancy linen on his lap. In front of him was a calotype menu listing eight courses. It would be a long night of fine food. He scanned the table setting with all the china and tableware. *Why not add a few things to the menu?* If his suspicions were right, one or both these men may have been involved. "If you're comfortable with the subject, ladies, I do have some things to share on the case and your association with the Moya family that might shed some light" replied Dolly.

Lester gestured to the ladies, in particular his wife, knowing his sister would not let go until she felt that the detective was doing his utmost to find the murderer. "Ladies?"

"Oh yes, please do, sir," Anne replied. Margret was being served the first course and turned from the footman to nod her agreement.

"Continue, Detective," said Sir Lester.

"Let me begin by saying I have a main suspect that has been corroborated by two independent sources."

"Someone saw the murder?" asked Lady Margret.

The detective continued. "Not an eyewitness, but reliable sources that have connected this person to the crime." The footman filled Dolly's soup bowl with a savory beef and vegetable broth. Dolly also started to serve up his dishes. "I had some questions for you, Sir Lester, about the night of Emilio's murder. Why did he want to meet with you?"

"He was asking to invest with Babbage and his lot and wanted to draw on funds," answered Lester.

"And you told him?" coaxed the detective, who was watching Randall.

He had his eyes down, more absorbed with the soup than the conversation. "That I needed to familiarize myself with the investment and the conditions of investment in the trust. The

Moya estate is complex, and the source and method of the investment would need to be evaluated."

"And how did he take your response?' asked Dolly as he finished his soup. "He was not happy with my answer. He said that he would think about who would be the best trustee for the estate and his personal inheritance now that my father passed," answered Lester signaling to have his bowl taken away.

Dolly followed with another question. "So he was going to hold the trustee position over your head?"

"I suppose, but it wasn't only his decision for the main trust. He would need his brother to agree," said Lester.

The footmen next brought out smoked eel, starting with the ladies then moving to the head of the table. "Mr. Strathmore, when you met with Señor Moya later that night, did he ask you to take on the role of trustee?"

"He did, and as we discussed earlier, we talked about other sources of overseas investment for Babbage," answered Randall.

"Randall, why am I hearing about this now?" asked Sir Lester.

Dolly wondered if the revelation would sow some distrust between the two and he would see the true colors of one or both men.

"With the news of his death, I thought it best to let it go and follow along with him to his grave. Lester, it may have just been his drink talking I met with him afterward to find out more about this Babbage opportunity."

Chilton stopped eating to give Randall his full attention. "Go on, Strathmore," said Chilton.

"There really isn't more, Lester. I have clients in the States with the funds and the desire to invest that don't give a tinker's damn about the mechanist guild and their quarrel with Babbage, and they have money to invest. I saw a chance for the firm to make a nice fee syndicating an investment," finished Randall.

"Strathmore, if Moya weren't dead, would you have entertained becoming trustee?" "Lester, I would not support Emilio's ploy to leverage control over the steward. However,

there is a certain logic that a family with almost all of their holdings in the western hemisphere should have a trustee in the same."

"The eel is delicious, Lady Anne," said the detective.

"Our cook has been here for decades. I don't know what I would ever do if she decided to leave us. Wait until you see what she has prepared for our dessert," replied the Lady. "Mr. Strathmore, you're not having any?"

"It does not agree with me, thank you," replied the Yankee.

Dolly thought to himself that at least he doesn't eat his own kind then he spoke. "When was the last time either of you talked with Hernando Moya?" The two men looked at each other, waiting for the other to answer.

Finally, Chilton committed. "I have not seen Hernando in over a year."

When he finished Randall, continued. "I have had some wires and letter correspondence, but I have not seen him for at least a year. I would need to look at my diary, but it would have been a visit to Haiti because of business."

"Well, I have what may be some startling news. French authorities have advised me that Señor Hernando Moya was murdered in April of this year."

The smell of smokey fish was overtaken with the buttery herb aroma of chicken fricassee presented with rice. Carrots and green beans served as a mixed vegetable dish. As the main courses were served Dolly, continued. "When we met before, Mr. Strathmore, you suggested that Hernando may have been behind his brother's murder out of envy and greed. Now that we know that Hernando was killed prior to his brother, who could benefit?"

"Lester, have you reviewed the documents?" asked Randall.

"I have" he replied.

Dolly watched the two men interact. He was looking for tells on either of the men.

Lester scrunched his chin and brow, thinking, then spoke. "There will be details for sure, small disbursements here and there, but the bulk of the fortune remains in the trust of Don Ernesto and goes to the benefit of heredity. While the holdings are international, the trust was formed under English law and will be adjudicated in the United Kingdom."

"This gets back to your question, Lady Margret, as to your father's murder. Evidence points to a woman that had dealings with the Moya family in Haiti. The French colonial authority believes that she was a runaway slave from the Moya plantation. If their murders were revenge for their treatment of her, that does not answer why she would murder Sir Francis.

And that begs the next question. Are other partners at the firm in danger of her revenge?" Dolly let that sit with the group and ate some more of his dinner. He called upon the footman. "Could I get another roll? You know the butter here is so much better than the rancid stuff in the city." The whole time he talked, his eyes moved about the table to measure reactions.

Lady Anne spoke. "Are my Lester and Randall in danger, sir?"

"I would say that depends on if the killer got what she really wanted out of that vault?" Dolly kept in mind the note the killer had left and her warnings to leave her to her escape, but he needed to know if she had help from within the partnership. Chilton's death was still a nagging question to him.

Sir Lester placed his utensils on his plate and took his napkin off his lap but had barely eaten his main course. "Gentlemen, please join me in the study for a drink and a cigar?"

Was that it? "That sounds like a terrific idea," said Dolly. *But I won't have that meeting unarmed.* "If I may be excused, I am going to go up to my room for a moment. I have some tablets I need to take for the pain, or I will be visited by a throbbing headache."

Lady Anne broke in. "Oh, Detective, you can't leave yet. There is a pavlova with summer berries for dessert."

Dolly sat back down and replaced his napkin. "I wouldn't want to miss the pavlova." Chilton's confidences could wait until after dessert.

~

10:30 PM, Meadhurst Manor, Sir Lester's Private Study

The gentlemen were in the study having cigars and brandy. Dolly did have tablets to take, but he also grabbed his two-barrel 0.47 caliber Lancaster and placed it in the small of his back in his waistband. He wanted to make sure if the meeting in the study revealed a co-conspirator he would be prepared. It was a horror to be sitting on the gun, but he had no other options to be safe and discrete. The pain of the pistol in his back was a constant reminder to pick up a smaller caliber gun he could also sport as a second.

Their talk turned away from the Moyas and focused on politics and who might be behind the explosion at Baden.

Randall Strathmore stubbed out his cigar in the ashtray then groaned and lifted himself out of the chair. "I smoked that fella way past where it lost its taste, but even bitter it was a fantastic smoke. I have an early day tomorrow to make my train to Birmingham. Good night, gentleman."

"Good night, sir," said Sir Lester, spinning his brandy in its snifter. This was his third, and the Scotch and wine over dinner had left Lester in his cups.

"Good evening, Mr. Strathmore, and safe travel on that airship of yours," said the detective.

Strathmore took the last swig from his glass and made his way out.

Dolly sat and waited.

"Strathmore is a good egg, Detective," said Sir Lester, slouched in his chair. He had taken off his dinner coat and was in shirt sleeves. "Mark my words, Detective. That man will become one of the wealthiest and most powerful men in the United States. You would do well to make him a friend."

Dolly decided he needed to press, given Lester would only get more drunk. "I'll keep that in mind. I think I will make my way to bed." He feigned getting up. That was all it took to stoke Chilton.

"One moment, Detective. Back at Chilton House, you asked if there were other documents missing. From what we could tell everything in the vault was in order other than my damn missing gold!" Lester came back to point after his rage. "Sims mentioned that my father did keep some files, not in the Chilton House but a strong box in a hunter's lodge on this property. I had never heard of the safe, and my father and I were very close." Lester's eyes were watery.

"I went out to the lodge to find this strong box. My father must have wanted me to find it, given he told Sims of its location. It only took a few tries to find the combination. It was my birthdate. While I cannot ascertain if anything was missing from the safe, given that a week ago I had no idea the box or its contents existed, what was in there was interesting."

"I will assume that you found something relevant to the case," replied Dolly.

"I think it may be." Sir Lester got up and stumbled over to a painting near his desk. The painting hung on hinges and swung to the side, revealing a wall safe. He fumbled at the combination, finally opening the strongbox after several attempts. Sir Lester removed a file and dropped the folder in the detective's lap.

Dolly began looking at the documents. They were the Last Will and Testament of Don Ernesto de Moya. Dolly looked up. "Can you tell me why you think these documents are relevant?"

"Those were the wishes of Don Ernesto when he was alive. That is how he expected his fortune and holdings would be distributed to his heirs. I was the trustee for Señor Emilio Moya. Therefore, I was quite familiar with holdings, inheritances and allowances. Those were not the documents I worked from for the past sixteen years since he passed. Look at the declarations and the disbursements in the appendix. If I were Hernando or Emilio, I would have taken issue with these documents," said Lester as he got up and grabbed the brandy bottle to refill his and Dolly's snifter.

"Why would your father have these documents?"

"I don't know, Detective," answered Lester. Then he continued, "I don't know why my father would have been party to this. Ernesto was his friend, and his wishes would not have cost the firm a pence in fees. It only served to help the brothers and their reputation. Why? Why would he hide this?"

"Would anyone else in the firm have benefited from the changes?" asked Williamson.

"No, no, no. The firm only collects fees for the management of the assets," Lester exclaimed.

"Mr. Strathmore told me at the club when I interviewed him that the Moyas, and specifically Hernando, had made your firm and other investors very wealthy. Would any of those investments be affected detrimentally by the revelations in this document?"

Lester sat back in his chair. His eyes went up to the ceiling, and his head rocked side to side. "Some, maybe all. Who am I to say? Character and reputation are important in the world of finance."

Dolly looked again at the declarations section of the will. "I think you have your answer, Sir Lester. This wasn't about the trust, but about Hernando and Emilio's other enterprises, and your father may have been complicit to protect all the firm's co-investments with the Moyas," said Dolly. *Your father's decision to hide these documents may have cost him his life.*

There was a knock at the door. "What is it?" Lester snapped.

"Sir, I have a wire-type for the detective," said the voice outside the door.

"Bring it in, Helmsley," said Sir Lester.

Helmsley entered the room and stood at Dolly's side with a silver tray extended. The wire-ype tape was coiled loosely on the platter.

Dolly uncoiled the tape and read the small type.

TRANSMITTAL 24061858 21:42
TO: MEADHURST T01
Williamson, Fredrick

FROM: Royal Teletype, Bethnal Station Ca
Caldwell Rose -Cash Acct

412 PILTON ROAD ALIAS BERTHA HELSTROM
LEAVING LONDON BY SHIP SUNDAY

CHECK YOUR POCKET WATCH I WILL BE THERE
AT 10 PM SATURDAY

Dolly looked up at Helmsley and motioned his eyes toward the baronet making a face. "Sir Lester, I think it is time you retire," said the butler.

"No, no. Helmsley. Williamson and I are just going to have another drink."

Dolly stood up to excuse himself. "As much as I would love to take you up on your invitation, I think I will catch the car with Mr. Strathmore and get to the station early. I have pressing business in London."

The Lodge was a nondescript somewhat run-down building in Surry Hill. The steam carriage idled to a stop, delivering Guild Master Gerrard and two Silver Seers in front of the townhouse. The necronists stepped out and walked up to the steps with energetic strides.

Poised on the stoop, Gerard took in a deep breath. Reaching into his left sleeve, he pulled out his malla beads to help him focus his energy and to center his formidable power. So formidable that all he needed was to think about the incantation, and the works began. He scryed the building and with his mind's eye saw the defenses the Lodge had erected to protect against forces from the outside and to contain spirits within.

Before he had a chance to knock, the door opened. Not a word was spoken as the three men entered. It was dark inside the flat, not yet fitted for gas light. Only candles were used for illumination, giving a hazy yellow-orange glow where light was cast. In the foyer, they were greeted by Madame Helen

Blatavsky, an Eastern European psychic. She had settled in London after traveling the world to augment her powers, now a trusted advisor to society ladies who dabbled in metaphysics, not looking to understand the true nature of the multiverse but to divine who their daughter might marry or if they might live to a certain age. Saint-Yves detested this use of the warp and woof of the universe and considered it a perversion.

"Welcome to the Lodge, Guild Master Saint-Yves," purred the woman with a Russian accent. She was dressed in a modest black gown as if mourning the loss of a loved one. "Follow me," she continued.

The gentlemen followed Madame Helen down a rickety wooden stairwell into the cellar. It was poorly lit, making it difficult to see the full size of the cellar. The dampness and mildew overpowered the senses. At the foot of the steps, they discovered an ornate candelabra set on top of a round table and chairs, set inside a sunken pool roughly dug into the cellar floor and lined with a tarp to hold water. It was an unsavory arrangement. The table was submerged in six inches of water, and as their eyes grew accustomed to the darkness, another object was present, a large circle of silver chain laying on the table. Two men waited in the basement, appearing out of the shadows when the necronists came into the candle light. Gerard grimaced. How pathetic the accommodations were. He would have to work with what he was given.

Blatavsky introduced her compatriots. "Guild Master Saint Yves, this is Lord Oswald the Grand Mason of the Lodge."

"A pleasure to meet you, sir," said Saint-Yves.

"Likewise," said Oswald.

Lord Oswald was thought of as a crackpot in high society, but

Gerard knew he was a man of talent and natural ability. He had been invited to join the guild, but Oswald was not prepared to give up his title and property as part of his fealty and devotion to the art and science of metaphysics.

"And this is Crosby Welch," stated the woman as she continued to introduce the party.

"It is an honor to meet you, Guild Master," replied Crosby.

"The honor is mine, Mr. Welch." Gerard had no idea who Crosby was. He was likely a high-ranking and talented Lodge member but of no consequence to the spiritual sciences.

"Let me just say how honored we are to have you, and while our terrestrial abode may be lacking style and substance, I am certain you will be impressed with our meeting hall," promised Lord Oswald.

"Shall we begin?" queried Madame Blatavsky.

Each of the attendees took off their shoes and stockings then stepped into the pool. All the attendees took a seat around the table, keeping their feet immersed in the water. The séance members grasped the silver chain in each hand to complete a circle of enchantment and began reciting the incantation.

Gerard closed his eyes and wriggled his toes in the ankle-high fluid. He could feel the electrolytes and tinctures in the water that would assist the group in conducting their spirits via astral projection to the locus amulet submerged in the pool. A slight smile crossed his face, enjoying the indulging benefits of the soothing foot bath for his tired feet. He then put his full attention to the incantation and let go of the terrestrial plane.

When he opened his mind's eye, the group had projected to an aetheris sanctuarii, a trans-dimensional sanctuary constructed by the Lodge for clandestine meetings. In contrast to the wretched townhouse in London, the Lodge members had conjured a fantastic spacious crystal dome with a white marble floor. It rivaled Joseph Paxton's Crystal Palace in Sydenham Hill, not in size but in complexity and beauty. Gerard was impressed with the faction's ability to project and sustain the construct in his mind. The crystal panes were fitted into a giant wrought iron frame, allowing those inside to look out into the astral plane where they had anchored the sanctuary, a floating aether observatory.

"Welcome. We can all speak freely here," encouraged Madame Blatavsky.

Gerard walked across the space to observe its construction as well as to show the Lodge members of his ability to move freely in his astral form. He peered out the crystal dome and saw the infinite expanse of the multiverse and the ever-changing nexus of the energy channels. It was like turning over a tapestry to see the warp and weave of its construction. You could still make out the coarse image of reality on the other side, and you could clearly see how reality was woven together. It was wonderful and humbling to view. "This is an impressive construct," commented Gerard. "I have asked for your help, Lord Oswald, to locate and capture a practitioner of metaphysics who is engaging in unsanctioned dark arts."

"A Haitian Witch," said Seer Moreau.

Gerard looked at him with a dismissive look. Gerard hated overt zealotry, and he couldn't hold the kind of animosity towards Angelica that Moreau did. His heart held admiration, respect and love for the woman. He thought, *don't be overconfident, brother.* "My guild's strength in London is limited. We seek powerful allies to help protect civilization and extend knowledge beyond the mortal realm. It is obvious from this construct that our choice in the Lodge was a wise one."

Gerard thought about what he had learned from the detective. Angelica was now strong enough to strip souls. She had done it twice in London. She either had an entourage to help her, or she had surpassed her master and could perform Pwen Hanaan as a solo practitioner. Either way, his group would be punching out of their spiritual weight class. Furthermore, she could maintain a controlling psychic connection for some distance and force the subjects to cross strong moral barriers, suggesting his group would be outclassed. Gerard knew he must devise and implement a strategic plan.

"I will leave Seer Moreau with you to scrye the location of Angelica du Haiti. Seer Thomas and one of your Lodge members will assist me in confronting Angelica. Once the scrying team deduces the location, the Seer will project it to me. Only then will we act," implored Gerard.

The guild master's plan was to split the group, with the stationary séance concentrating on divining the whereabouts of the enchantress. The second group would be mobile, and the necronists would connect telepathically across the aether, guiding them to the location.

Being physically closer to Angelica would leave her little time to escape from Gerard, if she detected the psychic search. The mobile group would be less noticeable to Angelica's psychic detection as they would be passively connected to the group that was actively seeking her location. The group understood the plan without speaking further as they all became mentally linked and the eldritch bonds of the séance strengthened.

The cluster uttered the incantation, "Inde aethere nunc revertetur ad terram santuary" The invocation returned the members to Earth and their places around the table. Gerard, Thomas and Lord Oswald each took two silver necklaces, wrapping one around the binding chain on the table and then placing an identical necklace around their own necks. The next step to binding the séance table to the hunting party would require the hunters to submerge an alabaster vial in the pool at their feet. Once full of water and the lids secured, the small vials were then attached to the silver chain around their necks.

Lord Oswald was the first to step from the pool after returning to the terrestrial plane. Guild Master Saint-Yves followed and then finally Seer Thomas. The Trio dried their feet, donned footwear and ascended upstairs out onto the street. The three ran to the waiting steam carriage as a torrential downpour began.

9:30 PM, Silkwood & Company

Jimmy stood alone in the recessed doorway of one of the shops. He breathed deeply to take in the scent of fresh rain. There was a short time after a good downpour in London that cleansed the air and freshened the city. He watched the rooftop horizon, looking for one of his triad brethren as he made his way to the furnace exhaust for that building. The furnace was churning so hard he could pick it out from the street by its large plume and the size of the pipe in comparison to the smaller heating chimneys hooked to coal stoves of homes and offices in the housing block.

On Thursday, Jimmy sent a triad affiliate, a regular at Silkwood & Company, to retrieve prices to recut stones from Simon. The real purpose was to confirm that they were working the smelter flat strap. As a bonus, his scout spied several packing crates from Venice lined up along the back of the cramped shop, validating that this was the gold he was looking for.

Jimmy observed the silhouette of his man against the moonlight as he knocked the cap off the exhaust pipe then stuffed a wooden plug into the pipe, giving it a good wallop with a mallet. As his man eased his way down, Jimmy looked at his pocket watch. Now he just needed to wait.

There was only one way in or out of that shop: through a large iron and oak door.

~

9:40 PM, the streets of London

In the back of the steam carriage, Gerard Saint-Yves sat in silent meditation, his back to the driver and the passenger partition open to allow the driver to hear the directions recited by the guild master. Oswald and Thomas contemplated in solitude, encouraging Gerard to concentrate. Each held awe of his ability to maintain a spiritual connection to the séance at such a distance and in a moving vehicle. Both had lost the connection miles ago.

Yet, in his mind's eye, the guild master and those at the séance were detached spirits floating over the city of London looking down for hot spots of arcane power. Seer Moreau and Saint-Yves hovered while Blatavsky and Welsh swooped over the city in astral form, searching for sites of intense arcane energy. Moreau acted as conduit to Gerard, feeding him the collective's results as it taxed both of their capacity to hold true the link.

Gerard watched as the astral forms flitted across the skyline, invisible to the human eye. When a street or building looked promising, Madame Blatavsky or Crosby Welsh would swoop down to inspect the location further. It was Crosby who spotted the house first and began to move toward it as he closed in. Gerard spoke, "Go across the river. Make haste."

The entire astral network sensed he had found a powerful locus of arcana. Madame Blatavsky stopped searching and altered her path towards the location. Crosby continued to investigate, having reformed his spectral essence in the middle of the street just as a horse-drawn handy passed. The horse brayed as it passed through his spirit form.

Gerard pleaded, *Get me the address.* His thoughts passed through the network to Crosby. He looked for landmarks and signs. Pilton Street, the 400 block, trickled back through the aether, bouncing up and down the spiritual network.

Crosby's projection looked down the street and saw a woman with short black hair in a long grey and red coat, observing the same address. As he began to move toward the dwelling, his ethereal form confidently marched closer to see who was the resident.

Gerard snapped out of his trance eyes, wide open with a gasp as if he had nearly suffocated. "Driver, get to 412 Pilton Road as fast as you can."

9:50 PM, Silkwood and Company

The steam lorry was stoked and ready to engage. It was parked facing away from the shop and perpendicular to the street Silkwood was located on. Jimmy approached the truck, pushing aside the canvas curtain covering the back end and jumped in together with the three other men. He quickly looked back between the canvas storage cover to confirm his man from the roof snuffed the gas lamps on the street to darken both roads.

They all waited for the Silkwood door to open. Still nothing. "What are these guys, fish? Don't they need air?" said Rooftop in Mandarin.

"Aww, fuck me dead," said Jimmy.

Rooftop and the others tried to push. "Get back, you cow cuds. It's a fucking copper," he whispered.

A single officer was strolling his beat. He walked leisurely down the cobble stone avenue, peering in shop windows. All the jewelers cleared inventory from the windows into strong boxes overnight so there was nothing to see. He looked closely to observe movement, like people in the shops that shouldn't be.

Jimmy turned to his crew. "If the copper gets in the way, don't kill him. Put a bag over his head and kick him in the pollywogs so he stays down."

They all nodded.

The bobby stopped and noticed that a street lamp was out near the shop. Glancing up, he pulled out his notebook and began to write down that lamp number, noting it's non-working condition. Just then, the door to the Silkwood's burst open by two men assisting an unconscious man out of the building.

≈

9:55 PM, Pilton Road

Rose stood at the street corner and gazed at the townhouse

two doors up the street. The street lights reflected in the puddles and sheen left on the streets from the recent storm. She donned scrying goggles and adjusted the lenses to check for wards. Rather than seeing the glyphs or symbols of both Western and Egyptian omens illuminated, she observed streaks and glimmers around the house.

At that moment, an astral form caught her eye, standing in the street just where a carriage had passed. It was the shape of a middle-aged man. He looked English, striding towards the home. Rose was impressed to see such a strong image. She had projected many times but only to other planes, momentarily and with extensive support from arcane instruments and objects. She changed her lenses and adjusted the resolution. The streaks around the house became spirit shades and apparitions of the dead, and the glimmers were dozens of flickering points of the aether breaching into the mortal realm. Angelica's defenses were pure, raw and unbreakable.

When the Englishman's apparition passed through the garden gate, the arcane defenses solidified. The entire front garden was filled with apparitions of those that had died at or near the location, men, women children of all ages in various states of decay. The randomly moving spirits coalesced to block the Englishman's path into the flat. An ancient Briton warrior grasping a spear and thatched shield stood resolutely in his way.

It was a surprise to the gentlemen when he tried to pass through the other apparitions but was blocked just as if he had walked into a material object. He tried to push through a second time, but the Briton warrior, showing a grin of rotting teeth, gave the Englishman the full brunt of his weight when he slammed into him with his shield. The English spiritualist fell to the ground.

For Rose, it was like watching one of those new moving stereoscope pictures silently flickering images playing out a tragic scene. She could do nothing more than stand by as the spirit guard of Angelica tore the astral projection to pieces, while all Rose could hear was the summer breeze rustling down the lane. What she observed on the man's face was terror and anguish. Looking back to the street, she saw a second astral projection. Rose recognized the woman who floated just above the street as Madame Blatavsky, a local spiritualist. Blatavsky looked in Rose's direction then flew away.

"Well, here goes plan B," Rose muttered to herself, pulling her goggles down around her neck and walking towards the residence. Plan A was to approach with stealth. She wore her long crimson coat, it's lining sewn with threads pulled from the death shrouds of sixteen saints and imbued with incantations of safe passage and protection. On past investigations, Rose had found the cloak to provide not only protection by camouflage from those wielding the arcane, but after what she just saw, she wasn't sure if the coat would afford any type of protection at all so she might as well just stroll up and announce herself.

As she crossed the street, she felt a vibration on her belt. It was her arcana circulata, a warning device and directional locator for supernatural energy. She opened the case and looked at the direction and intensity dial. The intensity was pegged. Not a surprise after witnessing the wards the priestess had erected. What befuddled her was that the directional indicator was spinning versus pointing at the townhouse. *Must look at that in the workshop.*

Rose opened the garden gate and stepped onto the property, knowing she was within the scope of the priestess' magic.

She slowly ascended steps up to the front door, expecting some type of snare or curse. Instead, as she made footfall on the landing, the front door creaked opened slowly.

Rose stuck her head in the doorway, taking notice of how nicely illuminated the rooms were all installed with the latest arc lamps.

"Come on back. I is in the parlor," came a female voice in a West Indies accent.

As Rose stepped into the ornate room, she saw a stunning woman with a deep brown skin tone and a perfect mix of African and European facial features. She wore a hand-painted silk kimono with a high-neck lace blouse underneath. Her hair was not pinned up but left down long, lush and flowing. The woman sat in a high-back chair. Resting against the chair was a primitive staff of warped and petrified wood decorated with feathers and beads. Five human skulls rested at the top, one above another, skewered by the staff.

"Please have a seat. When God created time, he made a lot of it," Angelica said as she shuffled tarot cards.

"You must be Ms. Angelica du Haiti?" Rose declared as she made her way to the chair opposite Angelica. She waited. "You are Angelica du Haiti?"

"Sister Caldwell, some know me by that name, but I prefer Angelica de Moya. Welcome. Would you please cut the cards?" the priestess requested, setting the deck down in front of Rose.

"Moya?" Rose said as she cut the deck.

While she laid out the cards face down, Angelica spoke." I am the only daughter of Don Ernesto de Moya and a Haitian woman. Years after Don Hernando's first wife died of yellow fever, he fell in love with my mother. Choose a card."

Rose turned over the Magician card. "Mastery of the material world, self-discipline and a willingness to take risks," said Angelica. A thoughtful frown crossed her face as she examined Rose, letting the meaning of the card settle in.

Angelica turned over the Priestess. Rose knew the meaning of this card—intuition, wisdom and secret knowledge.

"Pick another card, Rose," pressed Angelica.

Rose flipped over the Tower.

Angelica tapped the tarot as she recounted meaning. "A powerful selection, something remains yet to be revealed, but patience must be observed. Duality and mystery. Hidden influences, disruption. Conflict. Change. Sudden violent loss. Overthrow of an existing way of life."

Rose's hand was still on the card. Angelica placed her finger on the back of Rose's hand, and with that, she was sent to another time and place.

~

10:02 PM, Silkwood & Co.

Rooftop banged on the back of the van. The driver released the clutch and reversed the truck. Watching in the side mirror, the driver positioned the truck onto the sidewalk so Jimmy and his thugs could jump out right in front of Silkwood.

The bandits had wrapped scarves around their faces and wore

wool caps. Even Jimmy was dressed down, looking like a common cockney hoodlum.

The shocked officer saw the back of the truck barrel towards him, stopping a foot from him. Any comfort there was in not getting hit by the truck went away when Rooftop kicked the cop in the head, sending him to the pavement. He and another guy leapt on him, put a bag over his head then Rooftop punched the copper right in the solar plexus. The poor bastard was sucking so much air from the punch that the bag moved in and out of his mouth.

Jimmy's goons bagged the heads of the Silkwood workers, who dropped their unconscious coworker to fight off the thugs. Jimmy's gang were seasoned street fighters and quickly dealt with the jewelers, with one getting a knee to the groin and the other a blackjack to the head. Both hit the ground moaning and groaning. "Stay down or you'll get your head caved in. This will all be over soon, and you will be safe if you don't act a hero," yelled Jimmy.

The gang strode into Silkwood & Company.

"You two, grab a crate and get the fuck out. There is no air in here," said Jimmy.

One of the goons said, "We should have worn gas masks."

"Grab a box, sheep dip. Gas masks only filter out gas. If there is no oxygen in the room, you will still pass out," Jimmy growled as he slapped him in the back of his head.

When Jimmy walked in, they still had not completed smelting all the gold. There were four full crates, far more than the 1,450 the counterfeit paper work showed. Then the gangster realized they would strike the new ingots first before paying off the help with the gold. The gold was in various stages, some still guineas, some cooling in molds and more in a crucible in the furnace.

"Grab those crates," yelled Jimmy. He and Rooftop grabbed a crate by its rope handle and carried it out to the truck.

On his way back in, Jimmy stood on the cop's neck. "Any bloke looking to be a hero will get his medal posthumously."

"I hear ya, mate," moaned the cop.

The four men made the second trip from inside the shop to the back of the truck. Jimmy grabbed a handful of the gold guineas and shoved them in his pocket. After he threw the last crate onto the bed of the truck, he and Rooftop stalked over to the policemen and the workers on the ground and put a fuinea in each of their pockets. "Now you blokes may think about jumping up and taking the bag off your head... but don't do it. Not until you don't hear the rumble of my car boiler. Cause I'll be looking out the window with my pistol pointed back at you and will shoot whoever moves."

After leaving them with that thought, Jimmy jumped into the back of the vehicle. With a hiss of steam as the bypass vented and re-pressurized the piston, the lorry and Sir Francis Chilton's gold drove away.

~

10:05 PM, Pilton Road

Dolly waited, positioned in the driver's seat of the steam cruiser, and Detective Burton providing back-up in the passenger seat.

Dolly watched Rose walk across the street. It was hard to miss a woman wearing pants, let alone one striking such a confident stride, and then of course, there was the harness she rigged up to access her adventuring gear.

"Well, that one sticks out like dog's balls. Is that Sister Rose?" asked Burton.

"Indeed, it is. She sent me a wire-type of her discovery, the location of Angelica du Haiti at 412 Pilton Road," replied Dolly.

"Well, let's get in there," implored Burton as he went for the door of the carriage to get out.

Dolly grabbed his arm. "We are going to give her a little time to souse out the situation." On one hand, Dolly was being truthful. Rose was better suited to confronting the sorceress. On the other, he wanted to give Rose the time she needed to learn what she wanted from Angelica. He felt he owed her that, given that she tipped him off to the location. He would be feeling a lot more comfortable if he was sitting next to Keane. He rarely felt fear, or such a lack of control, but he was going up against an enemy who could bend people to her will and turn friend into foe. Maybe Rose would get further reasoning with her. He could give Rose five minutes before he went in to arrest Angelica.

The senior detective observed Rose as she stopped in the road then used her goggles to look up and down the street before continuing into the house.

Burton interrupted the silence in the car. "You know that we all think you a little batty and verging on the heretical consorting with her."

There's that judgment again, just like Keane. Maybe rather than conceal the truth, I should share it. Dolly opened up to the young detective. "I keep a confidential journal, mainly to check my sanity, but it also serves me if I am required to share some of the strange and fantastic things I have dealt with. Included are my notes from the St. Anthony Home for Boys."

"You worked the Milton affair?" replied Burton, who was the newest addition to the detective branch and not even a street constable when Dolly worked the case.

"I did. I was a Sergeant. This was before the detective's branch. We were pulling boys out of the rivers, all strangled, between the ages of eight and twelve. Strange thing was, no one was reporting any missing children. For months, we had nothing, and the frequency of dead boys was increasing. Finally, I had a break when we found two bodies in the same week, one on shore and a floater pulled out by a boat on the river. I had been plotting the body locations and drew a conclusion that the source had to be up stream. I figured it to be a poor house or orphanage, where there was no parent to miss the child. I canvased the city and began looking at two locations, St. Anthony being one. I interviewed Father Milton, and at the time, he seemed like a good bloke, even gave me access to his records, and everything checked out. While I'm there, I run into this young nun, and she tells me that I need to look further into Father Milton. I just assumed that she worked there so I start doing some digging and get a whole heap of pushback from the archdiocese."

"They were covering for the priest?' asked Burton.

"That's what I thought. I can't get any further access to church records, but I did have a list of his postings at several boys' homes. Obvious thing to do then was go to the local stations and see if there were similar murders. I saw a pattern of dead boys showing up strangled around the times and places he had been posted. Circumstantial, but a clear pattern.

"So, I go back to St. Antony's rectory, where Milton lives, to interview him, see if I can get him to crack. It's in the evening so I give the door a knock, figuring the padre should be home. No answer. I decide to have a look around, and I notice that nun prowling around. Now this is suspicious, a sister in her habit skulking around the rectory, and I see her go down into this cellar in the back of the house. I follow her down, and there is Father Milton, in the process of strangling a boy. I called out to him, but he doesn't even acknowledge I am in the room. I drew my pistol. In those days, I carried a Weiss brothers over and under. I took aim and gave the priest another chance to let go of the boy, but he kept choking him." Dolly rubbed his own throat now, knowing how painful that was for the boy, to be choked by powerful hands.

"I let loose a shot that hit him square in the chest with a fifty-caliber ball, and he didn't even turn to look at me. He was focused on the nun, who was carrying on with some mumbo jumbo talk. The shot should have dropped a bull. I could see the hole in his chest, and the wall behind him sprayed with blood from the exit wound.

"I had no idea what these two were up to, but Milton wouldn't stop so I tok two more steps closer and put a second shot point blank into his head. Bam! The shot was true, and the back of his head opened, brains and gore all over the floor, but the bastard was still grinning at the Sister.

"With no shots left and the priest with two bullets in him and half his head missing, I went into shock. Paralyzed, just standing there, like the village idiot. The nun proceeded to conduct an exorcism. Only then did Milton finally release the boy and descend into a fit, swinging and fighting at something in the room until he burst into flames. At least, that is what I thought I saw. Like I said, I was dumbstruck when my shots did not drop him.

"Next thing I knew, Sister Rose was pulling me out of the cellar. We both got out and the rectory was consumed in the flames along with Father Milton," finished the senior detective.

Burton gaped at him. "If you were there, how come the story is that Sister Rose started the fire that killed Father Milton?"

"That is just how the gossip-mongering has changed the story over time," replied Dolly.

"But they excommunicated her," replied Burton.

"From what I know, she caused too much of a stir during the papal inquisition. Those cowards booted her out to get distance from her, but she was fine with the outcome. It allowed her to focus on her war against the wicked. Adam, I'm only recounting this story so you're totally prepared for what you might see tonight. Rose Caldwell has shown me that far more exists in this world beyond what we can see and hear, and that there are forces at work on and off Earth, intending to do harm. Do you want to know what Rose told me went on in that cellar?"

"Hell yes. You can't tell someone something like that and not finish the tale," whispered Burton, his wool cap bunched in his hands.

"Rose Caldwell told me that Father Joseph Milton was possessed by the fallen angel Rabdos, now a demon that has the power to stop and alter the paths of the stars. He receives power from strangling humans. There is only one angel with the power to prevent him from succeeding, a seraphim called Brieus.

"What I witnessed was Rabdos enacting his plan to change the heavens and Rose summoning Brieus to aid her. The two fought, and Milton's corrupted body was consumed in the holy flames the seraphim used to triumph over his enemy. The sickening part is the demon's power is amplified by making an unwilling agent act against their own morality and nature." Dolly wondered if Milton was a good man infected and turned against his better nature. If it all began with one moment where he didn't do something overtly bad, but rather a sin of omission. Could any of us end up suffering the fate of Milton because we weren't vigilant?

"Bollocks!" cried Burton.

"Maybe. I could be mad as a hatter, or perhaps some time in the future you will be required to call on the services of Rose Caldwell because your intellect and a fifty-caliber shot are not enough to bring justice to the realm," finished the Detective.

"Well, what do we have here?" said Burton.

A steam carriage pulled up and parked in front of 412 Pilton Road. Several men exited the back of the carriage along with the driver and approached the flat. The three of them stood for a moment at the front of the house before entering the garden gate as the driver began walking up the street.

"Two of those blokes are necronists," announced Dolly. "That fella there is Guild Master Saint-Yves, one of the leaders of the necronist guild. I met with him earlier this week on this case, and he offered to help catch Chilton's killer. I agreed on the condition he inform me of her whereabouts and that I be on hand to arrest her." The senior detective paused. Dolly checked his pistol, making sure all the caps were in place on the cylinder then placed the pistol back in his shoulder holster. He had made his decision at that cafe table that as much as he felt Angelica deserved to die for what she did to Keane his purpose was to bring her to justice. "Looks like tonight the scales will be removed from your eyes, Adam. Let's check in and make sure that everything in there remains civil between this cast of characters. You go around the block and find the fella who went off on his own then meet me back inside the house."

Rose was no longer in London. She was channeled to a time in the past, in a place she had never been. She felt the immense power of Angelica coursing through her. Rose was the Voodoo priestess. She was Angelica, yet not in control, a passenger to see the scene play out yet feeling what Angelica felt and remembered. This wasn't the first time Rose had this type of out-of-body experience. Her life had been plagued by visions and dreams. The difference this time was it wasn't while she slept.

She was sitting at the Moya plantation in the office of Don Hernando. It was hot and humid with the frogs croaking and cicada droning in the trees outside. The windows were open but no breeze provided relief from the humidity. Above her head, a belt drive ceiling fan churned the air with no affect.

Hernando Moya finished signing the papers, and he handed them back to the solicitor.

The solicitor notarized the papers. "Don Hernando, that is the last of the documents you wanted drawn up," said the lawyer. He kept looking at Angelica, coveting her beauty. He likely assumed she was the house help for Don Hernando. Angelica met his gaze then looked back to her needlepoint.

"Please keep a copy and send the original notarized and witnessed last will and testament to the London and New York office of Chilton, Chilton, Owens and Strathmore," said Don Hernando without emotion.

"Very well," said the solicitor, collecting the documents, putting them in a folio then into his briefcase.

"Watson will show you out." Don Hernando rang a bell, and the house man came into the office.

"Yes, Don Hernando," said the butler.

"Show Mr. Foubert out, Watson."

"Yes, Don Hernando." Watson looked in Angelica's direction and gave a slight bow, not too much to be noticed by Moya or Foubert, but he wanted to be certain Angelica knew the respect he had for her. Watson had been with the house since it was under Don Ernesto and Angelica used to play here as a little girl. Watson was now a free man, liberated by the French government's decree, and Angelica had returned to her home as the witch queen of Haiti.

The two men left. Only Angelica and Don Hernando were in the room. She dropped her needlepoint to the floor, and underneath the fabric was the Voodoo fetish of Don Hernando she was using to control him. She walked over to him, pricked his index finger with a pin and used the blood to draw a mouth on the doll. He had control of his mouth again. "You won't get away with this. The trustee will see through those forgeries."

"Hernando, those documents are originals with your

THE UNTOLD TALES OF DOLLY WILLIAMSON

signature. They are now your last will and testament and precede these," she gloated while taking the old will off his desk. At that moment, she took a match from his cigar box, struck it and lit the papers on fire, throwing them at the foot of the curtains.

"The die is cast, my brother. You chose to go against our father's wishes. You chose to treat me and my mother as slaves. I am resetting the scales."

"You don't understand, you savage witch. There is a legal system to be contended with. The institutions handling these affairs will see right through this farce."

"Hernando, it is that very legal system that I plan to wield against you far more easily than the magic I just used to draft up those papers." It felt to Rose as if it was her saying the words, but it was indeed Angelica. This had already happened.

"Come, brother. Come out from behind your big desk and kneel before me." The curtains began to smolder at the flames from the burning documents.

Hernando gave every effort to resist. He was sweating and physically struggling against himself. His feet moved as if he wore shoes of lead. Hernando whelped in pain, but slowly moved closer to Angelica as she re-arranged pins in the cloth doll.

Rose felt the satisfaction of wielding power over this man who had started a string of horrors. First, when her brother showed up for the funeral, she and her mother were locked away in their rooms. She never was given the chance for a proper goodbye. When the doors opened days later, slavers came and took her and her mother away as slaves. Rose was plunged into the fear and pain of Angelica's two years as a slave, cutting sugar cane in the mosquito-infested fields, living in endless fear and abuse. The mix of her memories, Angelica's memories, and the experience of the events she was witnessing gave Rose a sick feeling of uncertainty and anxiety, unsure what was her, what was Angelica what was now and what was then. She wondered if this was how Preston felt during his possessions.

"Unbutton your shirt. Take it off," ordered Angelica.

Don Hernando unbuttoned his vest, shirt cuffs and shirt as commanded. He threw the clothing to the side, his eyes filled with fear and shock as he watched his body do unthinkable things no matter how hard he resisted.

"You know, Hernando, this is all your doing. If you hadn't disowned me as your sister and sold me off to that plantation, I would have grown up here as a privileged Catholic girl, with the guilt of being half-black and profiting from the work of slaves. Instead, my fate was to live as a slave and a savage in the jungle, and yours will be worse than damnation."

She walked over to her needlepoint bag and pulled out a spirit siphon, like those Rose had found in Moya and Chilton and a clear glass ball. "Do you have any idea what I am about to do, Hernando?" she asked as she held up the perfect glass orb and the primitive spirit siphon.

At that moment, Rose realized she could tap into Angelica's feelings and memories as well as her senses.

"No, please don't hurt me. You just said that it was your fate to go to the jungle ... to become so powerful. I beg your forgiveness and pity," whimpered Hernando.

Angelica moved in front of the overweight hairy man, soaked in the sweat of fear and no longer the picture of a haughty

Portuguese sugar magnate. "Hernando, do you know where you went wrong?

"I did not honor our father's wishes... I did not honor our family... You were family" said the Don.

"You're still begging, even in your answer," Rose heard Angelica speak to him. "No, your mistake was that you only saw my mother in me, never our father. You were blind to the half of me that is Moya and more than name. I have the Moya patience, intellect and determination, maybe more than you, and that is why father wanted me to have my birthright. I imagine it took you some time to plan. How long did it take you?

Hernando just looked up at her, gulping short breaths.

"How long? I asked," she repeated.

"The decision to send you away was a rash one. I did it and consulted with no one. Later, when Chilton asked about you, it was a few months to cover up the evidence of my transgression," answered Hernando.

"And your brother's part?" asked Angelica.

The situation was surreal for Rose. Her point of view was that of Angelica's, and she could feel her feeling sense what she sensed, but at the same time, experienced her own feelings as an observer, and she felt terrified for Hernando.

"It—it was easy to convince Emilio. He's so lazy and greedy. He was all for me doing what I could to grow and protect his inheritance," shared Hernando.

"Your selfish choice took two years of my life as a slave, then a month of running through the jungle to find the Village of the Falls. I did not know if the village was real or just a slave myth, but I decided I would rather die in the jungle looking for it then spend one more day cutting sugar cane," replied the queen.

"I'm so sorry. I see you are a Moya. You have our father's determination."

"Never mind your simpering. How did you convince the English bankers?" asked Angelica.

That was Emilio, really. I had sent you and your mother away. Chilton contacted him as executor and trustee of my—our father's estate. Sir Lester had a copy of my father's intentions and asked Emilio about you. He got him to agree to honor the preceding will and trust, or he and I would contest the will in court and our first order of business would be an injunction to move the trusts to the Rothschilds. He would lose the fees from the trust and our commercial relationships and the respect of his financiers for losing us to another banking house."

"Well, brother, we both have bankers that are prepared to bend the rules for their clients. Those papers you just signed will assure that all the Moya fortune flows to my birthright and that is your punishment for how you treated me. For you not honoring my mother, the punishment will be far worse. For subjecting her to the cane fields and whip, your soul will be ripped from your flesh and housed in this perfect glass orb, crafted by the Beaumont Glassworks in Shreveport, Louisiana,"

"Oh, God help me," he begged.

"Too late for that. What I can guarantee you is your immortal soul will not be punished in hell. It will stay right here on earth, in my purse. You will have the existence of a fish in a bowl." chided Angelica cruelly.

And then the incantation began. Rose was there as Angelica pressed the siphon against Hernando's chest and channeled his soul directly into the glass ball. Rose felt the anger, the sadness, the exaltation of the pure power and most importantly for her, the knowledge of the incantation.

SATURDAY, THE 26TH OF JUNE, WHAT REMAINS

10:25 PM, PILTON ROAD

When Rose returned to the room, she had the presence to discover the glass orb on top of the mantel, perched on a wooden pedestal. Inside the ball, ochre fumes swirled about. Emilio, Hernando and Sir Francis in spiritual limbo, she surmised. The spirit siphon was also on display above the hearth.

Rose got up from the chair, walked over to the hearth to examine the fetish wand and peered into the glass orb. "Do they have any sense of their fate?"

"The Pwen Hanaan. It's not meant to be pleasant, the ritual or the condition after," shared the Voodoo queen.

"I felt sadness but not remorse," said Rose looking at the fetish. "I mean, you didn't feel remorse. It was calculated." Rose could see a faint reflection of herself on the surface of the orb. She looked at and could see the tears running down her face.

"I have none. My upbringing was unusual. I was born on the Moya plantation; my mother was a house slave, but my father was the plantation owner. He loved my mother very much, and we grew up as his family, not as slaves. When Hernando completed university, he joined us in Haiti and learned he had a little black sister and was utterly disgusted with his father, my mother and me.

"He told my Papi that he was old and going senile to take up with my mother. He yelled about how the investors would lose confidence in their enterprises if they knew the life he was leading. Papi told him he was happy, and if Hernando did not approve, to leave. Don Ernesto was much older than my mother, and when he became sick, he signed papers that freed my mother and acknowledged me as a Moya and one-third heir. I was thirteen. I did not understand the significance of those papers or the fortune that one-third of his estate was worth, but my father knew his son's contempt. Should I care more that I killed my own blood? It was my brothers and Chilton that went to the extent they did to take my birthright and erase my existence."

"Thank you for sharing the experience," acknowledged Rose.

"Sister Rose, I see that you have summoned beings from the highest choir of Angels. You are steeped in the arcana of light. If you choose to apply what you have learned here today, you will break your covenant," Angelica explained.

"I don't take that decision lightly," said Rose as she contemplated the orb and its contents. Rose caught the reflection of a man standing in the archway behind her. She spun around to see a tall gentleman in necronist garb. Judging by his adornment, he was a Guild Master.

"Please continue, ladies," said the guild master.

"Gerard, have you met Sister Rose Caldwell?" asked Angelica.

Gerard held the stoic stance of a necronist, with both hands tucked into the opposite arms sleeves and his feet placed more than shoulder width apart to set a base of power to conjure from. "We have not met. A pleasure to meet you."

Rose looked him up and down. She had never met a necronist, let alone one of the six guild masters. "What's your business here?" she demanded.

"I could ask the same of you, but I'm sure that you, like me, were asked by Detective Williamson to act as a spiritual scent hound to find the murderer of Chilton and the Moyas, am I correct? One of us is the back-up plan."

Angelica flipped a new Tarot. "The Hermit, the law-bringer, is here."

"I don't need the power of premonition to tell you that the English detective is coming. She would have given him your location. We need to leave now and return to Paris, where we will have the protection of the Emperor," retorted Gerard.

"I have no intention of going to Paris," said Angelica.

"I am your way out of this mess you started. They will kill you."

"Gerard, that's the difference between you and I. You're so restrained and scientific, the son of the age of enlightenment, and I embrace the chaos and natural flow of the aether. How long did it take your city of Paris and solemn brothers to sap you of the primal power you discovered when we were together?"

His stoic stance melted. "Less than a year, but it wasn't the city that diluted it. It was no longer being with you. If you came to Paris, we could continue not where we left off. I know that would be too much to ask with what has passed, but we could start anew," replied Gerard.

"Gerard, it is your turn to pick a card," implored Angelica.

Gerard walked into the parlor and stood before her tarot table. "Angelica, I am not here to play games." Looking up to meet Angelica's gaze, something caught the seer's eye. It was the Voodoo King's staff and it had changed from the last time he swa it. "Is that a fifth skull on the staff? Is that Papa Lafayette?"

"He passed when France sent the Foreign Legion into the village. We had kept our side of the grand bargain, Gerard. We never left the Village of the Falls." Angelica touched his hand.

Rose assumed that Gerard was getting a vignette of the carnage in the village, just as she had experienced Hernando's death.

Without sitting down, he touched a card on the table with the hand that held his necronist beads.

Angelica put her finger on the card. "You broke the bargain."

Gerard lifted his finger "I had no part in that. I never knew until now."

Rose observed loss and sadness in the guild master as he spoke. "I left my heart there. it was our sacred place." He pulled his hand away. "I had no idea, Angelica."

Angelica flipped the card. "Death, the pale rider, the end of a phase of life that has served its purpose. How do you read the cards, Seer?"

The Voodoo queen stood up, grasped the Ju-Ju staff and made her way towards Rose, passing Gerard as if he did not exist.

Angelica stepped up to the hearth and looked at the orb, then at the spot where Rose had taken the siphon from. "Rose, you have played your part, and now you must go. The crossroads you face are of no consequence to what happens here. Please take your leave."

Rose advanced towards the parlor exit. She had what she needed and had to decide if she was prepared to take the consequences for using the ritual to free Preston. Rose looked back at Angelica and Gerard then turned to exit, only to be startled by the presence of another necronist standing at the front door.

Rose withdrew a reliquary from her belt sheath and incanted the invitation to Raziel, a guardian angel, protector of Adam and chief of Erilhiem. As the Enochian call rolled off her tongue, she felt in her bones that Angelica's wards dampened and hindered her summoning call. No supernatural power would intervene to help. She would be on her own.

"White witch, spare me your summoning," said Seer Thomas as he grabbed her arm and pulled her into the parlor. "Witness those that truly practice the craft."

Angelica turned to Gerard. "How did you see the conclusion, Master Seer?"

"Angelica, our offer still stands. Come with me to Paris, and we can continue our studies again."

"Our offer?" she questioned.

"My offer. My plead," Gerard begged, clasping his hands together.

"There is no going back to those young lovers in the jungle, and you can offer nothing I wish to learn. The best option for you, Master Seer, is to leave with your minions before there is more death by my hand." Angelica's tone invoked efficacy and resonated beyond the sound of her voice and into the aether as she began to glow with eldritch energy.

Rose watched in amazement as Angelica drew deeper upon her power. At the same moment, Lord Oswald phase-shifted through the parlor wall from outside of the house in hopes of surprising and surrounding the Voodoo queen. However, her defensive wards alerted her and slowed his ability to pass into the room. Still, it was a fantastic feat to phase-shift into the room, a sure sign of power and control of the arcane.

Angelica spun around to face the Lodge occultist, one arm outstretched with a subtle twist of her wrist. Her extended index and middle finger threw a hex that spewed an inky, smoky mass coating the wall with what initially looked like tar but transmuted into multitudes of spiders. Every type and size crawled all over Oswald and the wall he was passing through. It was enough for him to lose concentration and begin to rematerialize amid the cracked wall plaster. Blood splattered, as Oswald's internal organs were pulverized and intermixed within the parlor wall. Angelica's spider illusion disappeared, leaving a more horrifying vision of the dead Lord trapped in the wall.

Guild Master Saint-Yves desperately manipulated his beads, muttering an arcane incantation. Slowly, a sigil began to surround and glow on the floor around Angelica. Rose could divine from the arcane writing it was some type of defensive binding spell.

The Voodooist made a mopping motion with the Ju-Ju staff over the eldritch sigils Gerrard was conjuring. The sigil broke apart into a grey-green cloud of dust. Angelica slammed the staff down while uttering a chant to manifest the spirits of her predecessors. Gerard gazed in awe as the apparition of

Papa Lafayette spilled from the eyes of the dead Hougan's skull.

The phantom of Papa Lafayette moved across the room and grabbed Gerard by the throat. The guild master dropped his beads as his life force was drawn out into the apparition. The ghost let out a hearty laugh, pushed out his chest and stretched his free arm towards the Ju-Ju staff, channeling Gerard's soul into it. Gerard screamed as he began to wrinkle and age.

Angelica never saw Seer Thomas enter the room as she worked her spell. The Seer plunged a dagger between Angelica's shoulder blades with both hands assuring full penetration. With the blade buried to the hilt, he twisted the handle to actuate a mechanism. With that twist, a valve opened, releasing the contents of a crystal vial, a potion pressurized with aether. The soul serum was the name the necronists gave it. This potion was designed to inject through the center bore of the blade and into the victim, not a poison but an arcane reactive fluid that initiated the coagulation and collection of the spirit force back into the vial in the weapon's handle.

The instant the dagger plunged into Angelica's flesh, she released her staff, and the spell was broken. Gerard fell to his knees, racked with pain.

Rose stood frozen in silence. Torn and confused, Angelica had shared her memories with her moments ago and now she lay prone and lifeless on the floor. Seer Thomas hovered over the dead body of Angelica. Gerard arose to his feet with some effort. He was visibly older. He limped to the mantle and put the orb into his coat pocket. The ex-nun watched the guild master as he steadied himself on the mantle. Rose felt a tap on her upper arm. It was Detective Williamson standing behind her in the archway with his pistol drawn.

～

10:31 PM, Pilton Road

"Drop the knife," instructed Dolly, his gun pointed at Seer Thomas, who was still standing over Angelica and holding his dagger. As if in a trance, Thomas let the blade fall to the floor. Dolly quickly surveyed the room. Rose looked worn out but safe at his side, the woman on the ground had a stab wound to the back and there was Saint-Yves and one of his cronies with what had to be the weapon that stabbed the woman.

"Dear Detective, how timely of you to show up," said the guild master, who turned to face Dolly. He pointed to the floor. "The murderess you have been seeking. She was attempting to kill me when my colleague stopped her."

Dolly waved his pistol at the gruesome scene of Lord Oswald. "Christ, what the hell happened to that poor fucker?"

Rose spoke, "The remains of occultist Lord Oswald, who failed a phase-shift attempt, not a direct attack by Ms. Du Haiti."

Burton entered the hall from the back of the house with the driver in cuffs and his pistol drawn. "Detective Sergeant, I nabbed this guy going in the back door."

"Burton, get outside with that one and blow your police whistle to alert the uniformed constables and request a paddy wagon," barked Dolly, his attention back to the parlor where Gerard had moved from the mantle to the body of the priestess. He was reaching for the Ju-Ju staff.

"Dolly, don't let him touch that," yelled Rose.

"Guild Master, you just stop moving right now," ordered Dolly, realizing Burton had not left the hall yet. He looked to the young detective and saw him standing dumbstruck. At first, he chalked it up to the gruesome scene, but then he heard the murmuring of the two necronists.

He turned to see them both chanting then he felt something warm on his left-hand side. It was the amulet that Rose had given him. He could see it glowing through his pocket. He then saw Rose's necklace charm glow.

"You two shut your traps now."

They continued with the mesmerism.

"Rose, they are trying to hex us. Do something to protect Burton," yelled Dolly. She and Dolly were safe at the moment with the wards she had made to defend them, at least he thought they were since he felt like he was thinking clearly.

Rose turned, pulling off her coat. "This will afford him some protection," said Rose as she threw the coat over Burton, diving on him like he was a man on fire.

No way will I become a mind slave under someone's control or be made to fight Rose or Burton. "Alright, let's give this a try," he shouted.

He placed a bullet into Seer Thomas's thigh. Blood and gristle flew, and the necronist went down with a howl.

The report of the pistol broke Gerard's concentration. He bellowed, "You can't shoot him. We are diplomats, guests of your government!"

Dolly squared his gunsight on Gerard's head. "One more move from your lips, and I'll let this next chamber go." As Dolly stared at his head through the sight, he realized how ill and haggard the guild master looked. "Now, Guild Master, you look like you need a lie down. Why don't you just have a seat and keep your arms in the air and palms facing me. Don't say a word."

The detective lowered his pistol and looked at the other necronist. He was passed out and losing blood fast. "Looks like I may lose my badge ,but your mate's going to lose that leg. Burton, get outside and start blowing your whistle to get some uniforms in here."

Burton snapped out of his haze as he collected himself after Rose's body tackle.

"Rose, come here." He handed her the pistol. "You get close to the guild master and point this at his head. If he tries to summon anything, pull that trigger and conjure a hole in his head."

Rose took the pistol in both hands and stepped next to Gerard.

Dolly took off his belt and grabbed a candlestick to fashion a tourniquet. Thomas would certainly lose the leg. Staving off the loss of blood would be his only chance at living through the night. While he worked on the leg, he considered Saint-Yves seated in the chair, "I know what you're up to. You were trying to mesmerize me and Burton. You two are under arrest for the murder of Angelica du Haiti."

"So that's how the Metropolitan Police work? We do your dirty work, and now you arrest us?" retorted Saint-Yves.

"What's he talking about?" asked Rose.

"Never you mind, Rose. If he opens his mouth up one more time, you just pull that trigger. And point it a little more to the left. If you do shoot him, his brains won't be enough to stop that ball and you could hit me."

"Dolly, were you working with them?"

"In a manner of speaking, my boss requested I collaborate."

"The detective authorized me to hunt her down," replied the guild master.

"And I also told you to make sure I was on hand. Funny thing is that you weren't the one that tipped me off to Angelica's whereabouts. It was Sister Rose here that sent me a wire-type of the address." Dolly was struggling to get the bleeding to slow on the seer. It started to sink in that bullet might end his career. "So I'm prepared to bring you in and let the Crown decide if you were defending yourself or here to commit murder," said Dolly as he gave Gerard a smile while he twisted the tourniquet tighter.

Burton came back in with a constable. "Jesus Christ, has that guy been blasted through the wall? Bloody hell," the constable exclaimed.

"Constable, put some irons on the guild master."

MONDAY, THE 28TH OF JUNE

9:20 AM, KÖNIGSBERG, PRUSSIA

"Deiter, are the plans complete?" inquired Duke Gorber.

"Yes, Your Grace, as best as I can tell," the chief engineer replied.

"Excellent. When do you expect to get started on the construction?"

The engineer looked as if he wanted to speak but lost his words.

"When can I tell Prince von Bismarck that Prussia will have its first air dreadnought?"

"Your Grace, may I speak freely?"

"Go on." The Duke needed updated information on the progress, even if he had to listen to the engineer whine about his staff, materials and working conditions.

"While my engineers and technicians have the plans, we still need time to grasp the technology of the mechanists. I am informed daily that we require more documentation to unravel the complexities of a subassembly. That confounds us because we do not comprehend the process they use to craft a specific part. I know it pains you to hear it, but this is the most sophisticated airship ever to be built, and we need more time. Before we lay the hull, we need to understand the metallurgy process. For the ship to fly ,we need to master the design of the solar and stellar-scopic registers that drive navigation."

"What can I provide to make this project meet my schedule?" asked the Duke.

"I need a proper mechanist team and industrialist leaders such as Bessemer, Whitworth and Clooney. Likely I require intelligence from each of them," demanded the engineer.

"I will be back in one week's time, Deiter. I want your plan to have a keel laid by winter," demanded the Duke.

"May I make a suggestion, Your Grace?" asked the engineer. He wanted to provide solutions, not cry about poor resources.

"If it moves our plan forward, I will hear it. If it's more excuses, then keep it to yourself." Gorber was at the mercy of the Prussian engineers but did not want to show that weakness.

"If we were to follow these plans and build a replica of the British ship, it would be obvious that we have spies in the London works. Instead, my engineers can take the innovations and integrate them into Prussian designs. In fact, some of these concepts could be retrofitted to naval ships and ground artillery immediately," The engineer knew he had to deliver some progress given the risks taken to secure design drawings of the HMS Victoria.

The Duke was intrigued. "Continue."

"For example, we have the specification for Professor Honeysuckle's flexible armor. One of my engineers postulated that we could line the interior of our dirigibles an immediate improvement to the existing fleet," followed the Engineer.

"Deiter, strike my request. Upon my return, I want you to have a list of the upgrades and time frame for the implementation of the items you suggest." The Duke could use this idea to show progress. The Engineer did have a point that a duplicate of the dreadnought would leave no doubt there had been espionage.

"Affirmative, Your Grace."

The Duke left the factory located on the outskirts of Königsberg and returned to the city center to report to Prince von Bismarck. As the Minister for Internal Affairs, Duke Gorber's title was an innocuous term for his real purpose as the head of the Prussian spy service.

Operation Braunbär was the Duke's critical plot, essential for the game at hand of the Minister President of Prussia Otto von Bismarck.

Duke Gorber entered the Minister President's office. Kiefer, the High Elector Guild Baron of the Alchemists, was seated having a coffee with von Bismarck.

"Guild Baron, Minister President." The Duke greeted the two gentlemen with a curt bow and click of his heels.

"Have a seat, Gorber. May I call for a coffee or other refreshment for you?" queried Minister President von Bismarck.

"A brandy, sir. We should all have a brandy to celebrate the success of our operations in the British Empire," suggested the Duke.

"Very well. While we await the bottle, let's begin with a briefing on the home front. What can you report from the palace?" inquired von Bismarck as he walked to the door of his office and opened it. "Hans, bring three glasses and a bottle of brandy."

When Gorber knew he had the attention of Bismarck again he began. "The King's health continues to deteriorate. While none of the doctors have openly speculated on the King's demise, it appears there is little chance of him recovering from this stroke," replied the spy master.

"Very well. Do you have a summary on the Prince Regent?

"Not now."

"How about our Danish friends?"

"Nothing more than you read in the papers, I am afraid. The Danes are sensitive to our disputes to the hereditary claims on the two duchies."

A steward knocked at the door carrying a tray. "Excellent timing," said Gorber. "Pour the Minister President and Guild Baron a snifter, for we toast the success of our agents and the illustrious alchemists of Prussia." The men touched glasses and drank. "The Guild Baron and I are keen to be updated on the results of Braunbär." von Bismarck inquired.

"My agent in Scotland Yard has confirmed that the police are looking for saboteurs and do not believe the bombing was instigated by home-grown revolutionaries That being said, they suspect the subversives to be French, not Prussian," offered Gorber.

"What of the designs, Duke Gorber? I blew up my plant for your charade. Was it worth it?"

"Operation Braunbär was a success because of the sacrifice you made for the unification of Germany, Guild Baron. First, there is now a plausible reason for you to delay the supply of LQ to the British. Next, the explosion allowed us to destroy the drafting and records building to cover for the documents our agent stole. We have detailed plans of the Victoria to design counter measures to the warship. In addition, we have uncovered hundreds of innovations we can begin to include in the design of current and future airships and artillery," gloated Gorber.

"Minister President, it would mean a great deal to the guild if any of these innovations could be incorporated into our processes," added the Guild Baron.

"Minister President, I will need to conduct further operations on British soil to obtain additional industrial secrets. Some of what we have learned from the documents indicate other novel approaches in metallurgy and precision machining are needed to master and build at the level of Queen Victoria's mechanists," the Duke advised.

"We cannot rely on royal bonds of matrimony to secure alliances nor depend on those affiliations for our security. For decades, our borders have been subject to the whims of the French, the Russians and a pack of squabbling Germanic dukes. No offense meant to the present company," articulated von Bismarck.

"None taken," replied Gorber.

"Prussia will lead the Germanic people to a unified German Empire that will rival the French Russian and British monarchies. This empire will be fueled by alchemies of our most prestigious guild and finally bring peace to our people. No longer will our lands be trodden on by foreign invaders," von Bismarck declared.

Duke Gorber had no reason to doubt the Minster's mettle to make his vision a reality.

11:00 AM, NECRONIST GUILD HOUSE, ILE DE LA CITÉ PARIS, FRANCE

Guild Master Saint-Yves reached the shores of France with Moreau by his side and Thomas in a coffin in the hold of the ship. He'd made his way to the headquarters of the necronists and had been resting there for several days. He remained within the walls of the compound until he was certain that the French and English had settled any issues connected to Angelica's death. Of those that passed on Saturday, he still grieved the fall of Angelica the most. Thomas was devoted, but he was impetuous in stabbing Angelica and the necronist guild had its stock of rash zealots. Then there was Oswald, who Gerard knew for only a few hours, and there again he did not follow Gerard's aim to subdue Angelica, and for that he surrendered his life. There would be no further talk of the mission today for soon the Emperor would visit the guild hall. The necronist guild house ironically sat next to the Cathedral of Notre Dame on the Ile de la Cité, the site of a medieval hospital. The land stretched from Notre Dame all the way to the Seine. More than a house, it was a compound with multiple interconnected buildings and deep sub-levels that many of the guild did not rank high enough to enter. The site had been a donation to the necronist guild from the Emperor himself on the day of his coronation.

The necronists viewed themselves as savants of metaphysics seeking to define the science of the spirit. The Church saw his brother's exploration into the afterworld as heretical and counter to the beliefs and teachings of the Church. If it were not for the events that took place on Napoleon Bonaparte's expedition to Egypt and the work of one young necronist in particular, the guild may have become a footnote in occult history.

The accepted reason for Napoleon's expedition to Egypt and Syria fifty-nine years earlier was to establish France's leadership in Egyptology, but it was more to exert influence in the failing Ottoman Empire. General Napoleon sought to offset the expanding influences of England and the Russian Empire by leading a French scientific expedition with a military contingent for protection; the mission would show his ability to project a force into the Middle East. The research detachment included a metaphysicist and guild member, Sebastian Crocus, to lead the group that found the Rosetta Stone. The tablets provided the key to deciphering hieroglyphics and allowed for the origin of Egyptology through the translation of the symbols to ancient Greek and eventually to all other languages.

Another discovery was made in the royal tombs, the Oraculum, stones scriptures that allowed for decoding messages from the ancient oracle. The necronist seer translated the tablets and instructed the general on the uses of the Oraculum. Napoleon consulted his translated version for every significant political decision, finding it to be indispensable, It was the secret behind what the world perceived as military genius.

While the expedition devoted most of its resources to collecting antiquities and detailing the history of the ancient Egyptians, it was the Necronist Crocus who used the Rosetta stone to unravel the mysteries of the Egyptian priests and the experiments they were conducting to open and close gateways into the afterlife. These discoveries became the basis for the two areas of study in the necronist guild: divination and rejuvenation.

Ultimately, the guild became competent in prophecy through its research of the Oraculum and other works of antiquity. It was during a séance that the guild seers traced a thread of the future where Napoleon took Moscow but lost his army, not through conflict with the Russian Empire but by the savagery of the weather and desolate land conditions. The Grand Army never left Poland, held back by Bonaparte's obeying the warning of his spiritual advisor and confirmation by his own divination from the Oraculum. From that point, the fates of the necronists, France and Napoleon Bonaparte were inextricably linked.

Gerard was snapped out of his daydreaming by the appearance of Emperor Napoleon's entourage arriving at the necronist guild house. He was still depleted from Angelica's assault, but his presence was required when the dictator came to visit. The special detail of imperial guardsman rode on horseback, entering the courtyard then taking position to protect the area. The rest of the guard deployed around the perimeter of the necronist campus. Two steam carriages entered the gates of the campus. The first carried Dr. Phila, Gold Seer, Napoleon's personal surgeon.

The second car, an imperial carriage, pulled up in front of the large double-doored entrance to the guild house. An imperial guard stood waiting at the ready and opened the door for the

Emperor of France, who in the next year would celebrate his ninetieth birthday.

Dr. Phila made haste to reach the entrance before the Emperor exited his car to speak to his brethren. "Master Crocus, why wasn't I given more notice? I appear a fool to his majesty as I have no reason to insist he receive another treatment so soon."

High Guild Master Crocus was in the courtyard along with his assistants to meet the Emperor.

"Saint-Yves has made an impressive acquisition, and we decided it would please his Highness to receive this new medium directly," Crocus instructed under his breath.

Napoleon stepped up to the wyrding of necronists.

"How well you look, Your Majesty," crooned Crocus.

"Sebastian," acknowledged the Emperor. The two men looked at each other with genuine affection and exchanged a handshake that was almost a hug. No one else had this relationship with the sovereign of France. A cursory observer would guess that Sebastian was twenty years the senior to the Emperor, yet he was ten years younger. Crocus was prudent in his use of revitalization. He did not fear death like his monarch did.

The assembly made their way through the verdant garden. The blossoms were in full bloom. A placid summer day, it was a serene yet contrasting scene: the pleasant trickling of the fountain maintained by necronist novices dressed in black cloaks appeared to be in mourning of a loved one, not gardening. The inner forum served as a transition from the outside to the interior of the administration building among remnants from the medieval hospital built by the Church.

Savants and followers of the most powerful guild in France lingered at the entrance. The huge doors were open, letting the warm summer air mix with the cool interior atmosphere of the stone building. The large cast iron doors were covered in vignettes of the cult's history. The party's pace was deliberate, traveling through the solemn gothic hallways to the verticulator that led to the sub-levels.

Few were admitted beyond the entrance to the Cenaculum Mortale Rejuvination, the chamber of mortal rejuvenation. It was the crowning achievement of the necronists, where life could be extended and living tissue regenerated. The elite savants of necronist arts, known as the white wyrding under the leadership of Guild Master Hume, conducted research into the world of metaphysics and improved techniques to tap into and control spiritual energy.

Gerard was toward the rear of the retinue as they entered the ante-chamber. The guild had gone to considerable effort to represent the space as Egyptian to remind the Emperor of the expedition to Egypt that cemented the alliance between Napoleon and Crocus. Gerard knew better than anyone it was what Hume, and he and what they had studied in Haiti; that had provided the breakthroughs in divine energy transmission, not Egyptian tablets. What his dead paramour could manage with sticks and her incantations, the guild had industrialized to make the process reproducible by those that had limited spiritual talent, like Crocus and others.

Here the King's personal bodyguards took a position as sentries on either side of the double metal doors within the ante-chamber. They followed every movement of their liege with exception to his study and sleeping quarters and beyond this point at the guild house.

Inscribed above a small narrow archway that was the entrance to the most sacred space of the necronist guild was:

Through Death, I am Humiliated
Through Death, I am Exalted

The enclave moved through a narrow passage that compelled the company to move through in single file. Great effort had been made to leave an entrant with the claustrophobic quality of delving into an ancient mausoleum. This was another place where French imperial protocols were ignored. Crocus led the group into the chamber rather than everyone walking behind the Emperor. The inner chamber was simply constructed, a large pyramid-shaped vault of stone, with walls covered with carved inscriptions. Centered in the room on a raised dais were the Conoptic vessel, the tub where a subject was treated, and an ornate cantilevered armature that upheld the lid of the tub. Both the tub and its cap were sculpted out of alabaster.

Purposely hidden beneath the vessel were the piping, tubes and conduits that connected the tub to the complex process one level below. There beneath the tub was the machinery that powered the chamber. The necronists brought a scientific and industrial approach to the manipulation of supernatural forces but went to great lengths to hide the appliances to create mystery and to leave the Emperor with the illusion it was the guild masters themselves that imbued him with life-force.

Saint-Yves and the other guild masters took their positions around the tub. Only these few Masters and Dr. Philas understood the extent of the treatments and how dependent the Emperor had become on this secret process to his lively state at such an advanced age.

No one spoke until the Emperor started conversation. It was important to leave the King with an impression that the guild masters were subordinate and humbled in his presence.

"What happened to you guild master? An experiment gone awry?" questioned Napoleon, grinning at Gerard.

"My Emperor, this scourge was inflicted upon me while in service to you, my liege, and to the guild. It is a small price to pay to secure the medium we will use for today's therapy," replied Saint-Yves.

Crocus interceded. "My Emperor and dear friend, Guild Master Saint-Yves has made extensive sacrifices and was in mortal danger to secure this special spiritual medium to infuse into the healing bath, and your interceding on our behalf with the British government helped to secure his safety and assure we have the full complement of masters to conduct the infusion." *Crocus was more carnival huckster now that a metaphysical savant prepared to say just about anything to build illusion in the monarch's mind.*

"Your service to the empire has always been exemplary, Guild Master, and I hope that your brethren will provide you a similar treatment to reverse your unfortunate state. As to the English, you can be assured that your personal protection is a priority of the empire," stated Bonaparte as he removed his sash and sword.

"Thank you, Your Majesty, for my safe passage back from London, and soon, I too will have this mortal damage repaired," replied Gerard, wondering if the Corsican even could remember Gerard's name. Crocus and the other masters had gone to great extent to leave Napoleon with the impression that his treatments required a full complement of guild masters. *He might just think of us as important tools to extend his life.*

"Excellent. All will be right for you and I soon enough," said Napoleon. "I was wondering why you called for a treatment outside of the usual schedule." The Emperor's traditional treatments took place every three months.

Dr. Philas helped Napoleon out of his uniform, placing the items on a portable suit valet. The physician, a high-level necronist, was reduced to the duties of valet as he unbuttoned the Emperor's shirt.

"Saint-Yves, I appreciate all you have done for the empire. You sure you shouldn't take some time in the chamber first?" recommended Napoleon. Gerard was pleasantly surprised that the King remembered his name and offered to wait.

He had a different plan for his treatment. He touched the ampule in his coat. "Thank you, Your Grace, but the rejuvenation of a guild master is a different process and takes preparation," replied Gerard.

Crocus shot Gerrard a sly smile of approval for his comment. *I too can be a huckster, and the ringmaster approves.*

The self-coronated Emperor of France used the wooden steps near the conoptic tub to reach the edge of the huge stone vessel and lower himself into the ichor. "Can one of you discover a less foul and cold substance to be immersed in?" The King made a face of disgust as he limped into the viscous pool.

"We are constantly researching improvements, Your Majesty," replied Dr. Philas.

The High Guild Master used the cantilevered arm to lower

the massive lid of the tub into place. The other guild masters secured the seal of the tub. "All is in place" relayed Guild Master Hume, the Chamber Master. The entourage left the interior chamber once they were sure Napoleon was sequestered. Dr. Philas rolled out the Emperor's clothes, and Hume removed the steps, leaving the chamber empty but for the diminutive man in the tub. All the masters exited through a secret passage that led to stairs to the mechanical level. At the end of the treatment, the guild masters would approach the chamber through the antechamber, leaving the bodyguards wondering how the seers exited.

Hume signaled for the treatment to begin as the other guild masters left to fulfill other duties In the case of Gerrard, he had an interest in seeing how Hume had adapted the process to transfer the contents of Angelica's orb.

He followed Hume through the walkways that passed between the large pieces of equipment and had a seat by the main control station. He was easily tired in his current state.

The mechanical level was a hive of activity, looking more like the boiler room of a steamship than a spiritual sanctum. Lower order necronists of the White Wyrding monitored the equipment, worked the valves, adjusted the gas levels, read gauges and scurried to double check the various subsystems that made up the rejuvenation process.

"So, Hume, how did you deal with the material not coming in an ampule?" asked Gerard.

"I must agree with the man in the tub. You should get treated immediately," said Hume.

"After him, you can treat me."

"How bad is it?" asked Hume.

"Do you remember when Lafayette had poisoned us all with the soul worm and how bad you felt just before Huey returned and we were given the antidote?"

"Oh yes, all my bones hurt, and I was filled with such a fear because I felt my spirit waste away…"

"Well, it's like that again, but worse because I'm older with less constitution. I never thought I would live this long to feel this bad again." Gerard laughed at himself.

"Why didn't you have me go? I didn't have the same emotional connection the two of you had. It had to be horrible to see," said Gerard's friend.

"It was a complete, fucking failure, Arno, tragic. Just as I thought I was getting through to her, or at least felt we could keep talking, that nitwit Englishman comes through a wall like he is Merlin the Magnificent. Oh, the look on his face when she cast this illusion, and he realized he had lost concentration. I will never forget it. You should have seen her, Arno. She was ten times the Hougan Lafayette was. No entourage to augment her power, just her. Hell, she even summoned the old witch doctor to scourge my life force. I have spent my whole life with a hole in my heart because we were apart but always had the hope of seeing her again to offset it. Now that is gone."

Hume looked at Gerard for a few moments as if he was going to say something then he patted Gerard on his shoulder. "I can't fix that broken heart of yours, but I will prepare a nice bath for you later, guaranteed to take five years off your life. Or in your case, twenty. Look here. This is our traditional transfer chamber." He pointed at a metal chamber with a glass door. It looked sturdy and industrial.

Gerard was familiar with the design.

"Our ampules have metal contactors to allow a current to pass through the ampule and conduct the spiritual essence into the machine. The contacts slip into the four electrodes you see there. Of course, the orb does not have contacts, so we need to crack it open then conduct current through it without allowing the spirit to escape. Now look over here," said Hume as he pointed at a heavy bronze sphere with a large glass portal. It looked like a deep sea diver's helmet. "I crafted a special chamber with a holder for the orb. See how it holds the orb?"

Gerard looked and observed through the portal inside the bronze sphere. The glass orb was held in a set of prongs suspending it in the center. Within the glass, the swirling smoke could be seen.

"I throw this switch, and we now bypass the conductor through this chamber." Hume patted the bronze sphere. "To get the spirit essence into et viventem perpetua, the machine of everlasting life, we need to approximate what is going on inside the ampule's soul serum. To do this, I will now pump a gaseous coagulation agent. This gives the immaterial spirit something to cling to in the material world." He turned a faucet handle and pressed a button, and a pump reciprocated, pushing a pinkish fume into the chamber. "Gerard, go lie down. You look like you might keel over from the boredom of this technical session."

"No, please continue. This is a once in a lifetime treatment. I want to see how you are doing it," replied Gerard. He was not bored, just tired.

Hume pushed a button, causing green lights around the floor to signal the others to man their stations. "I begin now." Hume smiled. "This reminds me of the early days when we first began experimenting," said Hume.

The hall filled with the thrum of dynamos and the calls of men as they read off the variables from gauges and levels. Pumps started to recirculate the ichor.

"The electrodes will be pressed into the orb, causing it to crack and mixing the aether gas and spirit. After an initial reaction, the electrodes will have current applied and conduct the medium into the chamber." Hume watched the pinkish mist of the aether gas through the thick glass portal. He hand-operated a micrometer that slowly pressed the electrode prongs against the orb surface. Then he peered in to see when cracks appeared in the glass. With a sudden pop, the orb shattered instantly, starting the reaction. Hume lunged to the initiation button as fast as he could. His palm slammed down on the button. Current coursed through the viewing chamber, and the spirit form coagulated then caught on the current running from bottom to top.

"See how the essence caught on the current then was pulled up and out of the chamber?" Hume asked.

"I didn't. You blocked the view to the window. Hume, what do you think the punishment is for conducting untried experiments on the Emperor?" asked Gerard.

"I am not sure, but I would beg for leniency on Crocus' behalf," said Hume as he isolated the gas to the chamber and waited for it to clear. The spirit energy was induced into the ichor recirculation loop that flowed through the tub and would be absorbed by the Emperor. The guild master signaled to shut down the current and the dynamo system. He opened his pocket watch and squinted to make out the numbers on the watch face in the dim gaslight. "Gerard, he will need to soak for an hour then figure an hour to prepare your treatment. Why don't you have a rest in your office until then?"

Saint-Yves couldn't argue with the advice from his friend.

1:00 PM, Chilton House, City of London

"What's this, I hear? Strathmore is designated the trustee on the Moya trust?" barked Oscar Owens as he stormed into Lester Chilton's office unannounced, without even a cursory knock at the door.

Lester looked up from the documents he was reviewing, "Yes, Oscar. The wills of both Emilio and Hernando Moya were explicit that all the bequests and their estates were to be entrusted to Mr. Strathmore and managed in the New York office."

"There must be something awry with the documents. Have you advised our solicitors to review them?" huffed Owens.

"Why are you so upset about this?" asked Chilton.

"The Moya family have been long-standing clients and managed by this office for decades. Lester, they were your father's client, for God's sake. Why are we losing them?" Owens fired on his younger partner.

Lester stood up and leaned over his desk. "Owens, we're not losing them. They are transferring to our office in America. It's natural they be managed from that part of the world. Most of the holdings are over there." Owens was surprised by the heat in the tone of Chilton's voice. "Oscar, I want this whole affair with the Moyas behind us. If we were to take issue with the currently drawn documents, the trust could be put into question by half the people in Portugal looking to grab a share of the fortune. We would watch the estate dwindle and spend our days in court with every frivolous claim. Let it go quietly to New York."

"This is how it starts, Lester. They take our clients then one day London is reporting to America."

"And your name will still be on the door, collecting a partner share of the profits, including the fees charged to the Moya estate under Strathmore's supervision."

"Lester, I am not done with this matter." Owens had no argument. Chilton was correct. It was best to not stir the pot. "I have a client waiting, but I would like you to think about what I have said." He closed the door on his way out of Lester's office.

Outside in the seating area, a well-dressed oriental man lingered. "Mr. Lin, I am Oscar Owens, the managing partner. Please join me in our boardroom."

Jimmy Lin stood up, putting his gloves in his hat, and shook Owens' hand. "A pleasure, Mr. Owens. You have an impressive office, I must say."

The two men settled down at the end of the boardroom table. "I went over the documents, and there are a few items I would like to clear up."

While Owens talked, Jimmy set his leather attaché on the table and unlatched the leather clasps, removing similar documents. Jimmy beamed.

"Mr. Lin, Chilton, Owens and Strathmore is one of a select few merchant banks that a monarch calls upon in times of financial strain. We have been fortunate because of our reputation and the work we take on."

Jimmy stared at him.

"What I mean to say is that in the city there are many fine financial institutions that handle trusts, and while we are pleased that you desire to work with us, I don't believe we have the right trustee for your situation."

"Was there something wrong with the documents? I had them drawn up by Davis and Yorke." Jimmy knew where this was going. He would have fun with the fat man along the way. "Oh no. They are fine solicitors. In fact, Elton Davis started here in our council office," retorted Owens.

"That is what he told me," said Jimmy. "Then is it that I'm a chink?"

"Mr. Lin, Chilton has been banking in Asia for decades, with one of the first and now largest offices in Hong Kong," consoled Owens.

"That is good because I do a lot of business over there, and you can help." Jimmy pulled out a Mahogany box and set it in front of Owens and opened the lid. Nestled inside the velvet lining was a loaf of gold made up of ten 100-gram gold ingots slices. "I have a truck arriving in twenty minutes to deliver seventeen-hundred-sixty-seven 100-gram ingots to be stored in your vault and to fund these three trusts. So, you don't have a problem because I'm Chinese, the paperwork has been completed by the best solicitor in London and the funding will be here any moment." Jimmy continued, "That leaves only one issue I can think of. You may have heard a rumor, idle gossip of the ignorant, that my partners and I are involved in unscrupulous business. The word you may even be thinking of is gangster, and what if this were true? Now you might think I am a liability to your precious Chilton House, but no, on the contrary, I would be an asset. Once the streets of London know you are Master Lo's banker, no one would be foolish enough to steal from your vaults again. You could leave the door wide open and not one criminal would think to touch a shilling." He paused, "That's if the rumors were true."

Owen sat for several moments, looking at the gold. "Let me get a clerk in here to witness the documents and inform the doorman to expect the truck." Owens stuck out his hand to shake Jimmy's. "I want you to know how important your business is to Chilton House. Your bullion will be under my personal attention and stored in the partner vault. Only our top clients have this honor, and only partners have the combination. Be sure to let your associates know that is how much we value your business."

Jimmy shook his hand "You have lived up to your reputation, Mr. Owens. There is the matter of this one trust." Jimmy slid the documents across the table.

"Yes, the White Angel trust. I found that one interesting, and might I suggest that I personally take the role of trustee?"

"I couldn't think of a better person, Mr. Owens. As to the first matter of business, once the bullion is in your possession, I want you to liquidate enough of the gold to pounds' sterling then fund your investment strategy, leaving some cash liquid for the purchase of an appropriate residence."

"Consider it done," Owens replied.

"Excellent, and one final instruction. The beneficiary is never to learn that I am the source of these funds. If she does, and I hear it came from your lips then...well, I'm sure you understand that would be unpalatable for me." Jimmy just stared at the old man for a moment before continuing. "Can you put the gold in this box into the vault with the rest of the boxes? For your accounts, that will make it one thousand-seven-hundred and seventy-seven ingots."

The clerk knocked at the door. "Mr. Owens, I am here to witness and certify signatures."

"Come in, come in," replied Owens.

The clerk opened the box he carried and set out an inkwell, several pens and stamps. The clerk turned to Jimmy Lin. "You can begin signing documents at any time. Do you have a pen?"

◇

3:00 PM, Necronist Guild House, Ile de la Cité, Paris, France

Guild Master Hume entered Gerard's office. Gerard lay on a chaise lounge with a migraine and arthritic pains in his hands and knees. "How did the Emperor's treatment go?" inquired Gerard.

"Too well. I would say we stripped off fifteen years of aging. Doctor Philas suggested that the Emperor take a sabbatical to Versailles and limit his exposure to the public. I agreed," advised Hume.

"It will be interesting to see how long the effects are sustained." commented Gerard. His eyes closed as the light intensified the migraine.

"We have readied the chamber for you, brother," informed Hume.

"Can you help me up?" Gerard began lifting himself up but was lacking energy and strength to move.

"Yes, brother." Hume helped Gerard to his feet. His breathing became labored from the exertion.

As they walked through the mechanical room, Gerard stopped.

"Are you alright? We are almost to the chamber," said Hume. "I would like to check something. I will meet you inside." Hume continued down the walkway towards the stairs that led to the tub room.

Saint-Yves made his way towards the transfer chamber but ran out of energy. He looked around for someone to help that would not question what he planned to do. "You, technician, give me a hand."

With the assistance of the technician, Gerard made his way back to where he watched Hume transfer the spirits from the orb. The system was switched back to the traditional transfer chamber. The guild master opened the transfer chamber that held an ampule. Removing and slipping it into his pocket, he reached inside his jacket and held out the ampule that contained Angelica's essence. He gazed through it then placed the article between the electrodes in the chamber.

The technician watched as he changed the vials.

"What is your name, Acolyte?"

"Bertan," the young Acolyte replied.

Gerard closed the chamber. "Please help me into the inner chamber, Acolyte."

"But I am not permitted inside the sacred chamber," he replied.

"I need your assistance. Let me rest my weary body on your shoulder. It will be alright. Acolyte, you have no reason to mention what you think you might have seen," warned Gerard.

When they stepped through the inner door, Hume bellowed, "Bertran, what are you doing?"

"Hume, I asked him to assist me. It is not his doing," Gerard explained.

Hume moved to help Gerard. "Thank you, Acolyte. I will aid the guild master from here." Hume whispered to Gerrard, "We must get you treatment quickly. Your judgment has been affected."

"I have suffered from poor judgment prior to the attack. I was just able to cover better when I had energy," muttered Gerard.

Hume assisted Saint-Yves in disrobing, placing the garments of the guild master on the hanger of the portable valet. While hanging Gerard's jacket, Hume felt the ampule. He reached into the pocket, recognized the object and the number noted on it while looking back at Saint-Yves to see if he witnessed him discover the ampule. He had not. Gerard was occupied with steadying himself while removing his clothes. He slid it back into the pocket where he found it.

Hume assisted Gerard into the tub. The guild master already seemed to be receiving some relief just floating in the ichor.

Hume secured the tub, assuring that the vessel was sealed. The chamber master pushed the stand with Saint-Yves' clothes as he walked out of the inner chamber and sealed the door. He then removed the ampule from Gerard's clothes and walked to the conversion chamber to initiate the process. The vial in the chamber had no number. It had never been entered into inventory. He switched the unrecorded ampule for the numbered selected for the treatment. Safeties were released, cogs engaged and current applied with the push of a button.

Gerard would be rejuvenated from the life essence of another, but not the one he had planned on.

Hume slipped the unnumbered ampule into his jacket pocket.

WEDNESDAY, THE 30TH OF JUNE

10:13 AM, SCOTLAND YARD

Three days had passed since Keane's funeral and four had gone by since Dolly and Burton resolved the Chilton case. Dolly's face was almost completely healed. He sat outside Commissioner Mayne's office, waiting to prepare for an appointment at 10 Downing Street.

The door opened. and Dolly shot to his feet.

"You ready, Detective?"

"Yes, ready as I'll ever be, sir," Dolly said, tapping the back of his case journal that he held against his chest and wondering why he was called to the Prime Minister.

"Alright, then. I have a carriage out front waiting for us," advised Mayne.

Once in the privacy of the carriage, the commissioner was prepared to share more with Dolly. "Apparently, the Prime Minister and the Home Secretary have requested an audience directly from you regarding the Chilton Case," informed Mayne.

"The bleeding Prime Minister? Do you know specifically why? Is it an interest in the case, the victim or my performance?" queried Dolly.

"You did shoot a man who had diplomatic privileges in the country, who was assisting you in the capture of a murderer," replied Commissioner Mayne.

Dolly wondered if Mayne was coaching him on an inquiry regarding his behavior and not the case.

"Well, better you shot a silver seer than a guild master. That could have turned into a full-blown international incident," assured Mayne.

"Yes, sir," Dolly replied, staring at the floor of the carriage and searching for an answer to where this could go. There was the issue of how the Chilton murder case so gruesomely ended, loose ends like the missing gold, or it could easily be his treatment of diplomats.

The newspapers had had a field day printing stories of reports of spirits invading Lambeth.

"Tell them straight, Dolly, and we will get through this." Mayne explained.

Welch at the Guardian had been hounding Dolly for an interview on his phantom killer, the columnist's name for the murderer of Chilton and Moya. *Maybe it could be just a talk about managing the press.* "Thank you, sir." Dolly was worried. He was just the right level of authority to be made an example of between the governments. This had to be about the shooting.

The meeting was held in a drawing room, an informal atmosphere. It was just the four men in attendance: Dolly, the current Prime Minister, Edward Smith-Stanley, the 14th Earl of Derby, Mayne and his boss, the Home Secretary, Horatio Walpole.

"I asked you and Commissioner Mayne to brief the Prime Minister on the particulars of the Chilton case," said the Home Secretary, addressing Dolly.

"Before Detective Williamson gets into the case, I would just like to get on the record—" started Mayne.

"There'll be no record of this meeting, Commissioner," interrupted the Earl of Derby.

"Yes, sir." Mayne was on his back foot. "What I mean to say, sir, is the detective is one of our best men when it comes to sousing out the facts of a case and has always shown high character and tact when on a case."

"This tact and discipline includes conducting investigations with occultists and shooting French dignitaries," inserted Derby.

There it is.

"From what the Home Secretary has told me, we have a situation that has our national interest at stake, and I want to hear your side of this, Detective. Everything you know," Derby continued, ignoring Mayne's appeal.

"I was called on to investigate the death of Sir Francis Chilton, the financier. His body was found at his London home. He had not told his family why he was returning to London and no one knew of his whereabouts for nearly two days. The condition of the body was unlike anything I had seen before, and I requested the assistance of Rose Caldwell, a local occultist."

"Why did you call on her, may I ask? This city is full of fortune tellers," the PM queried.

"We have a history——"

"The Milton murders," Walpole interjected, looking at the Prime Minister in a way that left Dolly with the impression they had discussed them at some point.

"——and I trust her assessments," Dolly finished his sentence.

"Go on," prodded the PM.

"Over the following fortnight, the body of Señor Emilio Moyo was found at the Carlton in the same condition as Chilton—excuse me, Sir Chilton. Then two bodies were found in the vault at the Chilton House. In the case of the two guards, they had been shot.

"The Home Secretary requested a meeting where I was introduced to guild master Saint-Yves, a French diplomat and guild master. He shared that a similar murder had occurred in the colony of Haiti to Emilio's brother, Hernando, and that they suspected a Voodoo priestess named Angelica du Haiti. Sister Rose—sorry, Rose Caldwell—had an invention capable of detecting and imprinting spectral incidents on photographic plates. She showed me an image of an African woman in the room with Moya at the Carlton. I now had two independent sources pointing at Ms. Du Haiti, so while I had some certainty as to the identity of the suspect, I did not have a motive or an idea as to where to find her.

"I received a document from Sir Lester that his father had in his possession It was Don Ernesto's last will and testament. In the pages, Don Ernesto Moya declared he had an affair with a Haitian slave on his plantation after the death of his wife. He had his will changed to acknowledge the mother and his daughter and provide them an inheritance. There lay the motive of Angelica. Cheated of her inheritance by the Moya brothers in collusion with the elder Chilton, she sought vengeance.

"It appears Sir Chilton conspired with the sons to make Don Ernesto's will disappear and then Hernando ran the mother and daughter off the plantation. What they had not planned on was their half-sister becoming a practitioner of Voodoo."

"Voodoo, Detective?" asked Walpole, clarifying what he just heard.

The PM sat in silence, taking in Dolly's story.

"A practicing Voodoo witch, she used arcane methods to kill the Moyas and Sir Chilton. Her tactics were quite wicked. She did not just kill the men. She damned their souls to an eternal limbo. I suspect that she was stealing Chilton's gold to make up for what she was swindled out of by him and the Moyas."

"And that's when the guards were shot, not Voodoo'd?" asked the PM.

"There is that loose end. I surmise they were shot when they discovered the robbery. Given her abilities to enthrall victims, either it was by Chilton himself under her control or accomplices. What was taken was of a substantial weight. So, I suspect she or Chilton had help moving the gold."

"Have you retrieved the gold? We are receiving pressure from the younger Chilton to its whereabouts," voiced Derby.

"Actually the murder of the two guards and the theft of the gold is not my case. That happened in the city of London and is under their jurisdiction," replied Dolly.

"Tell us about the night of the Twenty-fourth at 412 Pilton

Road," requested Walpole. "Before you proceed, I want to revisit your comment that this woman was a Voodoo witch."

Dolly followed up. "To be specific, my understanding is that Ms. du Haiti was the high priestess of the Voodooists and a very powerful enchantress. Therefore, the necronists were intent on her capture."

"Or death," added Mayne.

"Yes, there's the matter of her death," said Derby.

"Very messy," interjected Walpole.

Dolly opened his journal and looked over his notes on the night of the 24th.

"On the night of the 24th, Detective Burton and I were surveying the address in question. We observed Ms. Rose Caldwell enter the residence. Shortly after her arrival, the necronists and Lord Oswald entered the home."

"Oswald, what a thunder there has been regarding his demise. His Lodge cronies are looking for justice on his part," accounted the PM.

"When I entered the residence, he was already dead. Might I say in a most gruesome way. She had mashed him into the wall," replied Dolly.

"So, it was Ms. du Haiti who killed him?" asked Derby.

"That is what Guild Master Gerard and Ms. Caldwell reported."

Derby pressed. "When do we get to the point where you shoot this Seer Thomas?"

"When I entered the room, I made it clear that I was with the Metropolitan Police Service investigating a crime in the process. I was gaining control of the scene. I observed that both Guild Master Saint-Yves and Seer Thomas were chanting an incantation. Earlier in the week, Miss Caldwell had given me an amulet to protect me against the magic of Ms. du Haiti.

"This amulet alerted me to the danger to myself and the safety of my fellow officer. I told the men to cease and desist so that I could ascertain if it was them or another source that was engaging the ward Rose gave me. They did not comply, so I could only assume that it was them who meant to do harm unto me and Burton. That is when I fired my pistol," recounted the detective.

"Do you have this amulet with you?

"I do."

May I examine it?" requested the Prime Minister.

Dolly removed the metal disk from his watch chain and passed it across the table to the Prime Minister, who regarded it thoughtfully, then handed it to the Home Secretary.

"We may all need one of these. What of its maker, this Rose Caldwell?" asked Derby.

"She assisted in apprehending the murderer and helped to protect me and Officer Burton. Rose is not a fanatic. She is a woman of faith but has found a different way to practice her beliefs," explained Dolly with admiration.

The Prime Minister leaned back in his chair. "Is there anything else you would like to add, Detective Williamson?"

Dolly thought for a moment. *Should I mention that Angelica might still be alive if he hadn't given Gerard and his companions the time? Or that Detective Keane was enthralled by Angelica, nearly killed me and I only escaped because Keane killed himself?*

"No, sir. I am prepared for whatever your decision might be," expressed Dolly.

"Decision? I'm not following you, Detective," Derby queried.

"The matter of me shooting a foreign diplomat and disciplinary action."

"What gave you that impression?" asked Walpole.

Dolly looked to Mayne. "I assumed that was the purpose of the meeting."

"Detective Williamson, I envy you that you have had the pleasure of shooting a Frenchman, particularly one of those grim-faced death worshipers. You showed restraint trying to just wing him," praised the Prime Minister.

All the men chuckled but Dolly.

"As far as the diplomatic impact, the French position is that if the Crown saw fit to drop charges against Guild Master Saint-Yves, they would consider Seer Thomas as a casualty in the apprehension of a murderess fugitive. I have settled the matter with Anou," the PM continued.

Walpole interjected. "Detective, the Prime Minister agrees that these home-grown occultists such as Oswald and his Lodge, the witch from the colonies or the necronists from the continent all have ill will for the Crown. It is our government's duty to put in safeguards.

"Detective, can I please see your journal?" the PM asked.

Dolly handed the leather-bound book to the Prime Minister.

The Earl of Derby set it on the table between Dolly and

himself. He leaned into Dolly. "Williamson, how does a man fall asleep at night knowing these types of dangers walk the streets of London? I for one have enough keeping me up," Derby inquired as he tapped his index finger on the journal.

Walpole continued. "Fredrick, we are in the nineteenth century now, and every day we learn more about how to bend the laws of physics and metaphysics to our will. You have been to the coal face and seen what those of mal intent are prepared to do with this knowledge. I want you to form a division of the Metropolitan Police Detective Branch to deal with those who practice the dark arts and choose evil ways."

"Ministers, are you authorizing Detective Williamson to lead a special branch?" questioned Commissioner Mayne. Clearly, Mayne had no idea what these two men were planning.

"I am. Detective Williamson would lead a branch of occult detection and prevention to protect our country against internal and external supernatural threats," concluded the PM.

Dolly could not believe what he was hearing. "How serious are you about this, Prime Minister?"

"Quite. This business with the Haitian and the explosion over at the gaswerks has drawn suspicion that our enemies and the weapons they are prepared to use against us are not the conventional weapons of war. We need to have some domestic defense that is also unconventional."

Dolly knew the test to determine the commitment they were prepared to make.

"Prime Minister, I will accept the position if Rose Caldwell can become a constable of the Metropolitan Police force."

FRIDAY, THE 2ND OF JULY

11:20 AM, ROSE CALDWELL'S ROOMS

Sister Rose wrote in her journal all the details she recalled from her out-of-body experience. The sounds, smells, the words Angelica spoke, everything she could remember, including the incantation used in the Pwen Hanan.

There was a knock at the door. Rose was not expecting a visitor. She closed the journal and placed it into a lockbox in the bottom drawer of her writing desk.

She peered through a view port she had installed in the door. It was Dolly.

Rose unlatched the locks on the door and let her friend in. He looked sour.

"What has got you in these parts? Looking for new rooms?" chided Rose.

"Could be. I had a meeting two days ago with the Home Secretary and the Prime Minister."

"What about?" said Rose as she locked the door and walked past Dolly. "Tea?"

"No, thanks. I had to explain how my murder investigation literally turned into a witch hunt and why I found myself shooting French diplomats."

"Why did you shoot him?" she pressed.

"Lower rank, thicker legs," Dolly replied.

"I must say, Dolly, it truly shocked me when that pistol fired."

"That is what shocked you? Not the remains of Lord Oswald mixed with the plaster wall?" followed Dolly.

"You can't imagine witnessing that scene, Dolly. It was fantastic how she used her powers." Rose put a kettle on over an alcohol burner she had for heating.

"You seem a bit taken by the sorceress," he suggested.

Rose paused, teething her lip. *Do I share with him what I was shown, how much I now know of her?* "We had a connection. I do not think she is all bad."

"I understand she was swindled out of her inheritance, but there is a better way to acquire justice. You murder people, the police come looking. Turning Keane on me was more than I could take."

"Her father waited until he died to legitimize her birthright. Her brothers sold her off to a plantation as a slave," Rose retorted.

"I didn't come here to argue the fine points of why a murderess was given the hard knocks of life. If being hard done by is a just cause, half all the convicts in England would be set free. You see, Rose, Angelica may have been alright knowing the consequences of killing her family were she would hang, and that was worth the satisfaction of getting revenge, but she never looked at the other lives lost in the process. Keane, those two guards, they didn't disown her. They never caused her harm." He was clenching the brim of his hat as he spoke.

"Dolly, the Scot has gotten hold of you. I'm not your enemy. I never said she was justified in her actions or even that Moya and Chilton deserved to die. I only said that she wasn't all bad."

"I don't doubt that any person is all bad or all good, for that matter. Anyhow, I didn't come here to argue about her. I came to tell you that you're right. The incident with Keane showed me the stakes are different—higher. These people aren't cut from the same cloth as you and I. They have power and are prepared to use it mercilessly. Du Haiti turned Keane on me, and I think if Saint-Yves could have, he and his seer would have done the same to you, Burton and me, turning us on each other like rabid dogs. Saint-Yves knew where she was hiding and didn't tell me. He had no intention of taking her alive."

"Dolly, I was invited to experience Angelica's past before the seers arrived. She was peacefully employing tarot. She saw how the night would play out. Angelica left me with the feeling that perhaps it was her last night on earth," whispered Rose.

Dolly moved into the single ratty chair Rose kept in her rooms. "Remember how we first met? Well, not the very first time, but in that cellar? I went down there with a lot of assumptions. I figured that you were helping Milton and he was some type of pedophile. I thought that all men could be brought down with the shot of a pistol.

"I came out of that cellar with less confidence in pistols and with what my eyes showed me. I am a bit more cautious in jumping to conclusions or that my allies have the same intentions I do," he finished.

"Alright then, if you didn't come here to rehash events, why did you come?" Rose asked as she poured the hot water over loose tea in her cup.

Dolly thought for a moment. There would be no going back, and he needed to know if this was going to work. It wasn't but a fortnight when he was here and Rose said she wanted to learn from the murderer. "Rose, I need to know what you and Angelica discussed before the necronists arrived. You were alone with her for some time, nearly a half hour. What were you two up to?"

"I may as well tell you. I need to share it with someone. She revealed to me that she killed her brother in Haiti. She channeled me there, back in time to witness the event. I was in her head, but it felt as if I was there—the smells, the sounds, the sight, her thoughts, the feelings of anguish and betrayal. This is when I sensed what was good in her and what drove her to act out and take life. The conflict of being in the home where she grew up, facing the person who sent his own blood away to the heinous scourge of slavery. I also experienced the power to damn him, and in the process, I learned what I wanted. I was brought back to that room with the full extent of her knowledge and power. Sadly, it's from such a dark place, just thinking of it makes me feel a deep despair."

Dolly left his chair and came closer to his friend. He pulled out the ward she had made for him. It was still attached to the end of his watch chain. Rose looked down at the amulet as Dolly encouraged her. "I trust it's still you in there, Rose. That you can process the evil and goodness of someone like

Angelica and have clarity of how the wicked was her undoing in the end."

"I do indeed, Detective."

"Does this thing still work, or did those blathering mystics foul it up when they tried to hex me?" asked Dolly.

Rose took the gemulet in her hand and looked at her craftsmanship. "No, the amulet is in perfect working order," replied Rose.

"Well, then, I have something for your protection. He drew a police whistle on a chain out of his pocket.

"It only works in London, but when you blow this whistle, your fellow bobbies will come straight away."

"Fellow bobbies?"

I told you. I had a meeting with the PM and the Home Secretary. Well, I thought for sure with the death of Seer Thomas I would be dangling in the wind on this one, but once again, I read the situation wrong. The explosion at the gaswerks and Angelica's gruesome deeds have the government preparing a domestic defense strategy against the metaphysical. They tasked me with forming up the branch, and I agreed on the condition that you were part of it.

"If all goes as planned, you, Ms. Rose Caldwell, will be our newest constable in the Metropolitan Police Department and the second member of the special detective branch for the paranormal."

Rose jumped up, kissed and hugged Dolly, tears of joy flowing. "Dolly, this means so much to me! You have no idea. To have what I do accepted."

"Well, Rose, I wouldn't go so far as to say what you do is accepted by the man on the street, but in the case of Her Majesty's government and me, it is certainly appreciated. Even if the bloke on the street doesn't accept you, he needs looking out."

SATURDAY, THE 3RD OF JULY

2:20 PM, STRATHMORE ESTATE, LONG ISLAND

Randall Wells Strathmore sat in deep contemplation, gazing out the window of his study.

The boy ran in the room and embraced Randall. Randall hugged and kissed him on his brown forehead just below his dark curly hair.

The governess hovering by the door spoke when Randall looked. "I told him to wait, but he was too excited to see you."

"That is quite alright, Ms. Meadows."

He crouched down to eye level with the boy. "Gerard, I do believe you have grown two inches since I left."

"Did you bring me anything, Uncle Randall?"

"In fact, I did." He walked behind his desk and retrieved a box. Before he could bring it back, Gerard had followed him.

There was a knock at the door. "Your guest is here sir," the footman announced.

"Lead him out to the gardens, and prepare refreshments. Gerard and I will meet him there momentarily."

A few minutes later, Randall walked up to the lean elderly gentleman that stood looking over the gardens in admiration. He wore a white linen summer suit and held a walking stick with a wolf head for the handle.

"Dr. Caiaphas."

Dr. Caiaphas turned to Randall. The two men shook hands. What always startled Randall about Warren Caiaphas was his Alopecia. Rather it was the terrible matted wig he chose to wear to cover his complete lack of hair. Initially, one would notice that he had no eyebrows, but that old hairpiece drew one's eyes to it quickly.

Gerard ran out onto the patio with a model airship. "Look what Uncle Randall bought me from his trip. He said he flew on one just like it back in England."

Dr. Caiaphas smiled at the boy. "Would you like to travel on an airship one day?"

"Oh, yes."

Randall again bent down to eye level with Gerard and then looked up at Dr. Caiaphas. "The doctor is a good friend of mine and Ms. Meadows. He has come to meet with you and ask if you would like to attend his special school."

"But I like it here," the youth cried.

"Of course, you do, but this is a very special school that very few are admitted to, and if you want to have a house like this someday, or perhaps your own airships, you need to go to school."

"But Ms. Meadow teaches me reading and maths," argued Gerard.

"I am a different type of teacher. I can teach you how to do tricks. Would you like to see one?" asked Caiaphas.

"Oh, yes, please,"

"Go grab a stone from the path, and bring it here."

The boy ran out on the garden path, searching for the perfect stone. Then after picking a few up and dropping them, he ran back to Caiaphas with the stone he selected.

Caiaphas took the stone. It was smooth, flat and grey in color. He held it out.

"Are you going to make it disappear?" asked Gerard.

"No, you are going to make it change color," suggested Caiaphas, closing his hand around the stone.

"Gerard, clasp my hand with both of yours and hold it really tight so you know that the stone can't get away."

Gerard grabbed his hand, "Your hand is cold, Mister."

"Now, Gerard, close your eyes and envision a color, only one color. I want you to think very hard and send that color right down your hands into mine. Don't tell me the color."

Gerard squeezed his eyes closed, as if his squeezing would pass the thoughts through to the stone faster.

Caiaphas looked and smiled at Randall as the boy concentrated. "Excellent, you can stop now."

The doctor opened his hand. The stone was as green as the grass in the garden.

"Oh, boy, that is a cracker of a trick. Can you teach me how to do that?"

"Gerard, you did it. I only helped boost your innate powers," the Doctor explained.

The young boy looked confused.

"Here, you keep the stone. When fall begins, you can come to my school and I will personally instruct you how to do that and many more things you can't learn from Ms. Meadows."

"Thank you, sir." Gerard grabbed the stone and ran back into the house.

"Let's walk, Randall." The two men strolled the gravel path of the expansive gardens. Not as grand as Versailles, but for America, this was a palace garden. As they walked, the doctor and Strathmore spoke.

"The boy is quite talented. With training, he will be like nothing this world or others have ever seen," stated Caiaphas.

"Doctor, I was thinking when the boy goes to Italy to study with you, I might come and spend time with the others?" asked Strathmore.

"What is your interest in meeting with others? I am the leader of our cabal. You have the ear of the master," said the Doctor.

"Well, it's just that I haven't met the others."

"Randall, this is how secret organizations work. In secret, far from the public eye and apart from each other to protect the cabal." Caiaphas stopped and turned to Randall with a smile and leaned to look him in the eye. "Are you lonely? Do you need companionship?"

"Well, I had been spending quite some time with Angelica,

helping with her plans. When the boy leaves, it will be very quiet around here." Caiaphas took Randall's hands and gave them a shake of confidence.

Randall thought, *The boy is right; his hands are cold.*

"All in good time, Randall. Before we worry about you meeting the others, let's discuss how we settled up in London. I checked, and from what I gather, Angelica never made it to the ship or Nova Scotia," directed the doctor.

"Hmm, I suspect the necronists never let her out of London alive, but I will keep an ear to the ground. She may still show up. She is very resourceful," Strathmore suggested.

"And the business with the Moyas?" pressed Caiaphas.

"All of the coroner's inquests are resolved, and the documents that Angelica forced the Moyas and Chilton to sign are in place. I expect the biggest stink to come from my partners at Chilton, Chilton, Owens and Strathmore will be about the trustee not being in the home office. If the documents see their way into court, they will stand up to any scrutiny. I am the trustee, and you are the boy's ward, as planned if Angelica was unable to make it back to the States."

"She understood the risks to exact her revenge, and now she has it, all of them dead and none the wiser. What else..." said Caiaphas, who seemed displeased by something.

Randall could tell by his curt speech and the ploy where he expected Randall to guess what he wanted to speak about. He wasn't really in the mood; his sleep was still off, and the last week had been quite stressful. "Doctor, as far as my observation, all has gone according to plan. Angelica obtained her revenge and the certainty that her son, now in your care, would inherit his grandfather's fortune.

"The gold," stated the Doctor continuing his inquest.

Strathmore couldn't believe his ears. Between the two of them, they had just gained control of the entire Moya fortune worth over seven million pounds. From what Strathmore knew of the doctor, he had no want for money. How could that small amount of gold make a difference? "The gold was stolen from the smelter before I could move it."

"Find out who is responsible. We can't have people thinking they can steal from us."

Randall's patience was all but gone. "The purpose of the heist was to cover up the search for copies of the revised will & testament."

"True. In part it was, but the fact is someone has stolen from us, Randall," declared the doctor raising his voice.

"Well, the thieves did not believe they were stealing from you. They don't even know you exist. At best, they thought they were stealing from Angelica," Randall explained.

"All the same, find out who is responsible. I don't like loose ends, and I had a purpose for that gold."

∽

11:40 PM, Rose's Apartments

Rose slipped in and out of sleep. Out again, this time realizing this wasn't a dream but someone at her door.

"One tick." She fumbled for the matchbox on her nightstand and struck a matchstick. She lit the lamp and replaced the wind glass once the wick had caught flame. After her eyes adjusted, she made her way to the door and looked through the portal.

She hadn't seen this face in years. Putting the lamp on a shelf, she worked the latches and locks to open the door.

"Violet?"

"Hello, Rose."

"What are you doing here?" Rose asked.

"I had nowhere to go. I left Chester after Pa passed, and I've been on my own. Well, sort of." Violet looked down at the baby in her arms.

"This is your niece, Rosie. Rosie, this is your Auntie Rose." Rose tried to recollect the last time she saw her sister. It was when Rose left for the convent ten years ago, and her sister was a little eight-year-old girl.

"Come in. Please, come in. How did you find me?"

"You were back in the papers again, and this time, I was in London. I just asked around Bethnal Green. I've been in London nearly two years." Violet reported as she did the mental calculation of the time. Since she was a little girl, you could tell when she was racking her brain. She would look up for the answer, as if it was on the ceiling or in the sky. "I've been living on the streets, and when I read about you in the papers, I just thought I would come see you and ask if you might be able to help me and Rosie."

"Oh, Violet, you are welcome to stay here. It's not much, but of course, you can stay. Here, let me see that little girl." Rose took the sleeping baby in her arms and looked at its precious face. Even being out on the street, the child looked peaceful while sleeping. "Close up the door and have a seat. Are you hungry? I have some bread and an apple. It's all I have, but you're welcome to it."

"Ta, sis, that would be most kind of you."

Rose handed Rosie back to Violet and took the few paces to her kitchenette. She reached into the breadbox for the loaf of bread and cut a few slices, and with the same knife, she cut up the apple. That was all the food she had. Placing it on a plate, she brought it over to Violet and set it on the small table beside the ratty chair. "Let me take her," she said, admiring the little one. Rose placed her niece on the bed behind the partition. When she returned, her sister had shoved a whole slice of bread into her mouth and was trying to choke it down.

"Violet, I am so happy you came here. It's so fortunate that you found me. I must let you know that the work I have been doing does not make ends meet, and this apartment..." Rose stopped herself. She didn't need to burden her sister with the fact of not having any money, being two months' arrears on rent and a pending eviction. "You are welcome to stay for as long as you want, and I recently had some good news. It looks like I am going to work with the Metropolitan Police Department, so we may be able to put more food on the table and find lodging better suited for the three of us."

Violet began to cry. "I would really like that."

THE ALCHEMISTS BOOK ONE OF THE GUILD CHRONICLES

CHAPTER ONE

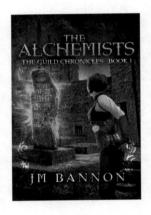

Need more Sister Rose?

What follows is the first chapter of the "The Alchemists"

FRIDAY, THE 25TH OF MAY 1860

5:30 A.M. KÖNIGSBURG PRUSSIA

Egon arrived at the research laboratory before daybreak. Holding up his ring of keys, the engineer turned to the faint but growing morning light to find the front door key. The heavy deadbolt threw open with a clunk when he turned the key in the lock. He pushed open the heavy door and stepped into the dimly lit building, Turning he pushed the door to slowly, and it closed with a soft thud. In deference to the surrounding silence he quietly made his way to the basement. Egon preferred the solitude of the early hours, in his domain in the mechanical room there was little quiet to be found.

He was the boiler superintendent at the Kraft Werks for the Illuminated Society of Alchemy, responsible for operating the latest technology in all of Europe. His chief responsibility was the supervision of Heiße Bertha the immense boiler designed to drive the dynamo the guild had commissioned Telegraphen-Bauanstalt von Siemens & Halske to make for them.

The direct current generator powered the experiments in the

upstairs laboratory of Doctors Maxwell and Traube. An added benefit of the massive power system was electric lighting throughout the building, the first in Königsberg. His initial task was to throw the breakers to the sub-panels, powering the illumination to the entire building. With one movement of a lever, the basement and the upper floor lights flickered to life and threw off more illumination as the elements in the glass orbs warmed. Another slice of modernity was the design of the condenser loop for the steam wheel, engineered to bypass through the building to heat radiators in the bitter winter months rather than just going to a condenser tank.

Yes, he was working in a boiler room, but at the private office park, not at the filthy Alchemy Werks near the railway station on the other side of town where he used to work. He would much rather conduct his rote tasks in a nice clean, modern boiler room any day rather than the fiery smelly hell that was the Königsberg Gas Werks, the largest commercial chemical facility in the world.

The boiler room was well kept. The room often had guests; dignitaries touring with the upper echelon of the guild. The Barron's and Electors liked to show off the Kraft Werks to assert the guild as the leaders of industry. Egon grabbed a broom to sweep up errant coal fines around the feed chute and storage bins while he waited for the lights to warm up. He had been advised by Doctor Maxwell that today they would run the magnets all day at full strength.

Setting down the broom he opened the firebox to Bertha and pitched four heaping shovels of coal into her fiery maw. The hot air blasted out into his face and murdered the morning chill of the basement. In a few hours, sweat would pour from him as he stood still in front of the controls. When Bertha was at full power, there was no escape in the mechanical room from her hot embrace.

He throttled back the bypass to apply full pressure and watched the gauge approach fifty bar, the prescribed setting. Producing a rag from his pocket, Egon cleaned the gauge face before making his way over to the dynamo and its complex control station. The man's trained eyes scanned the numerous dials and gauges. The instruments showed the right voltage, but the ammeter read as if there was a full load on the dynamo. *Are they already experimenting?*

Egon trudged up the stairs and upon entering the laboratory, could already hear the low purr of the bank of electromagnets. In addition, he detected a strange smell; something burning, unnatural. *Burning resin?* The thought sank in that there should be no hum as a faint gray smoke promulgated from the magnet housings transforming to fibrous black strands flitting into the air. The magnets were overheating, and the insulation was burning. Desperate, he ran to disconnect the lever to sever the circuit, as the hum increased to a bone jarring buzz.

The knife switch to power the pilot plant was closed and the ceramic handle smashed, the bits of porcelain lay on the floor next to a hammer. Egon knew not to touch the bare metal with his bare hand or he would be electrocuted. His eyes darted around the room he saw a pair of heavy rubberized gloves Dr. Traube used when working with vitriols and caustics. He donned the glove and gave the handle a tug; it did not budge.

The boiler man saw what appeared to be a tack weld on the switch, it would never move if welded. He choked on the growing smoke, his only option now was to get downstairs and shut down the boiler. Egon sprinted to the door glancing back one last time at the lab, only to see a fireball erupt and cascade toward him.

~

6:00 a.m. Königsberg Prussia

James Clerk Maxwell turned down the Physics Chair at King's College accepting a position in Prussia. His mates at the Royal Society reacted to the news across a continuum of amusement through ridicule, no one was celebratory. Some even claimed it treasonous.

It was not the obvious option to become a research scientist in Königsberg. His German was spotty, and Maxwell had his choice of teaching positions at any university in the world. Already a member of the Royal Society, and holder of the Smith's Prize, Adams Prize, and recently bestowed the Rumford Medal; Society considered James a savant celebrity in London.

Why then did his considerable scientific mind deduce that the next step in his career led to Königsberg? James chose the capital of Prussia because the Alchemy Guild's headquarters was in the city and they were prepared to build him a laboratory like none other, no expense spared. The Guild desired his expertise so much that High Elector Baron Keifer, head of the Alchemist Guild visited him to share that his stipend would be three times that of the college and he would have card blanche to pursue his theories on electromagnetism -that closed the deal.

The Guild threw in a well-appointed residence in the

Löbenicht district, a brief stroll across the Holz bridge to his workshop on the larger of the two Islets situated in the Pregel River. As he walked from his house to the office, Königsberg seemed fresher than London. It could be the sea air, or the sweet deal he secured doing what he loved. Maybe it was the Teutonic discipline that coordinated the industrial activities on the West side of the city, keeping the rest of capital quite cosmopolitan. His work would deliver the most significant advancement in alchemical sciences. Although not an alchemist, James had pushed the guild to move beyond the sourcing and refining of alchemical substances, to the ultimate alchemical goal of transmutation.

His tasks today were tedious, but required. Not a day of revolutionary research and innovation but running the crucible pilot plant to formulate and test recipes. He brought his lunchbox planning to work through the lunch hour to get through the humdrum tasks.

James admired the tulips and daffodils finally blooming in the late spring. The plants bordered the pathway of the office and research campus the Alchemists had built on the opposite side of town from the original gas werks. As he tread up the track he gazed at the first-floor windows of the lab building observing an orange - green light. His immediate reaction was to pick up his pace to see what was the cause, but before his foot fell again, the building erupted in a massive explosion, fire rolling out of all the blown-out windows. Glass and wood showered down and he saw a large object flying toward him. Turning away James put his arms up to protect his head. He cringed when he heard a heavy thud nearby. Slowly he turned and moved his arms down from his face to witness just a few feet away, Egon's smoldering body sprawled out in front of him.

～

10:30 a.m. Königsberg Prussia

Duke Gorber walked up to the chief of the local fire company, operated by the Hosliess Property Group. The brigade commander was busy conducting his company in the clean-up of the equipment. The Duke had several deputies of the Ministry with him to investigate.

"What is the situation with the fire?" inquired the Duke.

"You will need to talk with the proprietor," responded the brigade commander without giving the Duke even a courtesy glance. "Sir, let me be more direct. I am Duke Gorber the Minister of Internal Affairs, not a passerby, rather the investigator. I require your appraisal of the scene for my report to the Minister-President and the High Elector of the Guild." Now the Duke had the man's full attention.

"Your Grace, My brigade quenched the fire on the first floor, I cannot fathom what caused the fire but the damage is extensive. You will need to consult that engineer or scientist over by what is left of the building to understand what they were up to, it's not like anything I have seen." explained the leader of the fire brigade.

"Thank you. Inspector Segal here is with the Ministry and will take down your details, In case I have further questions" The Duke approached the smoldering building with his two other investigators. As he arrived, a commotion was unfolding. A youthful man speaking broken German with a heavy English accent, was gyrating hysterically in front of a massive piece of burnt equipment waving his arms and yelling at two of the fire brigade.

The Duke interrupted the group of men addressing them with his stern Teutonic tone. "Gentleman, as of this moment the building is under the examination of the Ministry of Internal Affairs by the order of the Minister-President and the High Elector of the Guild."

"Finally, someone who is talking sense. The machinery here is of the utmost importance to the Guild, as was the team in the building, God rest their souls," replied the Englishman.

"How many bodies have you found so far?" inquired Gorber speaking to the fireman. "Just the one but we are still working through the rubble, but this fellow wants us to stay clear of this equipment," replied the fire man.

"We must find out if Dr. Traube was in the building. She is diligent in her work and usually arrives before me," implored the Englishman.

"And you are?" asked the Duke.

"Doctor James Maxwell, the lead scientist in elementary prototransmutation, and you, Sir?"

"I am Manfreid Willhelm Gorber, Duke of Magdeburg and Minister of Internal Affairs. It is in my capacity as the eyes and ears of King Frederick William that I am here. Please slow down, I am grappling with your appalling German. First and foremost, who is this you are concerned about?"

"Doctor Traube, the lead alchemist on the project and my colleague. Certainly, you have heard of the Traubes." Of course he had, you couldn't go anywhere in Prussian society and not bump into a Traube. *They're a prolific bunch.*

"Go to Baron Traube's home and see if he is there." instructed the Duke to one of his attending inspectors. "And advise the local police we will need help going through the debris for evidence," directed the Duke.

"Doctor Lorelei Traube, the Baron's daughter was my colleague," James injected to correct the mistaken identity.

"Do you know her address, Doctor Maxwell?"

"Not off the top of my head,"

"Your coworker, when was the last time you saw her?"

"I have not seen her since yesterday."

"Doctor, If the case is that this was not an accident why would this building be targeted for arson?"

"The EPT." Maxwell gave him a look first of irritation then appeared to loosen up. "Elementary Prototransmutation, is the holy grail of alchemy. In antiquity alchemists sought the ability to change lead into gold. What we have achieved is that ability to take commodity feedstocks and convert them at the elemental level."

"Who might have knowledge about this important work?" inquired the Duke.

"We have the Electors of the Guild, then there is the architects and constructors of the production facility. You see this pilot plant was built to prove out the process then it was scaled up for the new kraft werks that will officially open in September."

"Beyond the Guild, have you spoken with others about your work, at the pub or through correspondence?" probed Gorber.

"Here in Konigsberg, I may be an unknown, living in

anonymity, but in the field of physics, I am a luminary. My writings are published in science journals internationally."

"Publications about this experiment?" asked Gorber.

"No, but my body of work is well known. That's my primary point, your Grace."

The only thing bigger than the Englishman's brain is his arrogance. "But not specifically this project?" asked the Duke.

"No, it is to be kept secret until the September unveiling of the production crucible at the International Convention of the Alchemical Sciences."

"I see. Would any rivals seek to foil your experiments? Maybe your decision to do the work in the Confederation of German States rather than your motherland had something to do with it?"

"While I have invariably suffered envy of my achievements and scrutiny of my theory given its advanced reasoning and my youthful appearance, I can think of no person prepared to go to this extreme to obstruct my work."

"Another angle is the commercial threats you may pose with your invention. Does this look to upset anyone's existing apple cart?" questioned Gorber.

"Yes and no. I reply yes because it will fundamentally transform how we make raw substances, and no because the new process just strengthens the Alchemists dominant position in feedstock production of the synthetic and alchemical."

"I will need to get your address in case I have further questions Doctor and please do not leave Königsberg."

"I hope you don't think I had anything to do with this?" replied Maxwell.

"I think nothing yet, if this is an accident even one that culminated in a death than I will step aside for the city guard to investigate. If a vital project to the Guild has been sabotaged, then I will have a keen interest in anyone associated with the project." asserted the Duke.

Continue Reading the Alchemists

MORE FROM JM BANNON

Want to know what Rose does with her newfound wealth?
Click here and get a short story as a free bonus

Want to learn more about Rose?

The Saints and Scoundrels of Steampunk Series is a collection of books that document tales in JM Bannon's Non-Newtonian Universe. The first book Awaken goes back to when Rose was younger and in the convent.

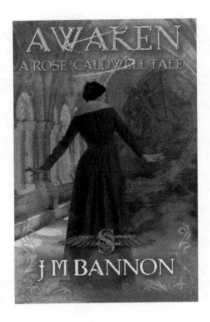

You can buy Book 1 Awaken: A Rose Caldwell Tale direct from JM Bannon. Use coupon code: Awaken to get the book in any file format for only $1.99 (a $2 savings) and get the exclusive content that only direct buyers get! This book is also available for sale at $3.99 on all bookstores.

You can also continue The Guild Chronicle series by reading for sale on Amazon or as part of your Kindle Unlimited subscription.

The Alchemists

The Necronists

THANK YOU

If you enjoyed this tale, please take the time to leave a review. Reviews help other like-minded readers to find new stories.

Click Here to Review

ABOUT THE AUTHOR

JM Bannon is the author of the Guild Chronicles. When not writing, his time is spent reading or walking the grounds of the sanitarium, where on a clear day you can see all the way to Prague Castle.

Feel free to reach out by email. All correspondence is reviewed by the staff of the Brookhaven Sanitarium and will be answered by JM Bannon or Doctor Gustav Kreppelin, the resident physician at Brookhaven.

If you too have witnessed strange events occurring in the non-Newtonian universe and would like to help others understand it's true reality, write JM and learn how you can contribute as an advanced reader or co-writer in the NNU.

Learn More:
https://cuxllc.lpages.co/jmbannon/
jmbannon@cuxllc.com

Made in the USA
Middletown, DE
11 January 2019